The
Maps
of
Memory

Also by Marjorie Agosín

I Lived on Butterfly Hill

The Maps of Memory

Return to Butterfly Hill

Marjorie Agosín

Translated from the Spanish by Alison Ridley

Illustrated by Lee White

A CAITLYN DLOUHY BOOK
Atheneum Books for Young Readers

New York London Toronto Sydney New Delhi

atheneum

ATHENEUM BOOKS FOR YOUNG READERS

An imprint of Simon & Schuster Children's Publishing Division

1230 Avenue of the Americas, New York, New York 10020

The Butterfly Hill Series

For information about special discounts for bulk purchases, please contact Simon & Schuster Special Sales at 1-866-506-1949 or business@simonandschuster.com.

The Simon & Schuster Speakers Bureau can bring authors to your live event. For more information or to book an event, contact the Simon & Schuster Speakers Bureau at 1-866-248-3049 or visit our website at www.simonspeakers.com.

Interior design by Irene Metaxatos

The text for this book was set in ITC Souvenir.

The illustrations for this book are rendered in in watercolor, ink, digital.

Manufactured in the United States of America

0820 FFG

First Edition

10 9 8 7 6 5 4 3 2 1

Library of Congress Cataloging-in-Publication Data

Names: Agosín, Marjorie, author. | White, Lee, 1970- illustrator. | Ridley, Alison, translator.

Title: The maps of memory : return to Butterfly Hill / Marjorie Agosín ; translated by Alison Ridley ; illustrated by Lee White.

Description: First edition. | New York : Atheneum Books for Young Readers, [2020] | "A Caitlyn Dlouhy Book." | Audience: Ages 10-14. | Audience: Grades 7-9. | Summary: After fourteen-year-old Celeste Marconi returns to Valparaíso from Maine, she decides to uncover the truth about what happened in Butterfly Hill during the dictatorship and find her missing friend, Lucila.

Identifiers: LCCN 2020011372 (print) | LCCN 2020011373 (eBook) | ISBN 9781481469012 (hardcover) | ISBN 9781481469036 (eBook)

Subjects: LCSH: Valparaíso (Chile)—History—20th century—Juvenile fiction. | Chile—History—1973-1988—Juvenile fiction. | CYAC: Valparaíso (Chile—History—20th century—Fiction. | Chile—History—1973-1988—Fiction. | Family life—Chile—Fiction. | Friendship—Fiction. | Disappeared persons—Fiction. | Dictatorship—Fiction.

Classification: LCC PZ7.A2686 Map 2020 (print) | LCC PZ7.A2686 (eBook) | DDC [Fic]—dc23

LC record available at https://lccn.loc.gov/2020011372

LC ebook record available at https://lccn.loc.gov/2020011373

*I dedicate this book to the
children who travel through life
without their parents searching for
happiness and a better world.*

—M. A.

To my son, Emerson

—L. W.

PART 1
The *Esmeralda* Returns

An Unexpected
Visitor

I wake from a restful sleep to the faintest sound of bells that seems to travel on the wind. It's not Sunday, so it can't be the bells of Santo Tomás Church on Concepción Hill, one hill over from Butterfly Hill. The enchanting sound comes and goes. As I leave my room to investigate, I see that Mamá and Papá are already awake. They're in their bedroom looking out the window, cups of coffee in hand. They've heard the sound as well, but the only things we can see are the same two birds as always sitting on the telephone pole having their morning conversation of "Chirp, chirp, chirp."

I run down the creaky stairs of our house, determined to get to the bottom of the mysterious noise. When I pull open the blue front door of our house, I find . . . a little mule on our front stoop. A mule! It looks dusty, like it's just stepped out of a cupboard of antiques. Around its neck is a trio of small bells that make the delicate sound I heard earlier. Each time the mule moves its tail, it also moves its head, making the *tinkle-tinkle* sound.

The poor animal looks lost and afraid. I stroke its fur, and puffs of what looks like ash sparkle into the air. "It's okay, little one," I murmur reassuringly.

Nana Delfina comes bustling out onto the stoop with a bucket of soapy lavender water in one hand and a sponge in the other. How did she know about this unexpected visitor? Nana Delfina, my surrogate grandmother, our housekeeper, and one of my best friends all rolled into one, has an uncanny knack for knowing about things before they happen! She's witchy that way.

"Nana knew someone was coming to our house today. The wind told me so in a dream," she says with a curious smile, talking about herself in the third person, as she often does. "Nana doesn't want any bad spirits floating into the house on the ash." She's also superstitious.

Mamá and Papá come to help. As we wash the mule, we can see that she—Papá, who's a doctor, has declared she's a girl—is a silvery brown, the same color as my morning coffee with frothy milk. The little mule looks at me with her huge brown eyes. My heart melts.

Seeing the look on my face, Papá says, "You can't keep her, Celeste. We have to find her owner. When Mamá and I go to our clinic this morning, we'll ask if anyone knows about a lost mule. Why don't you and Cristóbal Williams ask around too? It will give you something to do." He's hinting, not so subtly, at my laziness of

late. He says I spend too much time in my room "brooding," whatever *that* means.

Just then, Abuela Frida, my granny, magically appears in the garden, her wispy gray hair still in curlers. Her eyes, somewhere between blue and violet, go wide when she sees the mule, and she squeals in delight. "This mule is a sign of good things to come!" she says, and then, admiring the animal's coat, she adds in a dreamy voice, "She's the color of the stars just before they fall to earth." And she begins scratching the animal's long ears.

We take the mule to the back garden so she can graze and smell all the blooming flowers and the morning dew. She seems much more relaxed after her bath. Nana Delfina brings her a bucket of oats and carrots, and Abuela Frida brings her some plump figs. The little mule begins happily munching away. I rush back inside the house, put on my sneakers and a sweatshirt, and dash back outside, on a mission to find Cristóbal Williams.

Cable Cars at
Rest

The cable cars that used to take us up and down the hills of Valparaíso have been out of service for the last six months, so I have to walk into town. Since returning to Chile from Juliette Cove, Maine, where my parents had sent me until the dictator's death, I have noticed there's been one strike after another, and services like the cable cars have stopped running. Apparently the once magenta, blue, and orange cars—now a dull gray—haven't been renovated in decades and are no longer safe. Doors have actually come off their hinges! Thanks to the dictator, the whole country is now in a state of disrepair. No one knows what to fix first! Papá says it's going to take a long time to fix things because most of the people who have money do not want to help solve the big problems, and the people who want to solve the big problems have no money. So, for now, we all just have to be patient, and hope President Espinoza can begin to set things right.

If the buses or trains didn't run for six months in America, people would go ballistic! Here? It is what it is.

One day the cable cars will run again, and then we won't have to walk anymore. For now, we do what we have to. Jeez, I sound like Papá!

At least the houses on Butterfly Hill and the other hills of Valparaíso are still brightly painted compared to the more somber, run-down parts of the city. Some houses are orange and mint green, while others are canary yellow with blue trim. Nescafé cans that have been converted into planters hold magnificent bougainvillea plants that creep up fences and walls, showering the city with fuchsia and red blooms. I'm halfway down the hill when I see Don Alejandro leaning against his old taxi, the same one in which he took me to the airport on my way to Maine. "Don Alejandro, how are you?" I ask, giving him a hello kiss on the cheek.

He shrugs. "I'm fine, Señorita Celeste. I'm just waiting for someone to ask for a ride. Not many people take taxis these days. The rich people all have their own cars and drivers, and the poor people can only afford the cable cars . . . when they're running. And I stay right here watching the world go by."

"Any idea when the cable cars will be working again?" I ask. I personally don't mind walking, but I imagine it's hard for some people who have to carry heavy bags up and down the hills. Just then I see an old lady walking slowly, slowly with two canvas shopping bags overflowing with avocados, bread, and a bunch of violets.

"Well, it'll probably be a while longer. The government's focused on helping the people who lost their houses in the last earthquake." He shakes his head. "It's always something: earthquakes, tsunamis . . . So much damage. At least we, here, were spared. It makes you feel grateful for what you do have, even when you don't have a lot."

"You're right about that, Don Alejandro." This was something I started to notice when I came back from America: most people here look on the bright side, even after disasters. It seems to me we're a country of good losers.

Just then, Don Alejandro asks, "Say, how are your projects going, the ones President Espinoza gave you a prize for?"

I laugh. "I wish . . . I shouldn't have received that prize until I'd finished the work!"

"But you were doing so well—that traveling library you and Señor Williams came up with—people have enjoyed reading the books you two leave at the taxi stands and other places around the city."

"Really?" I feel a surge of happiness. "I'm glad to hear that. I noticed books being taken and replaced, so I hoped people were liking them, but I didn't know that for certain."

"Well, rest assured," he says with a smile, "the books have been a hit!"

"We still have more at home. Abuela Frida must have stored away a thousand of them for people during the dictatorship." My mind flashes to the hideaway under our stairs, once chock-full of "dangerous" books. If the dictator had known, he'd probably have burned our whole house down! Now Don Alejandro asks me something else.

"What's next? You'd talked about setting up classes so people could learn to read and write?"

"Ummm . . . yes, but I haven't started that yet," I reply sheepishly.

He looks surprised. "Why not?"

I hesitate a moment before saying, "Well . . . to tell you the truth, it's . . . it's been a bit more difficult than I thought, adjusting to being back in Chile. So much has changed." I sweep my hands down toward the city. "Everywhere I look, there are shops with names in English instead of Spanish. Restaurants . . . So many things I once loved seem to have disappeared . . ." I gulp, and go on, "Including friends who never came back. Sometimes I get so sad about everything." I take a deep breath. "I guess I've kind of been moping around. . . ."

"That doesn't sound like the Celeste Marconi I know!" exclaims Don Alejandro.

"I know!"

"We must all remember that the general is *finito*—his dictatorship will never return. To think he died of a bad cold, of all things!" Don Alejandro scoffs.

There are many stories about the dictator's death. Some people say he died of a terrible cold. Well . . . not really. They say he sneezed so hard that the walls of his house came tumbling down and squashed him. The true story is that he died of a heart attack. But don't you need to have a heart in order to die of a heart attack? Where was his heart when he made my best friend, Lucila, disappear?! Or so many other kids from my school. Or when he took my papá prisoner?!

Don Alejandro looks at me thoughtfully. "We have to stop thinking about how different things are and start making life better. As soon as you're in business with your classes, I will sign up to be one of your first pupils. I've always wanted to learn to read and write!"

"It's a deal!" I say, then I wave good-bye and fly down Butterfly Hill.

Clocks
Out of Sync

I arrive on Plaza Turri out of breath, but when I look up at the clock tower, it says it's only six o'clock. That can't be. I woke up at six and so much has happened since then.

In Valparaíso, there's actually a fabulous mystery related to clocks and time. Though the city is chock-full of timepieces, each one seems to tell a different time. For instance, the clock on Plaza Sotomayor runs fast, while the one on Plaza Victoria is always late by an hour. They're all out of sync! It's as though each one marks its own unique territory in the vast chronology of time. Nana Delfina says each one has its own voice, and we're the ones who walk out of step. Others say the out-of-sync clocks are a sign of decay, but I'm not so sure.

My parents tell me that during the dictatorship, time seemed to slow down as people tried to cope with their fear and what they had lost, living from one minute to the next, wondering if they would be the next to disappear. Everyone was a potential target—that's why my parents sent me to Maine—but especially students, poets, and people who worked for social justice and human rights. Being a political prisoner, like Papá, was apparently the worst. They were locked away, never knowing whether it was day or night. Time stood still.

Time was actually controlled by the dictator, and Chileans were subjected to his whims. Cristóbal told me an amazing story about how the general demanded that it be light for more hours than was possible in a day! That reminds me of one of the other tales about the general's death. When he tried to change time to make the days longer and the nights shorter, all the clocks stopped and an enormous one fell on his head. Finito!

I glance up at the clock tower on Plaza Turri again, checking it against my watch. Out of the corner of my eye, I glimpse a flash of lace and tulle. There's a beautiful young woman flying down the exterior stairs of the church. Is that . . . a bride? Where's her groom? She's all alone, running as fast as she can. Is she . . . ? She is! She's trying to make her escape! As she runs out onto the square, I shout out to her, "Señorita, there's a taxi driver just up the hill if you need a ride!"

"Gracias, niña," she calls back, and tosses me her small bouquet as she heads in the direction I'm pointing.

As I watch her float up the hill like an angel, I press the sweet-smelling roses to my nose, and realize the fugitive bride must have decided at the last moment that she didn't want to get married. She threw caution and fear to the wind just in the nick of time!

I make my way over to Señora Williams's flower stand. She and Cristóbal look just about done setting it up.

"Hola, Celeste," says Cristóbal. "What are you doing down here so early? I wasn't expecting to see you until lunchtime." Cristóbal has a new friend, a girl from France named Genevieve, who he wants me to meet. We're having lunch with her and some of our other friends today at a new restaurant called Stephen's.

"Hola, Cristóbal. Hola, Señora Williams. Cristóbal, I need your help. You'll never guess what happened this morning."

"Tell me," he says, wiping his hands on a rag after plunging a bunch of copihues—the national flower of Chile—into a green bucket.

"It's better if I show you. Señora Williams, can you do without Cristóbal for a while?"

"Sí, niña. We were just about to open. I can handle things from here."

Revelations

When we reach the house, Cristóbal is as taken with the mule as everyone in the Marconi household. He promises to help me find her owner. Mamá and Papá come outside to say hello and invite Cristóbal in for coffee and avocado toast. As we turn to go inside, Mamá gasps. We follow her gaze. She's looking out at the sea, where a magnificent sailboat is making its way toward the harbor.

"Is that . . . the *Esmeralda*?" I ask. "I haven't seen it since I've been back!"

No one answers, because Mamá has collapsed to the ground in a faint.

"Mamá!" I cry as I run to help Papá sit her up.

"Ay, Celeste," Mamá says, coming to, her face pale. "I knew I would have to see that ship again someday, but I wasn't prepared. . . . I'm okay. . . . Just give me a minute."

"Come, Esmeralda," Papá says. My mother shares the very same name as the ship. Cristóbal helps Papá take Mamá back into the house. As they lower her gently

onto the couch in the living room, it's as though Mamá
has entered a dark tunnel. Her eyes—a beautiful emerald
green—have gone flat, and she seems to be staring at
something only she can see. I move toward her, but then
stop, afraid. The air in the usually breezy room feels thick,
and it's hard to breathe. Cristóbal stands awkwardly, not
knowing what to say or do.

"Mamá, what's wrong?" I've never seen her this pale.
"Mamá! Can you hear me?!" Panic is building inside me.

Papá takes my hand. "Sit down, Celeste. I will
explain, but first let me get some chamomile tea to settle
your mother's nerves."

"Nana will fetch it," Nana says, and bustles out.

"Esmeralda, take a deep breath. Good. Now
another," Papá says soothingly, but Mamá's gaze is still
far away.

"But I don't understand, Papá. What's wrong?" I ask.

Mamá slowly returns as if from a great distance, and
she looks around, confused.

"How did I get *here*?" she asks, a sheen of sweat on
her forehead and upper lip.

"You saw the *Esmeralda*, querida, and you fainted,"
says Papá gently, and he wipes her brow with his handkerchief. Nana comes back with a steaming cup of tea.
When Mamá takes it, her hand trembles. "I want you to
stay put until you drink that tea," he tells her, motioning

for me and Cristóbal to follow him into the kitchen.

"What's going on?" I exclaim as soon as we're out of earshot of my mother. "It's as though the *Esmeralda* scared Mamá to death."

Papá looks out the window and back again quickly. "Ummm . . . Celeste . . . do you remember how each time the *Esmeralda* came to port, we would go down to the shore and welcome it home?"

"Sure, we used to go and wave to the sailors. You remember, don't you, Cristóbal?" My friend nods.

Papá sighs. "That ship brought us such happiness and pride in those days. Our finest sailors were trained on it. But what you don't know is that—and here's the hard part, Celeste—during the dictatorship, while you were in Maine, the *Esmeralda* and several of our other ships, were used for . . . other purposes." Papá's voice sinks low.

Mine goes in the opposite direction as I ask, "Other purposes? What do you mean? Do you know about this, Cristóbal?" He shakes his head.

Papá's voice goes even lower. "The *Esmeralda,* and other ships like it, were turned into detention centers where people who were considered the general's enemies were sent to be questioned."

"About what? Was it like a jail? What happened to them?" I ask, the questions spilling from my lips.

"We still don't know exactly. Most of the people the general forced onto the ships disappeared and have not returned, but some managed to escape and have begun to tell stories about"—he glances through to the living room, then looks back at me—"horrible acts of torture that took place on those ships."

"Torture? On the *Esmeralda*?" I glance out the window at the gorgeous ship with its sails full of wind. *Torture?*

Papá nods. "Yes, awful things happened on that ship, but until recently no one was ready to talk about it; because it's still too raw, even after all this time."

I think for a moment, back to when I was with Tía Graciela. Sometimes she would become very quiet and sit staring through the window at the falling snow. I would sit next to her and wonder what was wrong. One day, out of the blue, she told me about her former boyfriend Javier. She'd found out he'd been brutally beaten by the dictator's men before he'd disappeared. Tía Graciela was heartbroken. I ask Papá if he knew about Javier.

He nods slowly, so slowly. "Most people, like Javier, never came back after they disappeared . . . but some— a few—did. . . ." He pauses and seems to be searching for the right words. "Celeste, Mamá was one of those people. . . . She was a prisoner on the *Esmeralda*, but she managed to escape." He watches me carefully.

I gape at my father, speechless. But when I find my voice, I realize I'm shouting.

"WHAT? What do you mean, Mamá was a prisoner?! No! That can't be true! Why didn't you ever tell me? I've been home for . . . for . . . more than a year! Why didn't I know about that ship? Why was Mamá taken there? What happened to her?" The questions tumble out, and all of a sudden I'm crying. Cristóbal comes over and wraps an arm around my shoulders. All I ever knew was that Mamá went into hiding! But I should have *known* it was more than that—she hasn't been the same since she returned home.

"Hija," Mamá calls. She's standing in the doorway, flanked by Abuela Frida and Nana Delfina. She extends her arms toward me, her eyes glistening with tears. I go to her and she folds me into a tight hug.

"Celeste, we were trying to protect you from such awfulness, but the biggest reason is that it's still very hard for Papá and me to talk about what happened. When people experience horrible things, they have to take the time they need in order to be able to process everything, to speak from a place of peace rather than anger." She strokes my hair. "We know you will be patient and give us the time we need, and we promise to tell you more when we're ready and able."

I frown at my parents. I knew Papá had been

imprisoned, but Mamá? It seems unbelievable. They're doctors. They help people for free if people can't pay! What did they ever do to deserve being imprisoned? I shake my head and say, "Okay, I'll be patient, but you don't have to hide things from me because you think I'm too young to understand. I understand more than you think."

My parents look at each other. "You're right," Mamá concedes. "We'll get better at telling you things from now on." She hugs me again and, beginning to fulfill her promise, adds, "It was just such a shock to see the *Esmeralda* in the harbor."

"Where has it been all this time?" asks Cristóbal.

Mamá glances toward the window, then back at us. "Well, right after the dictator died, his men made the ships disappear just as they'd made people disappear, to hide the horrors that had occurred there. I heard the *Esmeralda* sailed halfway around the world. . . . Out of sight, out of mind."

"What exactly *did* happen on those ships?" I ask carefully.

Mamá's eyes cloud. "Well, you know that thousands and thousands of people disappeared, Celeste. . . . Only a few hundred, like your papá and me, managed to escape. Others are still missing. . . ."

"Like Lucila?" I say, my voice catching. Cristóbal

sucks in a shaky breath. Lucila was my best friend, but she was Cristóbal's friend too.

"Yes, like Lucila." Mamá's voice cracks. "Her disappearance was never even recorded. When her grandmother asked the authorities where Lucila and her parents were, they feigned ignorance. The dictator . . . he went to great lengths to conceal his actions. He knew what a terrible thing he was doing."

"But 'disappeared' doesn't necessarily mean *dead*, does it?" I ask, because I honestly can't let myself believe that Lucila and all the others might really be dead. They must be in hiding—in the mountains where no one can reach them. . . . But my father's next words tear those hopes to shreds.

"Not always, hija, but"—again my parents glance at each other—"in most cases . . . yes, that's what it means."

I pull away from my mother. Lucila, dead? Every time that horrid thought crossed my mind in the past, I banished it, refusing to go there. But now there is no escaping the possibility. "I think I'm going to throw up." I run for the bathroom just in time. Mamá follows and holds my ponytail away from my face as I heave and heave. Finally I sit back on the cool tiled floor. "But . . . but what did Lucila ever do to the dictator, Mamá? What did *you* do? I don't understand."

"None of it makes sense, m'ija. It makes no sense that a person could be taken away just for thinking differently from the dictator, or because their parents did. But I believe things are shifting. I heard that President Espinoza wants to turn the *Esmeralda* into a museum of some sort, as a reminder of the things that happened that so many people still do not want to admit. I didn't know if that was anything more than a rumor . . . until today."

"But . . . *why*? Isn't it better to try to forget?"

"I thought the same thing at first, but the president is right; we can't remain silent, and we must never forget." Mamá looks out at the sea again. The *Esmeralda* is just outside the harbor now. Then she looks back at me. "If we remain silent, we become the dictator's accomplices—what he's done disappears, and the disappeared people and the tortured will be forgotten." Then she adds, in a voice full of determination, "One day . . . one day soon, I will go on that ship again. I know it's the only way for me to truly heal. I want you and Papá to go with me. Will you do that for me, Celeste?"

I don't even hesitate. "Of course I will!" I hug her tight and realize with a jolt just how lucky I am. My parents both came home. So many others, like Lucila . . . it's as if they just dropped off the face of the earth.

The *Esmeralda*'s wake looks like black tendrils slithering across the water. Goose bumps prick my arms—what exactly happened on that ship? Nana Delfina is always telling me that things are not always as they appear, that I need to look beyond the surface to discover the truth. It's like what you have to do with the fog. You have to see through it or wait for it to lift to discover what lies beneath. I think I need to pay a bit more attention to the fog from now on. Just look at the truth that came sailing out of it this morning!

Don't Be Late!

After Cristóbal heads back to his mother's flower stand and Mamá and Papá leave for work, I retreat to the roof outside my bedroom window, my favorite place to write in my notebook of dreams. The *Esmeralda* is on the other side of the harbor now, but I still see it in my mind's eye, and I can't stop thinking about it. For my fourteenth birthday, my parents gave me a conch shell shaped like a snail. It's peachy pink and as big as my head. I keep it by my pillow so I can put it to my ear and hear all the sounds of the ocean and have soothing sea dreams. But now that I know the evil *Esmeralda* sails on that same sea, I'm sure all my dreams will turn into nightmares. I continue to write for a long time until a pelican caw breaks into my thoughts. I've been so busy jotting things down that I've completely lost track of time. When I look at my watch, I gasp, "I'm gonna be late!"

As I run toward the front door, Nana Delfina exclaims, "Celeste Marconi, is the wind chasing you? What's the rush? I've told you a million times—only ill-mannered people rush. Elegant young ladies like you should walk slowly, slowly."

Elegant? Not me! "Nana, do you know where my sneakers are? I need to get going or I'm going to be late!" I call out, trying to slow down and follow Nana's advice.

"Celeste, being early or on time is for people in other countries. Here we're all born late and everyone's watch is slow." Nana laughs as she hands me my shoes. "Sometimes I think you forget you aren't in the United States anymore. You'll get where you're going faster if you don't hurry." Nana Delfina is the calmest person I know, except for Cristóbal. . . . He's so calm, he sometimes falls asleep midsentence. *I*, on the other hand, am most definitely not calm.

"Here, take an umbrella. It's going to rain cats and dogs this afternoon," Nana adds, handing me an enormous black umbrella that's twice as big as I am. It's the same one she was carrying when she first showed up on our doorstep so many years ago. I take it, give Nana a kiss on the cheek, and race out the front door completely forgetting her advice about walking like an elegant young lady. I do, however, take an extra thirty seconds to go to the backyard and scratch the mule's ears.

Completos without Chimichurri?

As I reach Plaza Turri, I spy Cristóbal holding a beautiful bunch of jasmines in one hand and a huge black umbrella similar to mine in the other.

"Cristóbal! Hi! Are those for me? You shouldn't have," I tease, guessing they're for the French girl.

"They're for Genevieve," Cristóbal says, blushing. I've never been able to resist teasing him—he turns the most fabulous shade of red. I hug him and we walk together toward the restaurant. He's decked out in his nicest shirt, a yellow one, and his best khaki pants. His hair is neatly combed—well, neatly for Cristóbal. It only sticks up in a few directions, whereas usually it sticks up everywhere. I think he's totally crushing on Genevieve.

"You're here early," I say as a breeze swirls down and tousles his neat hair.

"No, you're late," he replies, and we laugh. Then he looks at me, concern furrowing his brow. "How are you?" But before I can answer, Marisol and Gloria arrive from the other side of the square. Marisol is fourteen, like me, but she's much taller and has long, curly brown hair and big brown eyes. She's wearing a pretty blue cotton dress and wedge sandals. She jogs over, grinning, and gives me a kiss on the cheek. Marisol is my best girlfriend after Lucila, who just happens to be Marisol's cousin. Gloria, however, eyes me warily. She and I have never been close, but we do hang out from time to time. She's shorter and rounder than Marisol, and she's wearing the most fashionable clothes. Her father, who was one of the dictator's men, is very wealthy. He buys Gloria anything she wants, and Gloria makes sure everyone knows it. Having the latest gadgets and clothes has never impressed me, though I don't let Gloria know that, of course. It would be rude.

Just then, someone with long blond hair runs up to us from the direction of Happiness Hill.

"Hi, Genevieve," Cristóbal says, awkwardly thrusting the bouquet of jasmines in her direction as she comes skidding to a stop.

Genevieve is short—about the same height as me— and she smiles a braces-filled smile as she beams at Cristóbal and accepts his gift, breathing in the sweet aroma. "Merci, Cristóbal. Thank you! They're lovely." Oh—her accent is so charming.

"Celeste, this is Genevieve," he says, his eyes bright.

"It's very nice to meet you," I say, and I give her the customary kiss on the cheek.

"Pleased to meet you, Celeste. Cristóbal has told me so much about you!" Then she kisses me three times, telling me that's how they greet people in France. I like her already. After Marisol and Gloria—who already met Genevieve—say hello, we head into the restaurant.

Inside, my eyes go wide—talk about a change! Stephen's, which used to be a cozy place called Quita Penas, is now ultra-modern. Everything is gleaming white, and the waiters are dressed in elegant suits. Gone are the squeaky mismatched chairs and the brightly colored tablecloths that the previous owner's grandmother made by hand.

"Hello, everyone. I'm Ernesto, and I will be your waiter this afternoon. What would you like to order?" a rather stiff-looking man asks once we lay down our menus to indicate we have made our choices. The waiters at Quita Penas used to chat with their customers: "Hola, Celeste Marconi," they would say, and even give me a hug. These new waiters treat us like strangers, which, I suppose we are.

I'm going to order a completo, which is like a juicy hot dog in the United States, only twice as big, and comes with my favorite Chilean toppings: tomato, avocado, and chimichurri—my favorite sauce, made of parsley, garlic, oil, and vinegar. I'm so hungry—yum!

"Could you bring me a coffee with frothy milk? And a completo with extra chimichurri?" I wriggle in anticipation.

"I'm sorry, señorita, but we don't serve chimichurri in this restaurant; most everyone asks for ketchup," says Ernesto, although he doesn't look at all sorry.

"What do you mean you don't serve chimichurri? How's that possible?" I ask in a challenging tone. I'm in Chile—how could any restaurant not have chimichurri? It's as if I'm back in the U.S., where everyone puts ketchup on their hot dogs.

He asks impatiently, "Do you want ketchup, or do you want to change your order?"

"Fine. I'll take the ketchup," I reply sullenly.

"Well, that was rude," says Gloria haughtily, looking at me askance.

"I know! I can't believe he didn't even try to explain why they don't have chimichurri."

"I didn't mean *him*, Celeste. I meant *you*. You didn't need to be rude to him."

"I wasn't the one who was rude, Gloria. *He* was," I say, glaring.

"Whatever," she replies, and begins polishing a little jewel set into her manicured nails.

"Okay, everyone, let's just try to have a good time,"

says Cristóbal, glancing at Genevieve, clearly uncomfortable.

I didn't mean to start anything with Gloria. The truth is, each new thing I find gone upsets me. No chimichurri isn't the biggest deal in the world, but . . . but, after what my parents told me about what happened on the *Esmeralda*—fury starts rising within me. Things just *keep* disappearing! Does anyone think about what happened to the disappeared? Does anyone know what happened on the *Esmeralda?* I notice Cristóbal staring at me—my face must be red. At least he gets why I'm irritable today. I have to calm down. I take a couple of deep breaths. Who am *I* to talk anyway? *I* didn't think much about those things until this morning either. What's *wrong* with me? I'm judging others when I've had my head stuck in the sand as much as anyone else. I think I owe everyone an apology.

Genevieve

Once I get over my embarrassment, I settle into getting to know Cristóbal's new friend—that's why I'm here, after all.

"Genevieve, where in France are you from?"

"A little town just outside of Paris called Croissy-sur-Seine," she replies with a smile that tells me she loves her town. I remember smiling that way when people on Juliette Cove asked me about Valparaíso. "I live there with my parents, my grandfather, and my little brother, Pierre. He's ten."

"Your Spanish is sooo good. How did you learn it?" I ask, impressed.

"Well, my father is Chilean! It's my mamá who's French. They met when Papá was sent to France for his job; he's an architect. My grandfather came to live with us just before the dictatorship. Papá has just accepted a new job here in Valparaíso. Mamá, my brother, and Grandpa are still in France, but they will join us soon. I came early to help Papá find a place for us to live. I can't wait to get to know more about Chile and to get to know all of you." The only word to describe Genevieve is "enchanting." No wonder Cristóbal likes her. Her big green eyes crinkle when she smiles; I think she and I are going to become fast friends.

"What about you, Celeste? Cristóbal tells me you have lived in America!"

Just then, Ernesto arrives with our completos and drinks. I sip my coffee, wondering where to start telling Genevieve my story. . . . There's so much to say. Stories are always longer than you first imagine, like Abuela Frida's colorful knitted scarf that goes on and on and never ends; that's why it's so beautiful. She's been knitting the same scarf since I was a little girl. It could probably wrap around all of Valparaíso by now!

"I live here with my parents, my abuela Frida, and my nana Delfina. My parents are doctors—they own a clinic down by the port where they treat everyone, regardless of their ability to pay." I eye Gloria, who I know doesn't share the same feelings about the poor. "I guess I'm like your grandfather. I had to leave Chile when the dictatorship started. I went to live with my aunt in the United States, in a state way up north called Maine," I tell her.

"What was it like there?" Genevieve asks in a way that tells me she's truly interested in my answer.

"Mostly it was cold," I say with a laugh. "I had never seen so much snow before! I made a few good friends, but I mostly missed my parents and my friends here. I spent nearly all of my time waiting for the mailman to bring me letters. Juliette Cove, the town where I lived, was really small—only about two thousand residents—and really secluded. Plus, people stayed inside for half the year because it was just too cold to go outside! Still, I was glad to spend some time with my aunt."

Genevieve takes a bite of her completo, sighs happily, and then asks hesitantly, "Do you mind me asking . . . Why did your parents not go with you to the United States?"

I blink a few times, wondering how to explain something so complicated. "I don't know, exactly. . . . All I know for sure is that they had to go into hiding at the beginning of the dictatorship, but they were both caught anyway and taken prisoner—" Genevieve gasps.

"They were really lucky, though, because they managed to escape. Now we're all back together." I take a tentative bite of my completo, red with ketchup.

Cristóbal looks at me with understanding eyes and says, "Genevieve, the general . . . you can't even imagine how terrible he was. He was like an evil king. The worst, of course, was how he made people disappear—"

Genevieve cuts in. "By disappear, do you mean . . ."

"Yes, usually murder," Cristóbal fills in, his voice husky, but he quickly recovers. "That was the worst, but he also had lots of insane rules, like forbidding people to laugh and giving everyone curfews. People even had to ask permission if they wanted to have a party! Those of us who stayed in Chile didn't dare complain because we were all afraid the dictator would come after us and make us disappear too."

Gloria is shifting in her seat as though something is stinging her, and I know why. When her father began working for the dictator in the early days of the takeover, she changed; she got mean—to anyone who didn't obediently follow the dictator's rules, as her family did. It's only since I've been back in Chile that she's been a bit more like her old self. I was starting to think she's sorry for how she treated everyone, but I'm still not sure I trust her completely. I've noticed she's become snippy again lately, so I've been inviting her out less and less, and she makes no effort at all to invite me to go anywhere with her group of friends. I guess you can't be friends with *everyone*.

"That must have been awful," says Genevieve, her voice bringing me back to the conversation. I remain quiet—images of Mamá being hurt begin to flood my mind. I shake my head hard.

"It was," Marisol chimes in. "The general—he made

my cousin Lucila and her parents disappear. No one's heard from them in three years." Her voice has gone wobbly.

I put my arm around her and, before I can stop myself, say, "Marisol, somehow we're going to find out what happened to Lucila." And, as I say it, I realize I really mean it. The image of that bride escaping from the clock tower flits through my brain again. Escape . . . She was escaping. My father and my mother, too. They escaped. So, why not others? Why *not*? My cheeks grow hot. Could Lucila have escaped? All of a sudden, I know what I'm supposed to do—I'm supposed to find out what happened to Lucila and the other children from my school who disappeared.

"How will you do that?" Genevieve asks carefully. Marisol has the same question in her eyes.

"I'm not quite sure yet," I admit, "but I'll try to think of something—no, I *will* think of something. Once I do, will you help me?"

"Mais bien sûr," answers Genevieve. "Oops, je m'excuse. I meant, of course I'll help. I'm still getting used to speaking only in Spanish!"

"If anyone can do it, Celeste can," Cristóbal says. "Genevieve, Celeste came up with a plan to find her father after the dictatorship. Then she and I went looking for him and found him."

"That's true, but it was as much your plan as mine. I couldn't have done it without you, Cristóbal," I say, poking his arm affectionately.

"Sacré bleu! Goodness gracious! Where did you find your papá?" asks Genevieve.

"We heard some rumors about where he might be, and with the help of an old man named Oviedo and a crazy Scottish fisherman named Fergus, we were able to find Papá. He'd escaped from the Prisoner Islands and had been living on a ghost ship, *El Caleuche*."

Genevieve looks at Cristóbal and me in awe. "Wait! A ghost ship! Really? Is there such a thing? Weren't you scared?"

As I think about her question, I take my final bite of completo, which, I have to admit, is pretty yummy, even with ketchup. Cristóbal turns to me. "Were you scared, Celeste?"

"I was and I wasn't. . . . When I first met Fergus, I was worried because he only had one good eye—the other was covered with a patch—and he insisted on only sailing when it was foggy. I remember shaking like a leaf as we went out on the rough waves in his tiny boat. I was certain we would flip over. But Fergus kept us right-side-up the entire time. When we reached *El Caleuche* was when I got really scared. It's known as a ghost ship because it appears out of nowhere from the fog like a phantom. They say that not everyone can see it, only those who believe in the time of magic. Anyway, that's exactly what happened; it was suddenly, impossibly, there in front of us, cloaked in fog. If Fergus hadn't been there, I might have died from fright," I admit, shivering all over. I rub my arms. "When I saw Papá, though, all my fear vanished. As we rowed back toward shore, *El Caleuche* once again disappeared into the fog, and to this day, it's never been seen again."

Genevieve's eyes have grown even wider. "Wow! I can't even imagine what that was like . . . And what about your maman?"

Just then Ernesto stops by the table to take our dessert order. I ask for suspiros de monjas, which are "nuns' sighs." I explain to Genevieve that they are delicious baked batter filled with cream and sprinkled with sugar. They have to be cooked at just the right temperature and for just the right amount of time to be crispy on the outside and light as air on the inside. Genevieve immediately says she would like the same.

"I'm sorry, young ladies," Ernesto says in a clipped voice. "We have hot fudge sundaes and banana splits for dessert today."

This time, I don't get worked up, and we order hot fudge sundaes all around. I tell Genevieve that one day I'll take her to Café Iris so she can try all the traditional

Chilean desserts like suspiros de monjas. "And you'll have to come to my house so Nana Delfina can teach us how to make a torta de mil hojas, a thousand-layer cake. I promise it won't take a thousand days to make!"

Gloria interrupts, "Celeste goes to Café Iris nearly every day after school, so you'll have lots of chances to try all of Chile's tasty treats."

"I can't wait!" says Genevieve, happily bouncing up and down a bit in her seat.

I'm glad the conversation has switched from serious matters to desserts, because it gives me a chance to decide how much to tell Genevieve, Marisol, and Gloria about Mamá and the *Esmeralda*. Nana Delfina always says to talk about what bothers you—so I go for it. "Genevieve, you were asking about Mamá," I say. I glance at the others. "Cristóbal knows this, but . . . I just found out Mamá had been held prisoner on another ship, called the *Esmeralda*—it actually arrived in the harbor this morning." Marisol's mouth falls open. Gloria suddenly starts wiping a coffee spill from the table, not looking at me. "Papá only just told me, so before you start asking a million questions, I need to tell you that I don't really have many answers. All I know is that the *Esmeralda* was turned into a prison and torture center during the dictatorship."

"That can't be true! Why, I just saw it this morning!"

Marisol cries out. "I—and so many others!—went down to the dock to greet it like . . . well, like we all used to." Then I see confusion in her eyes. "A prison? A torture center? But why? And why doesn't everyone know about this?! And . . . and it's back in *our harbor*?" Marisol sputters, outraged. Gloria rubs harder at the now nonexistent coffee stain. Cristóbal has hung his head low.

"I don't know, Marisol," I say. "I don't know if people don't know, or if they just don't want to know. Either way, Mamá is still too upset to talk about it." Genevieve squeezes my hand. I give a half shrug. "Anyway, that's my story."

Changes
Afoot

As I arrive home after lunch with my friends, Nana greets me wearing potato peels on her temples. Uh-oh! She only does that when she wants to scare away evil spirits or when she has a headache.

"Don't worry, Niña Celeste. Nothing's wrong. It's just a precaution after the news we heard this morning," she assures me when she sees my startled face. "How was Stephen's? Do you have room for sopaipillas, or are you too full?" she asks as she puts a plate of the delicious fried pumpkin pastries on the table in front of me. I'm still stuffed from Stephen's, but I know I can make room for at least two. . . . I missed them so much when I was in Maine. Nana Delfina always makes them when it rains— the perfect afternoon snack. My mouth is already watering. Just then Abuela Frida shuffles into the room, her eyes bright. "Do I smell sopaipillas, Delfina?" she asks.

"Yes, Abuela Frida. Come and have some with your lemon tea."

The three of us sit at the table, and I tell them about

what happened at the restaurant with the chimichurri sauce and the ketchup. Between bites of sopaipilla, I ask why so many restaurants in Valparaíso are serving American-style food.

"I thought you liked American food, Little Bean," says Abuela Frida, using her pet name for me, which suits me well, as I have always been small for my age, and I've always been skinny like a green bean, even though I eat *all* the time. "And now that the dictator's gone, lots of Americans want to invest in Chile, and that's good for our country."

"But pretty soon all our Chilean restaurants are going to disappear," I say in a voice that I know sounds whiny.

"Well, it's up to us to make sure that doesn't happen," Nana Delfina says decisively.

"Delfina's right, Celeste. We just have to keep buying bread and other things from the locals so they can stay in business. Not everything has to be Americanized if we don't want it to be," Abuela Frida says, taking a sip of her tea with her pinky finger stuck out like a proper lady.

"I'm just glad *you* still make all the traditional dishes, Nana," I say, scarfing down my second sopaipilla. How wonderful it is to be from a country that has a special food just for when it rains.

Up on the
Roof

Once it stops raining and I've had my fill of sopaipillas, I climb up onto the roof with my notebook, thinking about how to *do* something instead of just complaining about how things have changed. An owl that began visiting our house while I was in Maine approaches me cautiously. She spends most of her time on the roof outside my window, where she seems to wait for me. Olivia—that's what I've named her—comes within about two feet of me, fluffs her feathers, and settles in while I write.

Abuela Frida used to sit up here with me, but now she's too frail to climb out the window. Still, I imagine her out here with me sometimes. I'm not outside for ten minutes when she pokes her head out and asks me to come inside. I sit beside her on my bed.

"What else is troubling you besides ketchup, Celeste?" Abuela Frida asks, peering at me. She's always had an uncanny ability to know when something's wrong. Abuela Frida sees things with her heart, not just her eyes.

"Nothing in particular, Abuela. . . . I mean, of course I'm still upset about what Mamá and Papá told us this morning. Mamá . . . what might have happened to her on that ship! And how could something as beautiful as the *Esmeralda* have been used for such terrible things?" As Abuela Frida rubs my back, I have to ask, "Do you know what happened to Mamá while she was there?" Her back stiffens.

"No, Celeste. Your mamá's not ready to tell me yet either. All I can do is be here for her when she is. You must do the same. Her soul is the color of fog right now.

She needs to let herself heal some more before it can shine bright again." And for the first time ever, I wonder what it had been like for *Abuela*—to have her daughter and son-in-law missing, me many countries away, and with that monster in charge. I have been so wrapped up in myself and my own problems that I never stopped to think about how Abuela Frida felt. Now I rub *her* back and feel the tension slowly ease.

In an effort to make my abuela smile, I say, "Nana Delfina was asking me the other day if I thought hope had a color, and that got me thinking about the color of other things. For instance, happiness seems like it would be bright yellow or sky blue, and sadness probably an ugly gray, but I'm not so sure about our souls. What color do you think they are?"

"Well, in Italy, the soul is red because it's filled with passion!" she says with a chuckle. "But I think that, in general, souls are either blue or teal, like the sea . . . light like the breath of God. I also imagine they're brilliant like the sun. I think your soul and mine are the same color, because we're alike in many ways," says Abuela Frida. She pats my cheek, then stands on shaky legs to leave.

Even though I know Abuela is tired and wants to go to bed, I decide to ask one more question, one that's been bothering me for some time now. "Umm, Abuela, are you ever mad at Mamá and Papá for sending me away?"

She turns to me. "No, Celeste! Your parents did what was best for you. I never questioned their decision. And my heart was at peace knowing you, at least, were safe." She pauses and looks at me intently. "Is *that* what's been bothering you these past few months? You have been sort of . . . broody." That word again!

"In part . . . ," I say, glancing down. "That . . . and other things . . ."

"Celeste, querida, I can't tell you not to feel what you're feeling, but I hope you will talk to your parents. I won't say a thing, but *you* should. Talking always helps to cure what ails us. Don't let anger and sadness eat away at you. It will change you into someone you don't recognize and don't like."

More Questions
Than Answers

When Mamá and Papá return from their clinic even later than usual, I run downstairs in my pajamas to greet them. Their faces, which seem tired and drawn when they first walk through the door, light up when they see me. "How was your day?" I ask brightly.

"Celeste Marconi, it's nearly midnight. Why aren't you in bed?" they say in unison. Then they laugh and proceed to tell me all about the people who came to the clinic as they head into the kitchen for a late-night snack.

"Do you remember Señora Legumbres?" Mamá asks.

"The lady who sells vegetables and fruits down by the pier?"

"Exactly. She stopped in for a checkup and brought us the most delicious strawberry preserves and this lovely bread." She waves a slice of what we are currently eating—it *is* delicious! Many of my parents' patients can't afford to pay, so they bring food instead. We end up with lots of wonderful treats, everything from just-laid eggs to corn and potatoes.

Papá proceeds to tell me that one of their patients said the lost mule might belong to someone who lives in one of the neighborhoods at the very top of Butterfly Hill, a certain Señor Martín. Mamá and Papá know him and suggest I go up there with Cristóbal to see if the mule is his. Then I tell them about Don Alejandro and his question about the literacy classes, and about Genevieve, and my completo without chimichurri. I don't bring up what I *most* want to bring up, though . . . at least not yet. But Abuela's advice is weighing heavily.

After a while, Mamá says, "I need to get some sleep." She kisses me and heads toward the stairs that creak even more at night.

"Me too," says Papá, yawning.

"Papá, can I talk to you for a minute?" I ask, keeping my voice low so Mamá won't hear.

My father gives Mamá a little wave. "I'll be up in a bit, Esmeralda."

When we're alone, I dive in. "Papá, I have something important I need to ask you, and I want you to tell me the truth." He looks at me, perplexed. "Even though you've told me many times that you sent me to Juliette Cove because you thought it was the safest thing for me, I still don't understand why you and Mamá didn't just come with me if it was unsafe to be here."

"Ay, Celeste, we have been through this so many

times," says Papá. "I'm not sure what else to tell you."

"I've tried so hard to understand and not to be upset with you and Mamá for abandoning me, but—"

"We didn't *abandon* you, Celeste," he interrupts. "We did what we believed was best for you at the time." He's just repeating the same reason he always gives. So frustrating!

"Well, maybe it *wasn't* what was best for me," I reply. "I never told you this, but I felt like . . . like an orphan. I was scared and alone even though I was with Tía Graciela. It just wasn't the same without you."

"Celeste, you were never alone, even though you might have felt that way. But you're right in that we've never really talked about this the way *you* need to talk about it. So, here's what's important: Mamá and I *had* to stay behind. We needed to help our fellow countrymen in their darkest hour. We couldn't abandon them."

"But you could abandon *me*?" I brush back hot tears. "Why did it have to be you and Mamá who stayed behind? And, and, you never even wrote to me, not *once*!" I feel like a sulky child, but now that I've started, I can't seem to stop. I'm finally asking the questions I haven't dared ask since I returned home.

Papá looks at me thoughtfully.

"Celeste, when I became a doctor, I took something called the Hippocratic oath. Do you know what that is?"

"No, and what does *that* have to do with what I'm asking you?" I ask, becoming more and more frustrated with how this conversation is going.

"Now wait just a minute, young lady," says Papá. "I know you're upset, but don't be disrespectful. Mamá and I have taught you better than that."

"S-sorry, Papá," I say sheepishly. He's right. What's *wrong* with me? "So what is the Hippocratic oath?" Papá nods, accepting my apology.

"It states that a doctor will do no harm and will try to save lives. During the dictatorship, there were many, many lives that needed saving. You already know how people began disappearing. We were terrified that our family would be next. Our jobs as doctors to the poorest of the poor went against the general's philosophies. That's why we sent you away." Papá looks deeply into my eyes, making sure I'm hearing what he's saying. "We, on the other hand, *had* to stay, because of our *own* philosophies, our own sense of duty. It was our civic responsibility, and you should know we managed to help a lot of people in the first year of the dictatorship. It's true that we sent you away, but you must know in your heart of hearts that we never *abandoned* you, Celeste. We would have written you a dozen letters a day, if they could have gotten to you safely."

I hear Papá, but I can't stop myself from saying,

"Maybe I would rather have disappeared with you and Mamá than be sent to a strange country." I regret the words as soon as they leave my lips, but it's true, it's how I felt sometimes! But when Papá's mouth falls open, I try to backtrack. "I . . . I don't mean that, Papá. I'm sorry."

"I would hope not, Celeste. You have *no* idea how horrible and dangerous the fate of the disappeared was. You say you're grown-up and that you want to be a part of things, but you need to start acting more grown-up too. If you really want to know what happened, if you feel ready to know what happened, then ask questions and I will try to answer them for you, but do not judge me or Mamá without knowing the facts." He gives me a hard stare that makes me wince.

I've never seen Papá this mad; I've pushed him too far. Now sadness mixes with my anger, and I don't even know what to say. Papá's watching me, and he must be able to tell I'm about to burst into tears, because he says, "It's okay, m'ija. I get that you're angry. Perhaps you're right. In a sense we *did* abandon you, but sometimes you have to do things you don't want to do in this life. You may not understand that yet, but I hope you will. I just wish you had talked to us before now. In the past when we've told you we did what we did for your own good, you seemed to accept that explanation. We didn't realize you were bottling up all this resentment."

I look into Papá's eyes—eyes that are still clouded with pain.

"Okay. Okay, then. You need to tell me more, Papá. I need to know what happened to you and Mamá."

He puts his hands on my shoulders. "It's a deal. We will tell you more, and we'll work through the bad feelings together. Just please don't hold things inside anymore. You're the most important part of this family." He pulls me in for a hug that's as long as a sunset, then sends me off to bed. When I lie down, I put the conch shell to my ear hoping to hear comforting sounds, but the sea tonight is completely silent.

Curiosity
Calls

The next morning, I make a decision. I'm going to the port to see the *Esmeralda* up close. The ship has dropped anchor and sits like a floating statue in the sea, looking as regal as ever with its blue sails that seem to merge with the sea and the sky.

As I approach the ship, I think about how, while I was worrying about my broken English in Maine, there were people being tortured here. A shiver runs through me. The torturers could have been people my family was friendly with before. We probably greeted them on the streets and plazas. They were normal, regular people until the general arrived and turned them into beasts. Even though the general's men did such horrible things, nothing happened to them. Just look at Gloria's father; he was never punished for his part in the dictatorship.

A group of about twenty women is gathered on the dock. They're wearing white kerchiefs on their heads and carrying photographs and signs. They're chanting, "Where are they? Where are they? We want them back alive!"

I realize with a jolt that they must be the relatives of the people who disappeared. I participated in one of their demonstrations in front of the government building when I first returned from Juliette Cove. Have they been demonstrating *all year*? How did I not know that?

I spot Señorita Alvarado, my former history teacher, with the mothers and grandmothers. She's wearing a bright red coat and spiked heels—easy to pick her out in the throng of people. You see, Señorita Alvarado is as short as I am; if she didn't wear her famous heels, no one would be able to see her.

Cristóbal told me that Señorita Alvarado did what she could to keep the children at Juana Ross School safe when our principal, Señor Castellanos, escaped to Spain during the dictatorship, but I've never actually asked her what things were like back then. Come to think of it, I never even asked Cristóbal what things were like back then. How could I have never asked?

When my teacher sees me, she waves me over. "Celeste, what are you doing here?"

"I wanted to see the *Esmeralda*," I reply. "I . . . I . . . My parents just told me that the ship . . . well . . . that Mamá was a prisoner there. I mean, I've seen it my whole life, but . . . I wanted to see it up close now . . . now that it's back." I look questioningly at her. "I thought it would look different, but it looks the same as always.

How can it look like nothing happened there?!"

She inhales sharply. "Oh, Celeste, I didn't know about your mamá. What a miracle that she escaped! Most people . . . didn't."

I look around, taking in the signs that say THEY TORTURED PEOPLE ON THIS SHIP! and my insides turn to mush.

"Señorita Alvarado," I begin tentatively, "what *did* happen on the *Esmeralda*? I thought people were just questioned and maybe beaten, but Cristóbal, he thinks the people who disappeared were . . . murdered."

"Ay, Celeste, no one knows for certain. During the

dictatorship no one knew *anything* for certain. Only the general claimed to know everything. . . . But—the truth is, interrogation usually involves some kind of physical or psychological torture." Her face grows so sorrowful.

The images in my mind go quickly from bad to worse, and I can hear Mamá screaming in pain, crying out for faceless men to "Stop!" I go weak in the knees.

Señorita Alvarado notices and grasps my arm. "Come, Celeste. Let me buy you a hot chocolate and we can talk more, if you like." As she leads me away from the women and the ship, I turn for one more look. Off to the side, I notice a teenager, older than me, but not by much. I've seen him down by the dock before, staring out at the sea, always alone. I don't know who he is, but there's something oddly familiar about him. I wonder what he's thinking as he stares at the *Esmeralda*. On his face, I see sadness. Was *his* mamá on that ship as well? Is he imagining the same horrible things I am?

A Moment of
Truth

In the café—a small shop with only a dozen tables with red gingham tablecloths—I cradle a cup of hot chocolate between my hands, trying to erase the chill I've felt since I saw the ship. I can still see the *Esmeralda* through the window. Señorita Alvarado notices my gaze and says, "I can't tell you much about the *Esmeralda*, but I have an idea of some of the things that might have happened there. . . ." She pauses, swallows, then adds, "Because I too was sent to one of the dictator's prisons."

I nearly knock over my cup. "What?—You were?—Why?" I stammer. Cristóbal and Marisol never told me about this! Señorita Alvarado never told me. Did they not want to upset me? Did they not think I could take it? They may have been right.

"Well, some people, like your parents, angered the dictator because they always helped the poor and cared about human rights. Others, like me, angered him because we believe in education and ideas. It's said that the only things the general ever read were the fan letters people sent him." She scoffs and takes a sip of her coffee.

This doesn't surprise me, given all the books he banned or had burned.

Señorita Alvarado continues. "It was as if he hated anything good, anything beautiful. He loathed poets like Pablo Neruda and Gabriela Mistral. . . ."

"How . . . How did you survive?" I ask, steering her back to what I am most anxious to know.

My teacher hesitates, as if trying to determine whether she should continue. Then she gives a quick nod. "I'll start at the beginning. Do you remember how the general sent soldiers to our school—to all the schools in Chile—so they could monitor what we were teaching?"

I nod. "I do. It was pretty scary."

"Well, after you left, the situation got much worse. One day, late in the dictatorship, I made the mistake of quoting some of Señor Neruda's poetry. . . . Two children had been taken from the school that very morning, and I was desperate to bring some happiness to the other students. 'Today we are going to read "Ode to the Storm" and "Ode to Conger Chowder,"' I told them. No sooner had we started than a soldier stormed into the classroom, demanding, 'What are you reading?' My voice went wobbly when I told him. Red splotches appeared on his neck and crept up his face. He was practically spitting with anger. And I'll never ever forget what he said next: 'You have disobeyed the general's direct orders, and for that you will be punished! You know very well that Neruda is a subversive.'" My teacher takes a deep breath.

"But . . . but I don't remember anything subversive about 'Ode to Conger Chowder,'" I say, confused.

"Oh, it had nothing to do with the poems, Celeste. Poems are like food for our souls. It was about Señor Neruda's political opinions and how he felt about the dictator. Anyone who disagreed with him was considered dangerous and was silenced in one way or another. And because Señor Neruda wrote those poems, they too were considered dangerous." My teacher takes another sip of her coffee, and I wait patiently for her to continue.

"I was nervous all day, trying not to let the students notice. Then, as soon as the school day ended, two soldiers stopped me as I was about to leave the building and took me to the women's prison, the one over on Cárcel Hill. The minute I stepped foot inside that horrible place, I decided to stop speaking. Of course, my silence infuriated the guards, who continually interrogated me to find out if I knew *other* subversives who were enemies of the general. Some women in that prison would give up names of people just to make the torture stop, but I somehow managed never to say a word."

"Couldn't you have made up some names so that

they wouldn't hurt you?" I ask, thinking I've come up with a great solution.

"I thought about that, but . . . what if a name I made up really belonged to someone and the soldiers went after that person? I couldn't live with that possibility. Also, it was my only way to upset the guards, to not give them what they wanted . . . even if it meant they would hurt me. I realized that silence was my only weapon."

I look in awe at my teacher. "But didn't they punish you for that?"

"Yes, they did. . . ." She frowns. "Do you really want to hear this?"

"I do. I have to, señorita. I need to understand what happened, so I need to *know* what happened," I reply.

She looks out the window for such a long time, I think she's decided not to tell me any more. Finally she says, "Okay . . . okay," as though trying to reassure herself. "Well, one time, as a punishment, they stood me up against one of the walls and began to spray me with a fireman's hose. I kept choking on the water, and by the time the session was over, my body was black and blue from the force of the water. That was just one of their methods to try to get us women to speak. Then there were the electric shocks. . . ."

I have shrunk back in my seat, nausea creeping up my throat. I press a hand to my mouth to keep myself from gagging. Did the same things happen to Mamá? "That's so . . . awful! You must have been so scared," I finally manage to blurt out.

"I was terrified, Celeste, but I tried not to show it. I just kept thinking about all the things I love in this world, and that helped me survive."

"Señorita, I don't even know what to say! How long were you there?" I ask.

"Three months and eleven days. I was only released when the dictator died. I remember every single day. It was as though time stood still." She looks back out the window. When she speaks again, she says, "Can you believe someone can be tortured simply for reading a poem out loud?" She pauses and lifts her cup, then lowers it again, her hand trembling. "I don't know what happened to your mamá on the *Esmeralda*, Celeste, but I feel she and the other women and children who were held there must have gone through equally dark days."

My jaw drops. "Wait! Children? *Children* were kept on the *Esmeralda*?"

My teacher's face goes hard. "Yes, even children. If the general's men thought the children had information about their parents or other family members or friends, then they . . . underwent the same treatment."

I swallow hard. . . . Lucila . . . Was Lucila interrogated by big, scary men wearing black boots and dark glasses to hide who they were? I blink back angry tears and notice that Señorita Alvarado is doing the same.

After a long while, I ask my teacher in an unsteady voice, "Señorita, do you know what happened to the disappeared children from Juana Ross? Did some of them go into exile, like I did, or . . ."

"I honestly don't know. . . . Nobody does for sure. That's why these demonstrations take place." She gestures in the direction of the crowd on the dock. "But I believe President Espinoza is trying to find answers. She's organized something called a Truth Commission, and those people are investigating the crimes committed during the dictatorship. They want to make sure people know what really happened. That's why these women demonstrate. Perhaps some of their children or grandchildren are still out there somewhere, too scared to return home, even after all this time."

"So, there might be a chance . . . of finding people?" I hardly dare to say it, but then I do, a flicker of hope in my voice: "Do you think Lucila might still be out there somewhere?"

She must have heard that flicker, because she quickly answers, "Celeste, I don't want you to get your hopes up . . . but there actually *have* been stories in the news lately of a few people who went into hiding and who have only just begun to dare to return home."

"But the general's been dead for a year now—he can't hurt anyone anymore!"

"That's true, but fear is a very powerful emotion. Even now, I wake up in the mornings afraid someone will come for me, afraid someone in combat boots carrying a machine gun will knock at my door and drag me away. Fear still lurks everywhere, and people can't help thinking that if one dictator was able to come to power, another might be waiting right around the corner to take his place."

"You don't think that's going to happen, do you?" I ask, alarmed.

"No, but I understand why some people might think that way. Just like there are people—some people—who *liked* living under a dictatorship."

An image of Gloria fills my mind. "But why?"

"Well, dictators are good at making up stories. They make people believe that everything they're doing is good and right. They're also very good at hiding their bad acts and at convincing people that the so-called disappeared must have disappeared because they did something wrong and deserved to go away. Did you know that many of the general's supporters don't even *believe* that anyone disappeared during the dictatorship?" She shakes her head.

"But how's that possible?" I ask angrily. "It's so obvious—they're *gone!*"

"And that's why it's up to us to speak out about what really happened here."

I look out at the women once more and decide at that moment that I am going to join them; I'm going to do my part to help Chileans remember.

"Señorita Alvarado, can we go back out to the demonstration?"

"I think that's a fabulous idea," she replies, and we return to the group with renewed resolve. "You should talk to Principal Cisneros if you want to know more about the children who disappeared from Juana Ross. Perhaps you and your friends can do something to remember them."

"Now, *that's* a fabulous idea," I reply, already thinking about having a conversation with Principal Cisneros. He'd become principal after Principal Castellanos went into exile. Then I join the group chanting, "Where are they? What have you done with them? We want them back alive!"

PART 2
A Plan in the Making

No More
Moping Around

The next morning, after spending time talking to the mule and feeding her carrots and mashed potatoes, I have a big idea, probably a crazy idea, that I want to run by Cristóbal. He's my reality check. I head to his mother's flower stand. Señora Williams tells me he left home at the crack of dawn to go to Café Iris. When I arrive at the café, I find Cristóbal practicing magic with el mago, our resident magician, illusionist, and clown. Cristóbal has always been a fan of mysterious things, like the pendulum he used to carry with him to see the future. With that pendulum, he helped me find Papá after the dictatorship. These days, he focuses more on pulling bunnies out of hats, sawing people in half, and making things disappear, only to make them reappear again in the blink of an eye.

"Cristóbal," I say. "I need your help!"

My friend stuffs a seemingly endless multicolored silk scarf into his pocket and comes over to me. "You got it!" Ah, Cristóbal. He doesn't even ask me what it is I need him to do; he just says yes. What a great friend.

"When I was feeding the mule just now, I had an epiphany!" I say. Cristóbal grins at me. He's used to my epiphanies and wild ideas. "I realized that all I've been doing the last few months is moping around complaining about silly things like ketchup and rude waiters, when there are really important things to be thinking about, like what we found out about the *Esmeralda*." Cristóbal is nodding in agreement. "I mean, I've done squat this summer! After you and I got the traveling library going, I completely dropped the ball on the literacy project. So— I'm hoping—will you help me get it started?" And, before Cristóbal can answer, I keep going—I'm on a roll. "I also want to do something to help remember our classmates who disappeared, like the women on the docks do! I was there with them yesterday and, and . . . don't think I'm crazy, but—I want to find Lucila . . . if she's still alive, because she *could* still be alive! There's a *chance*, right? No one's said she isn't!" I say all this in one whoosh so there's no way I can back out.

Cristóbal is staring at me as if I've lost my mind. "That's huge, Celeste!" But then he taps the table with his wand. "Tell me more about what you're thinking," he says, interested—I can tell.

"I don't exactly have a plan yet. . . . But yesterday I was so inspired by the mothers and grandmothers. *They* are doing something! What about all the other people we know who are still missing? What about Javiera? Wasn't that the name of old-man Oviedo's daughter-in-law? She was *pregnant*! What happened to her, and her baby? And there are so many others just from our school! If there's even a chance, shouldn't we try? So other families can be as happy as I was when my parents came home?"

Cristóbal nods thoughtfully. "Let's pick up Genevieve, and we can start coming up with a plan."

"Sounds great! Remember we've got to take the mule back to her owner first, though. We promised my parents."

Awakenings

When Genevieve sees the mule, she coos, "Aren't you a cutie?" and begins scratching the animal's ears. "Who does she belong to?"

"Someone called Señor Martín. One of my parents' patients said he has been looking for a mule, so it must be him. He lives at the top of this hill."

"Allons-y! Let's go!" Genevieve says.

We tie a rope around the mule's neck, and as we lead her up the hill, Cristóbal and I explain how Valparaíso is divided into two distinct parts: the poor part, which we're approaching now, and the rest of the city.

"There was a fire up here recently," I say as we begin to see debris in the road—pieces of burned wood and lots of ash. Fires are a common occurrence in these neighborhoods. People can't afford to pay their electric bills, so they all use one electric cord for everything, and it gets overheated and starts a fire. And there have also been stories of people setting fire to the garbage, just to be nasty to the people who live here. It's not until we get to the very top of the hill—about twenty minutes later—that we see the extent of the damage caused by this particular fire. Some houses have been burned to the ground; others are barely standing.

"Where is everyone?" asks Genevieve, moving a little closer to Cristóbal.

"I don't know. Maybe at work?" I guess.

"We have to do something to help," says Cristóbal, horrified.

As I look around, I nod my head in agreement. "How could we not have known how bad this was, Cristóbal?" I ask, embarrassed at my ignorance, and upset that my parents didn't fill me in more. They come up here all the time to tend to patients who are too sick or old to make their way down to the clinic. *I*, on the other hand, have never even *been* to this part of my hill. And I live so close!

We walk a few hundred yards up the road, seeing bits and pieces of people's lives: soot-covered and singed clothing in heaps waiting to be taken to the dump; old chairs and tables with legs burned off; children's toys, melted and broken. . . . Suddenly the mule stops short in front of what used to be a house, bobs her head up and down, and says "Hee-haw!" A heartbeat later, we hear someone calling in a hoarse voice, "Milui, is that you?" We turn to see an old man hobbling toward us. The mule pulls at the rope and trots over to him, presenting him with her muzzle. "There you are, my sweet Milui. I thought I'd lost you," the old man croons. "Niños, thank you for returning my Milui. Where did you find her?"

"She showed up outside my house a couple of days ago. Are you Señor Martín?" I ask.

"I am. But—forgive me—how do you know me?"

"I don't, but my parents do. One of their patients told them they thought this mule belonged to you."

"Ah! Are you the daughter of the Marconi doctors?"

"I am. I'm Celeste, and these are my friends Cristóbal and Genevieve. It's very nice to meet you. When did you lose Milui?"

"It was last week, during the fire. I've been trying to find her ever since. I went to the place by the beach where she goes with me to sell the wooden carvings I make for the tourists. I also asked around, but . . ."

"Oh, you should have put up signs! Then we would have been able to bring her back sooner," I say.

Señor Martín turns his attention to patting Milui's rump, then says, "It's not so easy. I don't know how to write." Darn. Why do I always put my foot in my mouth? I shouldn't just assume everyone knows how to read and write.

"Was this your house?" Cristóbal asks, changing the

subject and pointing to the skeletal remains behind us.

"It was," he says sadly. "But luckily, my neighbor's place didn't burn; he's letting me stay there until I can rebuild." He pauses for a minute and shakes his head. "Unfortunately, all the materials I use to make my crafts—the wood, the tools—were destroyed, so I can't get back to work right away. And now I also don't really have a place to keep Milui. . . . The small shelter I built for her was also lost in the fire."

Before I can even think it through, out of my mouth comes, "Would you consider letting us look after Milui for you until you get back on your feet? She can stay in my garden. There's plenty of food for her there."

The old man blinks at me. "You'd do that for me?" I nod enthusiastically.

Señor Martín scratches Milui's snout, and she nuzzles his arm. "Now, now, Milui, you go with these young people. I know they'll bring you to see me when they next come up Butterfly Hill," he tells her. I swear I see something pass between owner and animal—a moment of understanding and affection—and Milui turns back to Cristóbal, Genevieve, and me.

"We will, Señor Martín. We'll take really good care of her," I assure him.

"I know you will," he says. Milui lets out one loud bray, and lets us lead her away.

A Spark of an Idea

We are deep in thought about what we've just seen when, all of a sudden, Cristóbal says, "Did you hear what Señor Martín said about not being able to write?" Genevieve and I nod. "Well, what if you start your literacy program at the top of Butterfly Hill, Celeste? Señor Martín probably isn't the only person up there who might need help."

I only have to think for a moment before saying, "That's a great idea, Cristóbal, but how would we get people involved?"

"Perhaps Señor Martín would be willing to spread the word. And didn't you say that Don Alejandro wants to learn? Perhaps they can be our first two pupils."

"I hadn't thought of starting with grown-ups," I muse. Although, interestingly, the first person I ever taught to read and write was, in fact, Nana Delfina.

"It wouldn't be too hard to start something," chimes in Genevieve. "Marisol told me the other day that she wants to be a teacher. Perhaps she could help us? N'est-ce pas? Don't you think?"

"Great!" I say. "You guys are brilliant!"

As we approach my house, Nana Delfina comes out to greet us.

"Didn't you find her owner?" she asks, wiping flour from her hands onto her apron and looking at the mule with affection.

"We did! Her name's Milui," I say, and we fill her in on Señor Martín and our budding plan for the literacy program.

"If you get it started, I will provide snacks for your classes," she says. "Let Nana know how she can help."

"Thanks, Nana! Is Abuela Frida awake? I have something I want to ask her," I say as another idea flits into my mind.

"She is. Come in, niños."

We leave Milui in the garden under the big shade tree, tell her she's a good girl, and head inside. Then, to my surprise, Olivia the owl flies down from the roof and perches on the mule's head! Milui acts as if owls are always landing on her head. We all laugh, and the two of them stay there in companionable silence for the rest of the afternoon.

Abuela **Frida's**
Secret Books

Abuela Frida has hair the color of the moon, with silvery rays of sunshine thrown in, as well as shimmers of violet. She's also as light as a feather. Sometimes it seems as though she floats around the house, always carrying her giant magnifying glass with its beautiful blue handle and frame made of lapis lazuli, looking at things that interest her. "You have to look at things closely, Celeste, and appreciate them for what they are," she likes to remind me as she glides around the house spying a speck of sand on the stairs or an errant firefly.

Abuela Frida is also the smallest person I know. Sometimes when I feel like teasing her, I say, "Abuela Frida, you're so tiny, you could make friends with the ants!" We giggle at the image of her greeting the ants and inviting them to tea. She may be small, but she has a courageous and feisty spirit. After all, she saved hundreds of books from the general's bonfires, even though she, too, would have disappeared had the general found out.

When Cristóbal, Genevieve, and I enter my grandmother's room, we find her knitting the same blue and silver scarf as always, which is now so long that it snakes out of her bedroom and all the way down the stairs like a magic carpet. The knitting needles are almost as big as she is, and she's working them at amazing speed!

"Abuela, we've figured out a way to start our reading and writing program, but we're gonna need your help," I announce, sitting beside her on the bed. Genevieve and Cristóbal look at each other, perplexed—they don't know what I'm about to ask. "Would you let us use the books you still have under the stairs to help with our lessons? We're gonna start at the top of Butterfly Hill."

Abuela sets down her needles. "I think that's a fine idea," she says. "Come with me." And she floats toward her hiding place with the three of us in tow. To my happy surprise, there are more books than I remembered hidden behind an assortment of brooms.

As we pick up one book and then another, Abuela Frida says, "Celeste, did I ever tell you about how the dictator would walk around day and night wearing dark glasses?"

"No, but, come to think of it, in every photograph I've ever seen of him, he's wearing sunglasses. How come?" I ask.

"Well, I don't think it had anything to do with the

weather. He just didn't want us to see his eyes, because our eyes always tell the truth. The general's eyes would have shone with hatred and fear."

"Fear?" asks Cristóbal, confused. "Why would the general be afraid? He had all the power."

"He did, but he was also afraid. Afraid of ideas that

weren't like his own. You see, ideas are powerful, niños. They allow you to be free, and dictators don't want people to be free."

"From everything I've learned so far, the general seems like a monster. Did you ever meet him, señora?" asks Genevieve.

"Call me 'Abuela Frida,' child. Everyone does," says my grandmother with a kind smile. "No! Had he come to my front door, I would have hidden in my knitting basket." The impish smile comes back to her lips as she adds, "I'm almost small enough to fit these days."

"Weren't you afraid of getting caught for hiding these books?" Cristóbal asks.

"Of course, but I couldn't just do nothing. Hiding these books was my small way of rebelling against the dictator, of saving ideas." She raises her eyebrows and adds, "It felt good to do something . . . sneaky."

"Did soldiers actually come here looking for books?" asks Genevieve, and I can tell she's blown away by the idea of having to hide books.

"Yes, they had a habit of dropping by unannounced. They would ask if we had any 'dangerous' books in our possession. The first time they came, Nana Delfina told them she didn't know how to read, which satisfied them. However, they always managed to find some books on their rounds that they would burn in their giant bonfires on the plazas. It was awful to see all those books going up in smoke," she says, holding a hand over her heart. "It made me sad—those soldiers, some of them so young, did not appreciate the value of our national literature. They were like robots. When things got scary here, I knew I could always retreat to these books to feel safe. Delfina and I spent many a night reading together in this little room." Her violet eyes remain fixed on her treasures.

I pick up a worn copy of *Don Quixote* that I hadn't noticed before. "Do you remember who dropped this book off, Abuela?"

"I do. I had only just begun to spread the word that I was willing to hide books, when early one morning a very old man struggled up the front steps of our house to give this one to me. It was wrapped in an elegant blue silk scarf. As he handed it to me, he said, 'Señora Frida, please don't let them burn this book. It has taught me everything I need to know about how to dream. It must be saved.' And with that, he ambled off. I never saw him again." She stares toward the front door for a moment as though hoping the old man might walk through it this very moment.

"What about this one?" asks Genevieve. "I love its velvet cover. It makes me think of a forest." She turns the book over and strokes it.

"Ah! Now, that one has quite a story. A lady came by one day wearing glasses with lenses so thick, they made her eyes look like saucers. She handed me a straw-berry cake and said, 'Here's a small treat for you and your family.' Then, she turned and left. When I cut into the cake, this book was hidden inside wrapped in plastic! People came up with ingenious ways to hide their favorite books."

"Have many people come back to claim them?" Cristóbal asks.

Abuela Frida's eyes go distant. "No. . . . No more than a dozen. I don't think the others will ever return. . . . They either went into exile and don't plan on coming back, or they are among the disappeared. After all, people with the most 'dangerous' books are probably the ones the general wanted to silence. If the owners ever do return, though, we will know that their books are either in the traveling library or up on the top of Butterfly Hill. . . . Now it's time for my snifter of limoncello." Then she whispers to us conspiratorially, "Don't tell anyone, but I have a bottle stashed under my bed!" And she begins to giggle like a schoolgirl.

A **Bull** in a
China Shop

When Papá and Mamá arrive home from work, I meet them at the door. Without even giving them a chance to take off their shoes, I start in. "Cristóbal, Genevieve, and I found Señor Martín today. You were right. . . . The mule—she's called Milui—*is* his. But he's letting us keep her until he can rebuild his house. So many houses up there were destroyed by that fire! It's a disaster!"

"Hello to you, too, Celeste," Papá says, laughing.

"Sorry! It's just . . . I was super upset by what I saw on the hill. It's like the mudslide all over again! You helped those people rebuild. Can't you help again?"

Mamá sits on the couch, takes off her shoes, and rubs her feet. "We *have* started to do something, hija—"

"What? Why didn't you let me know? I could've helped!" I say without letting her finish.

"Calm down, Celeste," says Papá. "We've only just begun to put a plan together. You *can* help us. We simply haven't had time to do anything yet."

"Oh . . . okay," I say. "Well, let me tell you what else

Cristóbal, Genevieve, and I decided today. We're going to start our reading and writing classes at the top of Butterfly Hill. We found out that Señor Martín doesn't know how to read and write, and probably there are others who would like to learn. We'll use Milui to take some of Abuela Frida's books up the hill. We'll start by reading to people, and then we'll teach them their ABCs, just like I taught Nana Delfina." I announce all of this proudly, not even giving my parents a chance to tell me about their own plans. "I was hoping we might be able to build some kind of an outdoor school, perhaps a tent like the ones they put up at weddings?"

"That's all good, Celeste—it really is—but we need to think first about what those people need immediately: housing and fresh drinking water. We learned today that their water supply has been temporarily cut off and there's no electricity—"

"Don't you like my idea?" I interrupt Papá.

"Celeste, listen to yourself!" Mamá says. "It's not about you and your ideas; it's about helping the people at the top of Butterfly Hill! Try to be a little more sensitive to other people's problems!" She leaves the room in a huff and heads upstairs.

I feel like Mamá has slapped me. "But, Papá! I *do* want to help those people. That's *why* I wanted to do the literacy classes in the first place!" I exclaim indignantly.

"I know, hija, but sometimes you're a bit like a bull in a china shop. You make assumptions before thinking things through. Why would you automatically think Mamá and I hadn't done anything to help the people on Butterfly Hill? And then, why did you automatically assume we had excluded you? It's like we can't win with you these days! Didn't what we told you about Mamá and the *Esmeralda* make a difference in the way you've been thinking about her? About us?" he asks, a note of hurt in his voice.

I stop in my tracks. Do I really do that? Do I speak without thinking? *Am* I selfish? I don't want to hurt my parents. I slowly turn back to Papá. He looks exhausted. "Papá? I'm . . . I'm sorry," I say timidly. "I don't mean to be insensitive. . . . I guess I get excited and speak before thinking sometimes. I love you and Mamá. Please don't be upset with me."

"It's okay, Celeste. Just promise me you will try harder to give us the benefit of the doubt."

"I will," I say, my head hung low.

"Look, let's start from scratch," Papá says. "I think the tent and the lessons are excellent ideas. Mamá and I will help with both. In turn, we would like *you* to help *us* gather supplies so we can begin to put our own plan into effect. Just today, we began asking our patients to bring whatever supplies they could spare to help us rebuild the

83

damaged houses. We're asking for bricks, wood, nails, hammers, cement, but also clothing, food, and blankets. A group of our medical students and some fellow doctors have agreed to help. Mamá and I were hoping people from your school might as well."

"Okay," I say, getting excited again. "I can get people to help, and I will ask Cristóbal, Marisol, and Genevieve to go with me to ask local businesses to donate supplies too, if that's okay."

"That'd be terrific, Celeste. Now let's get some sleep. There's a lot of work to be done in the next few weeks."

"Good night, Papá."

"Good night, Celeste of my soul."

All Is Forgiven

"Sorry about last night, Mamá," I say as I enter the kitchen early the next morning.

"It's okay, Celeste. I'm sorry too. I was tired. I shouldn't have snapped at you."

"No, you were right. I was being a brat," I say, smiling.

"Well . . . you *were* being a bit of a brat," she replies, laughing, and I know instantly that everything's okay between us. She bites into a slice of bread slathered with strawberry jam and says, "Papá tells me you're going to help us get donations for the houses damaged in the fire."

"Yes. I'm on my way now to pick up Cristóbal, Marisol, and Genevieve. We'll try to visit a dozen or so businesses today."

"I like that idea, hija. Nana Delfina has agreed to organize everything, so tell anyone who wants to donate to drop supplies here at the house. You could also spread the word that we'll need volunteers on Saturday to transport things. . . ." She looks at me thoughtfully. "Papá and

I also think we should take the first round of books up the hill on Saturday, and we can begin to build a shelter where you can hold your literacy classes."

"Really? Thank you, Mamá. That would be great. I love you." I hug her tight.

"I love you more, my darling, bratty Celeste."

Painful
Truths

Cristóbal and Genevieve offer to talk to business owners on Happiness Hill and Concepción Hill, which sit right next to each other, while Marisol and I take Butterfly Hill and Barón Hill.

Marisol and I go into Pan de Magia first. It's everyone's favorite bakery on Butterfly Hill. My family has been coming here ever since Abuela Frida and Abuelo José arrived in Valparaíso some forty years ago. At the counter, one of the sisters who owns the place is putting a loaf of bread into a bag for a customer. The smell in here is amazing because they bake bread all day long. My mouth is watering. When I explain our request, Señora Harina agrees immediately. "Of course, Celeste. We had already been thinking about what we could do. A dozen loaves a day until people can get back on their feet—how does that sound? When do you want to start collecting? We would bring them ourselves, but we have to stay here to run the bakery."

"Thank you! We can start on Saturday and then

come by every morning until school starts up again. We really appreciate your help."

"You're welcome, niñas." She wipes her floury hands on her apron and hands us each a cheese empanada. Yum! Marisol and I leave the bakery munching on our treats and floating on air. *This is going to be a breeze*, I think.

However, at the next place, we receive a very different response. It's a hardware store that opened shortly after the end of the dictatorship. I've never been in here before. When we make our request, the owner's face grows red and angry, and with spittle flying from his mouth, he says, "Get out of here! I'm not helping *those* people. They need to help themselves!" Then he runs us out of the shop, slamming the door behind us! Marisol and I look at each other, stunned. That man was so hateful and mean! Why wouldn't he want to help? I loop my arm through Marisol's and we walk in silence, rather than float, to our next stop, Café Iris.

When we enter, I ask Miguel, one of the waiters, if we can speak to Señora Colibrí. My family has known the owner for many years, and I hope we'll get a better reaction from her than we did from the ugly man whose shop we just left.

A few minutes later, Miguel returns with Señora Colibrí, a plump woman of about sixty with rosy cheeks and a kind smile. Marisol and I are still reeling from our encounter with the hardware store man. "Celeste Marconi and Marisol López, how lovely to see you. Would you like to order something?" she asks. I'm already stuffed from my two breakfasts!

"Maybe later, señora. . . . We're here for something else . . . ," I say tentatively.

"Well, tell me what I can do for you." When I hesitate, she says, "You're not usually this shy, Celeste. Speak up!"

"It's just that . . . we had a scary encounter just now with the man who owns the hardware store. We went there asking for donations and volunteers to help the victims of last week's fire up on Butterfly Hill, and he literally chased us away," I say, the words tumbling from my lips. "He was *really* mad."

Señora Colibrí purses her lips. "Ay, niñas, I'm sorry that happened. Some people . . . well, they think the poor people of Chile are just lazy. The general thought the same way. That's why he tried to make them all disappear. It's actually a miracle that neighborhoods like that one managed to survive. President Espinoza has been trying to get them more aid since she took office, but change can be slow." Marisol and I nod.

"Now, don't fret about Señor Ferretero. He's just an old grump who needs to catch up with the times. *I* will definitely help you. What do you need?"

Relieved, Marisol blows out the breath she's been holding as Señora Colibrí, tapping her finger against the side of her head, cries out, "I have an idea! Why don't I buy nails, hammers, and wood? I'll buy them from Señor Ferretero, but I won't tell him what the supplies are for. That way, we can make him help the effort without him even realizing it." She grins devilishly. We grin back. Señor Ferretero will be no match for Señora Colibrí!

The **Trek up**
Butterfly Hill

It's Saturday morning. I look out the window, then look again. Though it's still early, there must be thirty people standing outside my house! I blink hard—I can't believe it! Have they all come to help rebuild houses? Yes, it must be! I can see Cristóbal, Marisol, Genevieve, Señorita Alvarado, Señor Castellanos, six of Papá's medical students, so many people, even that teenage boy I saw down by the dock the other day.

Nana Delfina gave Milui an extra large serving of oats this morning so she would be ready for the work ahead. After strapping two baskets onto her back, my friends and I fill one with picture books and the other with hammers and nails. The boy from the dock wanders over and checks the straps on Milui's baskets, then gives her ears a scratch. As he steps back, he looks at me and smiles. I'm suddenly overcome with julepe, that feeling of excitement and nervousness all rolled into one. I'm paralyzed. He probably thinks I'm a complete dork! "Thanks," I finally say, but he's already moved on to help with something else.

I must have a strange look on my face because Cristóbal asks if I'm okay.

"Y-yes," I reply.

"She's fine," say Marisol and Genevieve in unison, laughing. Am I *that* obvious?

The medical students are carrying gallon jugs of water. Señor Castellanos—who became my English teacher after he returned from Spain—along with some of the other teachers from my school and the entire soccer team from a local high school, are carrying about a hundred planks of wood between them. Señorita Alvarado picked up bread from Pan de Magia on her way over. Papá and some of his friends have filled wheelbarrows with bricks and bags of cement. You may wonder why we don't just drive up the hill with these things. Well, first of all, only a few of my parents' friends have cars, and none of them have trucks. Second, the road, such as it is, is impassable by vehicles in some places. By foot is the only way to get to the top right now.

Other people's arms are filled with blankets and baskets of food. Between them, Cristóbal and Genevieve are carrying the canvas tarp that will be used to build the reading tent. Mamá has both her and Papá's medical bags. Nana Delfina and Marisol have a gallon of water in each hand.

I take a couple of the bags of bread from Señorita Alvarado and pick up some blankets. I'm also in charge of guiding Milui, although she probably knows the way better than I do!

Mamá takes the lead and we all start up the hill. It's a cool morning, but by the time we reach the top, everyone's panting and sweating. Well, not everyone. . . . Milui acts as though she could go up and down another ten times. After we catch our breath, we spread out, heading up and down narrow, twisty streets delivering water, food, and blankets. We leave all the wood and bricks in one spot until Papá can find out who most needs their house worked on first.

On one side street, a boy of about eight runs up and begins petting Milui.

"Hi, Milui. Where have you been?" he asks the mule with a smile.

"Oh, you know her?" I ask, and then think, *Duh! Of course he does, Celeste. He just said hello to her!* "What's your name?" I ask.

The boy pushes too-long bangs out of his eyes. "I'm Paco."

"Nice to meet you, Paco. I'm Celeste. Here, would you like some bread? It's nice and fresh. Did your house get damaged in the fire?"

He takes the bread. "Just a little. I live over there with my tía and my cousins. We only lost the back part where our kitchen was." He stuffs a chunk of bread into his mouth and chews. He's ashy with soot, and I wonder when he was last able to wash up, or brush his teeth. I am suddenly embarrassed—I can brush my teeth anytime I want or take a shower. . . .

Paco points to Milui's basket. "Can I have a book, too?"

"Of course! How old are you?" When he tells me—yes, I guessed correctly, eight—I rummage around in the basket and pull out a picture book version of *Platero and I*.

Paco looks at the donkey on the front cover and laughs. "What does it say?" he asks.

"Oh, *Platero and I*. Do you know how to read yet?" I ask.

"No, I've never been to school. I look after my little cousins while my tía goes to work in the city."

I hold back my thoughts from the boy, but I'm instantly steaming. When President Alarcón was still in power, all Chilean children could attend school and there was even day care for working moms. The dictator put a stop to all that. It has taken a long time, but President Espinoza finally got the votes she needed to change the rules back to how they were before. Soon all children will be able to attend school again. But until then . . .

"Hey!" I say. "If you'd like, my friends and I could teach you." Paco looks at me skeptically. "No, really. I'm starting a reading and writing group for anyone who wants to learn." I think on what else could entice him. "Your cousins could come too!" I add quickly. "What do you think?" He nods slowly. "Did you know that the president is going to make sure you all can go to school soon? And so, when you do, you'll already know your

ABCs. Won't that be great?" At last, a smile appears on Paco's face. He's still petting Milui. "If you like Milui, you're gonna love this book, because it's all about a man and his donkey, Platero."

"Gracias, Celeste," he says, and with a final stroke of Milui's soft fur, Paco dashes off to his aunt's house yelling, "Primos, look what I have," waving his book in the air.

Up ahead, Cristóbal and Genevieve are handing out books and food to the dozen or so people who have gathered, curious. My friends have put the canvas down by a magnificent fig tree, ripe with fruit, and we decide it will be the perfect place to put up the tent. Then I see Mamá and Papá re-dressing minor burns on people they must have seen earlier in the week. Señor Martín is helping them. I go over to him, and when he sees Milui, he exclaims, "There's my girl!" to which Milui gives an enormous sneeze. "Salud! Bless you!" says her owner, and he scratches her head.

"Señor Martín, Milui has been a big hit today. Thanks again for letting us borrow her. The children love her," I tell him.

"I know," he says. "Most of them already know her. They used to come to my house and play with her." His face clouds over.

"They'll be able to do that again soon," I assure him. "Papá and his friends are going to rebuild your house and lots of other houses," I say, looking over at my father for confirmation.

"We plan to start this very afternoon, Señor Martín, and we'll come up every weekend until we've finished," my father tells him.

Señor Martín turns to Milui. "Did you hear that, girl? We're going to have a home again! Can you say 'thank you'?" And to our delight, she give us a drawn-out "Hee-haw."

Groups of people are sitting together on the sooty ground. Even though things are pretty bad up here, everyone's smiling. I think again about Chile being a country of good losers. Just then, I glimpse the boy from the dock—he's spreading a tarp over the bags of cement, in case it rains, I imagine. I feel julepe once more. I decide I'm going to say hello to him, but when I try to put one foot in front of the other, I can't move. I stand there trying to convince myself that I can do this, but by the time I'm finally able to move, the boy is no longer there.

The Start
of Something
Beautiful

The next day, Genevieve, Marisol, Milui, and I excitedly head back up the hill with the things we'll need for our first class: a fold-up beach chair for Señor Martín, a few more books, paper and pencils, and a basket of empanadas that Nana Delfina prepared for everyone. Cristóbal has a magic lesson with el mago at Café Iris, so he can't come with us. Genevieve and I are comfortable in jeans, sweatshirts, and sneakers, while Marisol is dressed in sensible shoes, a skirt, and blouse. She's nailed the teacher look!

As we reach the top, Genevieve and Marisol head to where we stacked the books yesterday under the white canvas tarp by the fig tree. Papá promised that the reading tent, along with a couple of shelves, a table, and a few chairs, will be set up soon—some of his buddies have offered to do it.

With Milui in tow, I go to invite Señor Martín to join our first class. I'm struck by how small the house where he's staying is. . . . It's really more of a shack than a house, and I marvel at how everyone fits in there. It's barely the size of my bedroom!

"Celeste, Milui!" Señor Martín exclaims when he comes to the door.

"Ready for your first lesson, Señor Martín?"

He reminds me a bit of old Oviedo. He's got a gray beard and little tufts of gray hair by each ear. His eyes are bright and he has lots and lots of wrinkles. I wonder why he lives alone, and, without thinking, I ask that very question.

"Ah, Celeste. I have no family. My wife died long ago, and my son, Daniel, who lived in the city with his wife, Juana . . . Well, they disappeared." His blue eyes look off to the distance.

"Oh, I'm so sorry, Señor Martín," I say, biting my lip. "Perhaps I shouldn't have asked."

"No, please—I like to talk about Daniel and Juana; it helps me remember them. I was so proud of my son. I made him go to school and then university, because I never could. He became a civil rights lawyer, and Juana . . . beautiful, kind Juana . . . she was a social worker. I was living with them when they were taken."

I can't begin to imagine how hard that must have been for him, but before I can say a word, he continues. "I actually went quite mad after Daniel disappeared. I couldn't work, I couldn't sleep. I . . . I fell apart. I lost my job . . . even my will to live. . . . I just didn't care any-more, and no one cared about me. Then, one day, out of the blue, the man who owns this house approached me—I was sitting alone on a park bench—and he invited me to come here for a meal with his family. He had next to nothing himself, but he shared it . . . with me. I never returned to where I had lived in the city. My friend helped me build my little place here. There's nowhere else I want to be right now." I nod thoughtfully. Everyone seems to have known someone who disappeared, I'm realizing.

"Thanks for telling me, señor. My best friend, Lucila . . . she disappeared as well, and I like to talk about her, too. It . . . it keeps her close in my heart, if that makes sense."

Now Señor Martín nods in understanding. He places a gnarled hand on my shoulder. "Okay, Celeste. Let's start teaching me my letters. I'm not getting any younger!" he says, laughing, and then he has a coughing fit.

"You should let my parents check that cough. It sounds bad," I say, again forgetting my filters and not minding my own business.

"Oh, they're busy with more urgent cases," Señor Martín says, waving the idea away.

"Señor, my parents find a way to help everyone," I say proudly, and realize that, in fact, this is true. Hmmm.

"Well, maybe I will, then. Now, to my lessons!"

We head to the fig tree, where Genevieve and Marisol

are already reading to a small group of children, including Paco and a few new faces.

"Señor Martín, have a seat here," says Marisol, indicating the beach chair. "We were just about to start the alphabet." The old man settles down tentatively next to a girl called Luci. As Marisol pronounces the individual letters, Genevieve points to each one on big pieces of paper where she's drawn them in bright colors.

"Now, can everyone think of a word they know that begins with the letter *A*?" Marisol asks. She's soooo good at this!

"Amor," says Paco.

"Ayuda," says Señor Martín.

"¡Ay!" says Genevieve, melodramatically placing the back of her hand to her forehead, and everyone laughs.

"Only the students, please," says Marisol in a teacherly voice, and everyone laughs again.

Pretty soon, we're singing the alphabet song together. Other people are wandering over to join us.

We end the day's lesson by reading a chapter from *Platero and I*, turning the book to our class to show them the pictures. Paco looks at Señor Martín and says, "This story is like you and Milui."

"Indeed it is!" says Señor Martín. "I can't wait to find out what happens next!"

A Gift from Juliette Cove

A couple of weeks later as I'm returning from a morning of lessons—nearly everyone can write all the letters now!—I see Abuela Frida on the front stoop waiting for me with an airmail envelope in her hand. A letter? Could it be from Tom, my old friend from Juliette Cove?

"Who's it from?" I ask. A shot of julepe jolts through me.

"It's from your tía Graciela," she says, handing me the blue envelope. I'm momentarily disappointed, but then quickly recover. I look at my aunt's bold script. A letter from Tía Graciela is just as good . . . just in a different way. I rip open the envelope, take out the letter, and start to read aloud so Abuela Frida can hear Tía Graciela's news too.

> *Dear Celeste,*
>
> *I'm writing to you on a clear, dark night on Juliette Cove. I'm sitting here by the wood-burning stove where you and I used to spend time together*

waiting for Mr. Carter to arrive with letters from
Chile.

I know you hoped I might return to Chile,
because you worry about me being by myself
with only the silence and the icicles to keep me
company. Well, I wanted to tell you that I've
met a new friend. His name is Charlie Deveny
and he's a fisherman who lives nearby in Perkins
Cove. I met Charlie one day when all the residents
of Juliette Cove and Perkins Cove were holding
a vigil for two of our neighbors who went missing
when their boat was lost in a terrible storm. Even
though Charlie's a man of few words—like most
people who have become accustomed to living in
the solitude of the coves—he's a good man who
likes spending time with me. Of course, no one
keeps me company like you used to, not even the
icicles on the trees!

Anyway, I told Charlie about your literacy
project, and he organized a fundraiser. I'm
enclosing a traveler's check that you should be
able to cash at any bank. We hope this donation
helps. I remember how much you loved to write
the word "solidarity" in your notebook of dreams,
Celeste. With this small gift, we're sending you
some "solidarity" from those of us here on Juliette

Cove and Perkins Cove to those in need on Butterfly Hill.

I'm proud of you and I love you very much. I want you to know that I still dance by the light of the moon, but I no longer dance alone. I hope you will meet Charlie one day soon.

Love,
Tía Graciela

I pull out the check and my eyes go wide. What a wonderful gift! This money will be a big help. I'm so glad Tía Graciela has found someone, but I'm also sad she has decided not to return to Chile. I notice that Abuela Frida's eyes are glistening. She misses her daughter so much. I hug her, and we both imagine Tía Graciela dancing with Charlie under a moonlit sky.

PART 3
A Time of Discoveries

They're **Alive!**

"Celeste," Papá yells from downstairs on a foggy morning in late summer. "Come quickly! There's something you have to see."

I'm still half-asleep when I wander into the kitchen and Papá thrusts the newspaper at me. "Look at this," he says, pointing to a headline on the front page that says WHAT HAPPENED TO THE CHILDREN OF THE DISAPPEARED? Suddenly I'm wide-awake.

"What does it say?" I ask.

"Well, read it. It's an eye-opener!"

I rub my eyes and begin reading.

Everyone assumed that the children of the disappeared met the same fate as their parents, most of whom are thought to have perished. However, this reporter recently learned, thanks to President Espinoza's appeal to all citizens to share any information about the disappeared, that some of the children may have survived.

According to one source, who wishes to remain anonymous, a number of children were rescued from detention centers in and around Valparaíso and were taken to safe locations by soldiers who did not agree with the general's actions. My source knows of one such child who is now living on Chiloé Island. The child does not want to return home because the rest of his family was killed and he has nothing to return to . . .

I blink up at Papá. "Why would they have gone there?"

"Well, it's secluded, and it's also difficult to reach. It would have been easy to hide children there. The people of Chiloé are . . . different, because they live apart from everyone else. The island actually scares a lot of people because it has its own mythology that most don't understand. I'm guessing the general didn't waste his time with Chiloé; he focused his attention on the mainland instead."

As Papá is explaining this, I'm only half listening, because I'm still stuck on *some of the children may have survived*. Señorita Alvarado suggested the same thing.

"Do . . . do you think it's possible Lucila might be there?" I whisper, hardly daring to ask.

"I don't know. I suppose it's possible, but I think it's

unlikely. . . ." I can tell he doesn't want to give me false hope.

"But . . . she *might* be! Right? But if she is . . . if she is, why wouldn't she have contacted someone by now? And why are we only finding out about this now? Who's this 'source' and why have they taken an entire year to speak up? I don't understand why the children weren't sent home right away after they heard the general was dead! And—" The questions tumble out, and Papá can hardly answer one before I ask another.

He finally gets a word in. "We don't know their stories, Celeste. . . . Perhaps, like the child mentioned in the article, their families were killed and they no longer have loved ones to return to. We also don't know what happened to them while they were prisoners. It could be that they were abused and are still too afraid . . . or ashamed . . . to come forward."

I go quiet. I can't bear to think that Lucila—no, I *won't*! Instead I think of Mamá and Papá. What did *they* go through? "Papá, were you . . . hurt?"

This time, Papá doesn't avoid my question. "Oh, Celeste, I suppose someday you should know. Perhaps this is the day." He shifts his jaw back and forth, then says, "When I was a prisoner, I was beaten . . . every day. Had I not escaped, my captors would surely have killed me."

I frown hard, pushing back tears. "Papá, what did they think you did to deserve that? You've never hurt anyone!"

"I know, I know," he says soothingly, but there's a quiver in his voice. "Neither did any of those poor kids who . . ." And he stops, giving me room to figure out the rest for myself. The thought of little kids being beaten sickens me, and I press my hand into my stomach.

"What about babies! Did they . . . ?" I ask hesitantly.

"No. Apparently, the babies and toddlers—they were illegally adopted by the general's men and given new identities," Papá explains.

"So, they don't even know who they really are?" I ask, outrage creeping into my voice.

"No. There's no way they could. . . . The good news is that, according to this reporter, the government has launched an inquiry into the illegal adoptions. Officials are working with family members of the disappeared to see if there's a way to start identifying those children."

I chew on that for a while, nodding, and then ask, "So . . . So, Lucila wouldn't have been adopted?" I don't wait for Papá to answer. "You said before that the children may have been abused or feel *ashamed*. Why would they feel ashamed? Because they were beaten? That doesn't make sense; it wasn't their fault! Was Mamá beaten?" Papá goes quiet for so long that I begin to feel scared. "Papá, tell me!"

Just then, Mamá comes into the kitchen. She looks at our faces and stops in her tracks. "What's going on?"

Papá hands her the paper and says, "We were just talking about Lucila and what might have happened to her and the other children who disappeared . . . which led Celeste to ask about what happened to you."

"Oh . . . ," says Mamá, and I can see she's struggling with what to say. "Are you sure you're ready for the truth, Celeste? It will be hard to hear, and for us to tell, and once you hear it, you can't un-hear it. It will always be with you."

"I'm ready, Mamá," I say. "I need to understand."

"Okay, hija. . . . Well, first of all, I don't know for certain what happened to the children who were on the *Esmeralda* with me, because we were all taken to the . . . ummm . . . the . . . torture rooms separately. I only know what happened to me, but I can assume similar things happened to the others as well. Everyone, regardless of age, was forced to feel pain and indignity. . . ." She stops, holds up her finger, and walks out of the room. I look at Papá, but he only shrugs.

Esmeralda's
Story

Mamá comes back moments later with Abuela Frida and
Nana Delfina; she must have decided it's time for us all to
hear what happened to her. Abuela Frida wears a worried
look on her face. Nana Delfina makes coffee and we sit
around the kitchen table with its aged embroidered table-
cloth that made the trip to Chile from Austria in Abuela's
suitcase so many years ago. The sounds of the ocean
and the pelicans' caws reach our ears through the open
window. It's almost as though the birds have gathered to
hear this story as well.

Mamá clears her throat, and Papá takes her hand,
gives it a squeeze. "Ready, Esmeralda?"

Here's a terrible new thing: now, every time I hear
Mamá's name, I think about that ship. I wish they were
not called the same thing. I need to concentrate on all
the beautiful esmeraldas in the world: my mamá, the
emerald, the vibrant shade of green . . . Mamá pulls her
hair, long and glossy, back away from her face, then nods
and begins.

"After we sent you to Tía Graciela, Celeste, Papá and I hid in a remote area called Retoque, which can only be reached by the road that runs along the coast. We weren't the only ones hiding there, but we never exchanged names with those other people so that, in case we were captured, we would not be able to reveal one another's identities. We stayed in abandoned buildings designed by the architecture students at the University of Valparaíso. We didn't think anyone would ever look for us there. After a while, we began to feel safe. Papá and I would sneak away and visit our patients, wearing heavy disguises so we wouldn't be recognized. One day, however, Papá saw soldiers approaching our hiding place, and we decided to leave . . . separately. We . . . we agreed it was better not to be together, because . . . had they captured and killed us both, you . . ." Mamá can't say the words I know would come next. Tears fill my eyes as I think, in horror, of a life without my parents.

"You see, even though you didn't understand why we sent you away, we were always thinking of you." Mamá takes a sip of her coffee, collecting her thoughts. I blink a few times but stay silent. I need to hear the rest.

"Papá headed south to a place where he had friends who were also doctors and political activists, and I went to stay with our friend María Fernanda, the seamstress, who lived on Concepción Hill. I continued to disguise myself by wearing big glasses and different-colored wigs. The red ones were my favorites." She smiles wanly. "The only possessions I took with me were a few clothes and books. It would have been too dangerous to have photos, letters, or addresses. The most important thing back then was to protect your loved ones, so I took no trace of any of you with me, but I always had you in my heart."

"You mean . . . you were right *here* in Valparaíso?" I cry, swinging around to the others. "Did *you* know?" Abuela Frida and Nana Delfina both shake their heads.

But then Abuela Frida admits, "I knew you were close, hija. I could feel you, but I didn't tell anyone I thought you might be near."

"And I couldn't risk coming to the house," says Mamá. "Except when I was helping patients, I spent my time reading and trying to stay out of sight. It worked well for quite some time, but then one day, the general's men came. . . . They didn't knock; they just kicked down the door and stormed inside. I didn't have time to hide. . . ." Mamá takes a deep breath.

Nana Delfina has taken hold of Abuela Frida's hand, and she's mumbling something under her breath . . . perhaps a prayer?

"I . . . I was so scared," Mamá continues. "I tried to run, but they grabbed me by the hair and yanked me

down to the ground." My hand flies to my mouth. I see tears in Abuela Frida's eyes.

"Do you want me to stop?" Mamá asks.

"N-no. . . . Please keep going," I say shakily.

"Okay, if you're sure . . . At least María Fernanda wasn't home, so they couldn't arrest her, thank goodness. I didn't dare resist when they blindfolded me, but when they took me outside and I heard a car door open, I began to fight—I had always heard that when they took you away, you never came back. The men grabbed me and began spinning me around to make me dizzy. Even though I was wobbly, I still fought back, and that's when they . . . became violent. I must have passed out because the next thing I remember, I was in a moving car, sandwiched between two large men. I could smell coffee, garlic, and cigarettes on their breath. I sank back in the seat and tried to disappear into the darkness, as though I could hide from what was happening."

By now I'm gripping the tablecloth. "But . . . how did they find you? Where did they take you?" I ask in a trembling voice.

Mamá's eyes grow dark. "I never found out who turned me in, but it wasn't unusual for neighbors to tell on neighbors, because everyone was scared . . . terrified, actually, that *they'd* be taken. Some people snitched because they thought the soldiers would leave them alone

115

if they appeared to be supporting the general, while others actually believed in everything the general was doing and openly searched for his supposed enemies. As for where they took me initially, I'm still not sure. . . . You see, time stood still during those hours or days. . . . They never took the blindfold off, so I didn't know when it was day or night. Not being able to see was . . . well, it was terrifying. All I know is that I eventually ended up on the *Esmeralda*, although I didn't realize that was where I was at first. I remember being shoved down some stairs and then being pushed forward. I heard a door close behind me and a key being turned. The voice of a woman came out of the darkness telling me not to be scared. Someone pulled my blindfold off. Once my eyes adjusted to the dim light, I saw that it was one of my patients, Petra Sálazar! I was so relieved to see a familiar face. When she told me where I was, I remember thinking, *The* Esmeralda? *Why?* Then I noticed there were other women in the room. Some I knew; others I didn't. I thought I must have been dreaming."

Mamá pauses, and I say in a soft voice, "You must have been so scared!" It's almost as if I'm hearing some terrible story about someone else, not my mother. It can't be about Mamá!

"I remember that it was cold." She gives a grim smile. "But I didn't understand what cold was until later. Before Señora Sálazar had a chance to warn me about what was going to happen next, the guards came back, put the blindfold back on me, and took me up onto the deck. I could smell urine and blood, but I didn't know where those smells were coming from. . . . I was ordered to take off all my clothes. . . ."

"W-what? . . ."

I notice that Mamá is shivering. "When I shook my head, a guard slapped my face so hard, I saw stars. He was yelling at me to do what he said, or else. I obeyed, and then I was tied to what must have been one of the ship's masts. . . ." Mamá pauses, tipping her head back as if to gain strength from the sun pouring through the kitchen window, then starts again. "I was left out there for . . . I think it was for two days and nights, without food or water. The ocean water spraying up onto the deck was frigid. . . . I still get so cold whenever I think about it. I had only the sun and the moon to keep me company, even though I couldn't see them. I was certain I would die from exposure and starvation. . . . The truth is . . . there were moments I hoped I would."

Now I'm shivering too, even though it's warm in the house. I wonder if this is why Mamá has worn long sleeves ever since she came home—because she's always cold. I never thought to ask. I glance at Abuela Frida and Nana Delfina. My grandmother has grasped Mamá's hand. Nana looks like she's about to get potato peels for us all. We sit in silence until Mamá is ready to continue and we're ready to hear more.

"At last they untied me and took me back belowdecks. Señora Sálazar tried to comfort me. She explained that all new prisoners were given the same treatment when they first arrived, to get them ready for the *real* torture to come." Mamá must anticipate my next question, for she says, "The guards hoped that hunger and fear would force the prisoners to talk."

"But what did they want you to tell them?"

"Mostly they wanted names: names of people who were supposedly the general's enemies. They asked me many times where they could find Papá. I was always honest with them when I told them I didn't know, but they didn't believe me. They would scream at me, call me a liar, and hit me over and over again until I passed out." Now I'm quaking with anger.

"At least once a day, the guards would come and get us one by one to interrogate us. That's when things got even worse. . . ." Mamá eyes me carefully.

"Go on, Mamá. I can take it," I say, sounding so much braver than I'm feeling.

She looks at Papá to see if he thinks she should continue. He gives her a slight nod.

"They . . . they would burn us with cigarettes and spray us with hoses. On a few occasions, when they were especially furious, they shocked us with electricity. Then, sometimes the guards would . . . touch us. There was nothing we could do. . . . Nothing. . . . I would just remain silent and try to lose myself in my imagination. And after a while I didn't feel the pain or humiliation anymore, because I was able to transport myself to other places in my mind. I would think of you and Papá and Abuela Frida and Nana Delfina. I even thought of happier times when we all used to go to see the *Esmeralda* when it arrived in port. I tried desperately to disconnect myself from the evil *Esmeralda.*"

Now Mamá is rolling up the sleeve of her blouse. She holds out her arm. It's lined with small round scars. Cigarette burns. . . . She also shows us some of the places where the general's men shocked her with electricity. Then I realize her long sleeves were not only protecting her from the cold; they were protecting her from terrible memories too.

I suck in a breath. "Does it still hurt?" I ask, gently touching one of the red marks.

"Not anymore," says Mamá.

Abuela Frida is moaning, "Ay, mi hija, my poor daughter." Mamá squeezes her mother's hand.

"Now when I look at these scars, I see them as a sign of my survival. Those men tried to break me, but I was stronger than they were. They did *not* destroy me."

She says this with a forcefulness that surprises me. Mamá is so brave!

"How did you get away?" I ask—I can't stop looking at those scars.

Mamá seems to be searching for the correct words. "After one of the . . . the torture sessions," she says at last, "the guards chained my hands and feet—it's what they always did when transporting prisoners from the cells to the torture chambers. The chains were all secured with a padlock. That night, one of the guards, one who I had noticed never participated in any of the torture sessions, looped the padlock around the chains but didn't secure it. He looked me in the eyes, gently placing my hand over the padlock while his fellow soldiers were looking the other way. Then I remember him whispering, 'Try not to be scared, Esmeralda Halpern,' calling me by my father's surname. Just then, the other guards grabbed me by the elbows, but instead of guiding me back to my cell, they took me up on deck. At first, I thought they were going to tie me to the mast again—and I quaked inside. Instead . . . instead . . . they took me to the edge of the ship and said 'Any last requests?' And . . . and . . . they pushed me overboard, laughing. They meant to kill me." A single tear slides down my mother's cheek, but she goes on.

"You see, the chains weighed people down and kept

them from using their hands and feet to swim. I hit the water with such force that I still can't believe I didn't black out. I sank so quickly, but my body knew what to do—it began to struggle desperately. That's when I remembered that the guard hadn't secured the padlock. I fumbled with it and somehow managed to unhook it from the chain wound around my ankles and wrists. I desperately needed to breathe, but I knew I had to continue holding my breath and swim as far away from the *Esmeralda* as I could. If I rose to the surface too soon, the guards would surely see me . . . surely shoot me . . ."

My heart is beating so fast that I begin to gasp. Papá rubs my back. "Breathe, hija, breathe," he says.

I ask shakily, "What . . . what did you do?"

"I swam until my lungs burned. I thought of you and Papá, because I didn't know if I'd be shot as soon as I came to the surface. As I surged out of the water, I looked around frantically, expecting bullets to hit my body at any moment. But then I realized the current had moved me far enough away from the ship that I couldn't be seen. It seemed so impossible to have such good luck that I actually thought I must have been dead or just imagining that I had escaped. Slowly, though, I realized it was true—I was free! I began to swim again, this time less frantically, quietly, quietly heading toward the shore."

Now I'm staring in awe—and I have so many

questions. "Thank goodness for that guard," I cry out. "Do you know why he helped you?"

"I don't, but I do believe there were many people working for the general who didn't agree with what he was doing. They were in a difficult position, because any indication of compassion would have been deadly for them. That guard obviously knew it was the day I was supposed to die, but he made sure I had a chance of escaping. I owe him my life." She shakes her head ever so slowly. "What irony . . . I was saved by one of my captors," she says, mirroring what I was just thinking.

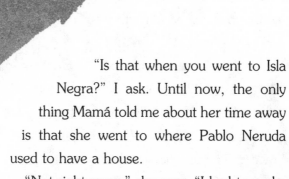

"Is that when you went to Isla
Negra?" I ask. Until now, the only
thing Mamá told me about her time away
is that she went to where Pablo Neruda
used to have a house.

"Not right away," she says. "I had to make
sure I was safe first. I didn't know where to go or
who to trust. I couldn't go home, and I couldn't go back to
María Fernanda's."

"Do you know what happened to her?" I ask hesitantly.

"No. . . . I hope she found out I had been taken

and didn't go back home, but no one has heard anything from her. She was probably arrested and taken to one of the other detention centers. I fear she became one of the disappeared who did not survive, just like Petra Sálazar." And only now does she begin to sob. "María Fernanda would not have gotten into trouble if she hadn't helped me!" she cries out.

Papá tries to comfort her. "Now, Esmeralda, we've talked about this before," he says in his calmest voice. "María Fernanda helped many others before you. You know that. She knew the risk she was taking. She was a brave and honorable woman . . . a hero, really."

"I'm so sorry, Mamá," I say, nestling against her, regretting how difficult I've been lately, how thoughtless. "I'm really sorry." We stay like that in a Marconi huddle, all five of us, for the longest time.

Between the *Winnipeg* **and** the *Esmeralda*

It's late now, and I'm out on the roof because I can't sleep. Olivia looks at me with her huge unblinking owl eyes, keeping me company. I stare out in the direction of the *Esmeralda*. Mamá was kept on that ship in the darkest of darks, as dark as the deepest ocean. I can't see it now, but I feel its presence like a cold wind that tears through me and leaves me breathless and afraid.

I take out my notebook—writing my fears sometimes helps. As I write by starlight and moonlight, tears spill onto the pages and smudge my words. I wonder how many tears Mamá cried while she was a prisoner.

Then I begin thinking of Lucila again. Did they tie her to the mast of some ship? Did they dump her into the ocean? I swallow a sob as I think of all the terrible things that might have happened to her. How can people have such hatred in their hearts? I don't understand. *Lucila. Where are you?* I look up at the sky again and call to my friend, "If you're out there, please send me a sign. . . ." But the only thing I hear is the sound of the wind.

Another teardrop falls, landing right on Lucila's name. As the letters blur, I begin to cry in earnest.

Even though I'm trying to be quiet, Abuela Frida hears me and pokes her head out my window. "Celeste of my soul, come back inside." I do as I'm told and sit next to my granny on my bed. She takes my hand and says, "Try not to look at the world with sad eyes. I know it's hard, but it's important that you try to rise above your sadness." I look at my grandmother and hitch in a breath. "I'm horrified by what happened to your mamá, but we have to fight against the bad things that happen rather than letting them control us. Feeling hope instead of despair is a powerful way of fighting against evil. Your mamá and papá are trying to do that, and I want you to try as well," she says, patting my cheek. "I've told you this before, but I'll tell you again that there's much more good than evil in this world."

Even with Abuela's soothing words, I can't stop crying. I bury my face in my pillow.

"Shhhh, niña. Shhhh . . . ," says Abuela Frida. "There are so many things I want to tell you, Celeste, but my memory is sometimes hazy. It gets away from me like the wool threads at the hem of my skirt that unravel and float down Butterfly Hill in search of the fragrant sea. Other times, when I think back to specific events in my life, my memory is as clear as day. But . . . I have remembered a story that I want to tell you, a story that will help you." I lift my tear-streaked face.

"You may know that there was a civil war in Spain in the 1930s. Well, that war left Madrid in flames, people in the countryside without food, and lots of other people—like my favorite poet, Federico García Lorca—dead. The people who managed to escape fled to France, where they were housed in internment camps. That's when the most extraordinary thing occurred. When he heard about what was happening, our beloved poet Pablo Neruda rented an old beaten-up French cargo ship and convinced everyone to chip in and paint it and fix its cabins and bathrooms. That ship was only supposed to hold a couple of dozen people, but Señor Neruda saw to it that the boat could hold many, many more. In 1939 the ship, the *Winnipeg*, sailed from France across the ocean to Valparaíso with the blue flag of hope flying high. That ship held twenty-two hundred refugees, and *every one of them* made it to Chile safe and sound! When they arrived, they were welcomed by the Chilean president to their new home."

"More than two thousand! That's amazing! I had no idea Señor Neruda did that. How *did* he do it?" I ask, swiping at my wet cheeks.

"I think it was love and determination that made it possible, Celeste. Señor Neruda was an extraordinary and courageous man." Abuela taps my chin and says, "I want you to remember this story, because it reminds us that not all ships are evil. Some ships, like the *Winnipeg* and the *Ship Called Hope*, the one that brought *me* to Chile, saved people's lives."

I nod thoughtfully.

"And perhaps when the president has turned the *Esmeralda* into a museum," Abuela says, "you will see that it can once more serve a good purpose: to remind us all of what must never happen again."

Four Heads Are Better Than **One**

The next morning, I'm still thinking of what Abuela Frida said about Pablo Neruda—what he managed to do, because he had hope. . . . How Mamá managed to survive, because she had hope. They, I realize, *did* things, because of hope! I have a sudden urge to go to one of Señor Neruda's houses to get inspiration for how to turn my hope of finding Lucila into reality. So, I call my friends and ask them to meet me at La Sebastiana, his house that looks out onto the Pacific Ocean. It's tall—four stories— and is covered on the outside with murals of birds, flowers, and the ocean. We can't go inside because the house is still being restored; the general's men ransacked it after Señor Neruda died, and left it in a total shambles.

Genevieve and Cristóbal arrive together. As I watch them approach, it occurs to me that Cristóbal hardly ever falls asleep in the middle of things anymore. He used to be famous for nodding off anywhere and everywhere. Since Genevieve came into the picture, Cristóbal has been *very* alert.

"Bonjour, Celeste," Genevieve says, kissing my cheeks. "It's beautiful up here. You can see so far!" Her long honey-blonde hair blows in the wind; she pushes it back from her face to get a better look at the ocean.

"Hi, Celeste," says Cristóbal, giving me a hug just as Marisol comes up to us, huffing and puffing.

"Sorry I'm late!"

"You're not, amiga—we just got here."

She wipes sweat from her brow. "I was with my abuela. She wasn't feeling too well, so I wanted to make sure she was okay before I left."

"Is she okay now?" asks Genevieve, concern furrowing her forehead.

"I think so, but her blood pressure has been really high lately." Marisol loves her grandmother as much as I love Abuela Frida.

As we lean against the fence in front of La Sebastiana to look out at the sea, I decide I don't want to tell my friends about Mamá just yet. I want to focus on something else.

First we grumble about having to start school tomorrow after two months of summer vacation, while at the same time assuring Genevieve that she'll love Juana Ross. Then, after a couple of minutes of silence, Cristóbal says, "The reading program is going really well, so you can't want to see us about that, Celeste." He looks at me and

starts to laugh. "Ah, you have other plans for us, don't you?" Marisol laughs now too.

"What?!" I ask innocently.

"Celeste! We know that look!" says Cristóbal. Then Marisol turns to Genevieve. "That's Celeste's *I've got an idea* face."

I give a teensy shrug. "Wellll . . . There *is* something else I'd like to do, and I need your help. . . . I still want to come up with a way to remember Lucila and the other kids from school who disappeared. We talked about it, but we haven't *done* anything. Will you guys help me?"

"I'm in," says Cristóbal.

"Ditto," says Marisol, and Genevieve nods her agreement.

"You all are seriously the best. So, ideas, people?" We fall silent again, thinking about where to start. Waves crash below, sending fine sprays of water onto our faces. Cristóbal is the first to speak.

"We should probably start by getting a list of the students who disappeared—then we'll know who we're trying to remember. There's Lucila and the other kids from our class, but there must have been others from other grades. . . . I have no idea how many. . . ."

"You're right! One of us should go and ask Principal Cisneros for that list," adds Marisol. "I think it should be you, Celeste." She wiggles her eyebrows at me.

"Why *me*?" I ask.

"Why *not* you?" she replies. "Unless you want one of us to go with you to hold your hand," she teases.

"Fine," I say. "I'll do it, but what if he doesn't want to give me the names?"

"Make him understand that it's important," says Cristóbal. "You've always been able to persuade people to do things"—he jabs me in the ribs with his elbow—"even when they really don't want to!"

"Jeez, am I really that bad?"

"No, you're really that *good*!" answers Cristóbal, laughing once more. I smile, not entirely sure whether he's paying me a compliment or not.

A **Request**
and a Story

The next morning, I head to Juana Ross half an hour before the first class to speak to Principal Cisneros. I knock on the big wooden front door, and through it I hear footsteps approaching. I'm in luck! Principal Cisneros cracks open the door and peers outside. He's a short, portly man whose clothes are always rumpled. Abuela Frida would say he's "harried," because he always seems concerned about something. But he has the kindest eyes. When he opens the door all the way, I see he has a pile of papers and books in his arms.

"Señorita Marconi, what a surprise. You're here awfully early. Come in, come in. I'll make us some café con leche. I was just getting started on the day's work."

While Principal Cisneros heads to the kitchen to make coffee, I sit in front of his desk that's made of reddish wood from the Canelo tree, the sacred tree of the Mapuche—one of the indigenous peoples of Chile. There are papers and coffee cups everywhere, and it dawns on me that teachers and principals must not get long summer breaks like I do! A few minutes later, he returns with a small tray and two cups of coffee. He hands me one and then settles into his chair, searching for his glasses, which are perched on top of his head. I point at them and he slips them down.

"Now, what can I do for you, Señorita Marconi?" he asks.

I blurt out, "Principal Cisneros, I need a list of the students who disappeared from our school during the dictatorship." A strange expression comes over his face, and he begins drumming his fingers on the desk.

"Can I ask why you need it?" he says, a hint of steel in his voice.

I'm a bit taken aback. "Well . . . my friends and I want to do something to remember the children who disappeared, but we can't do that if we don't know who they are," I explain.

"I see. . . ." He pauses, takes a sip of coffee, before at last saying, "I will get you the list, but I want you to be prepared. . . . It's long."

"I know. . . . Last year I saw the empty seats in my classroom," I reply.

"Yes, but you were only seeing the empty seats in *your* classroom, not in the *whole school*."

Huh. Cristóbal mentioned the same thing yesterday.

"I just want to understand what happened to my

classmates. I'm worried that no one talks about them anymore, as if they didn't just disappear . . . but never existed at all!" I say, a hitch in my voice.

Principal Cisneros looks thoughtful. "It's interesting you say that, Celeste. This summer, we received a letter from President Espinoza encouraging us to have conversations with students about the dictatorship and its effects. Apparently every school in the country did. So, I've instructed our history and literature teachers to begin those conversations in their classes this year. Too many people, for various reasons, have chosen to push what happened out of their minds."

I nod. "I know. My parents are only just beginning to tell me about what happened to them when they disappeared—and they've been back for more than a year! I didn't understand why they wouldn't talk to me before, but I think I'm beginning to get it. It was too difficult to talk about . . . and now I know they were trying to protect me as well."

"I'm sure that's the case," he says pensively.

"I've been thinking a lot lately about how, when I returned from America, I was so glad to be back that I didn't spend much time thinking about the disappeared. I was so, so sad that my best friend, Lucila, wasn't here anymore, but I didn't really *do* anything about it apart from write to her in my diary, hoping I could give it to her one day. . . ." I take a deep breath, wondering if I *want* to tell him what I tell him next. "I found out recently that my mother was a prisoner on the *Esmeralda*." The principal looks at me solemnly and shakes his head. "I realize that, up until now, I've been burying my head in the sand like everyone else. . . . Now, though, I want to know, and I want to remember."

We both sip our coffee, and then I decide to ask one more question. "Principal Cisneros, what was it like at Juana Ross after I left?"

He begins drumming his fingers again, harder this time. I'm sure he's going to send me away—I've pushed my luck for one day. Finally, though, he sighs. "I suppose I need to practice what I'm telling my teachers to do . . . so, here goes. . . . Soon after you left, men—looking oh-so-smart in suits with carnations in their lapels—would come to the school practically every week and read the names of the latest group of children who were to be taken away. If we didn't identify the children right away, the men beat us. No one was safe," he tells me. His Adam's apple bobs up and down as he swallows several times.

"One day, when the men came looking for your classmate Sergio Marino, I covered for him, saying that he was out sick that day. The men began to hit me, but I kept saying, 'He's sick. He didn't come to school today.'

It gave Señorita Alvarado enough time to sneak out of the teachers' lounge and find Sergio. She pushed him out the back door into the garden and told him to run. Señor Caléndula, our gardener, saw Sergio, grabbed him, and took him to the potting shed, where he quickly decked Sergio out in a gardener's hat and smock. He put a bag of soil into Sergio's hands and walked with him back to the flower garden, where Sergio hid in plain sight for the rest of the day. At the end of the day, Señor Caléndula had to pry the trowel out of Sergio's hand, because he was too scared to stop digging."

"You were all so brave," I can't help but exclaim.

The principal shakes his head sadly. "Sergio was only one case, Celeste. We managed to get him into hiding, and then he went into exile with his grandparents. But most of the other children were not so lucky. The men would take away two or three students at a time. We never saw them again," says Principal Cisneros, clearing his throat over and over.

"The other teachers and I—we feel a lot of guilt for not doing more to prevent the children from being taken. Had we intervened, though, we surely would have been killed. It's an awful feeling to want so badly to act, but to be too afraid to do anything," he says, and a sob escapes his lips. I've never seen a teacher cry, and I'm momentarily at a loss for words. Beads of perspiration break out on the principal's forehead.

"Can I . . . Can I get you a glass of water or something?" I ask.

"No, I'm okay. Thank you, though." He mops his forehead with his handkerchief. As the first bell rings, he says, "Celeste, I'll get you that list."

A **Lesson**
to Remember

As I head to my first class, the halls feel different some-how, now that I know what happened within them. I feel like I'm beginning to put together a giant puzzle. Pieces are missing, like what my friends who stayed here went through. . . .

My first class is with Señor Molina, our ninth-grade history teacher. As I enter the room, I take in the walls covered with world maps and a copy of the real Chilean constitution, not the one the dictator created for his own benefit. I remember how, before I left for Maine, these walls were plastered with pictures of him, looking so proud, so imperious. I'm more glad than ever to see our constitution on the wall.

"Hi, Celeste," Gloria calls out, a smirk on her face. What's her problem? "I heard you visited the principal this morning. Are you in trouble *already*?" She laughs.

"Hi, Gloria. No, I just had something I wanted to ask him."

"Whatever," she says, and turns away from me to

talk to her group of friends. Since the lunch at Stephen's, she's not been in touch with me at all. Maybe she's upset because we didn't invite her to help us with the literacy classes? I decide to push her out of my mind, and I realize it's pretty easy to do. She's just not that important to me anymore.

"Hey, Celeste. How was your summer?" asks Pedro Álvarez, who spent the break with his grandparents in Spain.

"It was okay, Pedro. How about yours?"

"I had a great time, but I'm glad to be back. Soccer practice starts this afternoon, and I'm ready to kick some major butt on the field!"

I like Pedro, but he has a *huge* ego. He's a great athlete, I must admit. And . . . I think maybe he likes me, but all he ever talks about is sports. True, it's practically unconstitutional not to like soccer in Chile. And it's not exactly that I'm anti-soccer. I'm just not soccer 24/7.

"I bet you are," I say. "I'm sure you'll do great," I add cheerfully.

"What was Pedro saying to you?" asks Marisol in a singsong voice, wiggling her eyebrows suggestively as I make my way over to the cluster of desks where she, Cristóbal, and Genevieve are sitting.

I give her a look. "Just saying hi. You *know* I'm not interested in him."

Cristóbal, completely oblivious, asks, "How did it go with Principal Cisneros this morning, Celeste? Did you get the list?"

"Not yet, but we should have it soon." Then I begin to tell them about my conversation with the principal. Before I can finish, though, the door swings open and Señor Molina strides in. All conversations come to an abrupt halt.

Señor Molina is a skinny, serious man of about fifty who rarely smiles. Actually, everyone's a little afraid of him. He sets down a big red binder on his desk with a loud thud, and we all jump. Then he looks at us with such intensity that we sink lower in our chairs, and he launches right in. "Welcome back, estudiantes. I hope you had a pleasant summer. . . . This year, we will be studying contemporary Chilean history, including the dictatorship."

My classmates and I glance at one another. Señor Molina pauses and then continues. "History has many layers, like an onion. You have to peel back those layers carefully to be able to distinguish truth from lies. You will learn that there are different versions of what happened during the dictatorship: the 'official story'—the one that was published in the press by the dictator and his followers—and the other story, the one lived by the people who did not support the general. This year, we're going to talk about both so we can begin to understand what really happened during those two long years. You have your own stories, and I want you to contribute those to our discussion—whether you were here, or in exile, whether your family supported the general, or not—because you are *all* part of the overall story." I look around. Everyone's eyes are as wide as mine.

Señor Molina continues. "Many students from this very school disappeared. They can't tell their stories, but *we* can. I want you to think about them and remember them every day when you enter Juana Ross, even if you didn't know them. . . .

"The conversations we will have may be difficult, but we are going to make every effort to come together around the facts, to reach a balanced understanding of what happened." He looks at us again. "Do you have any questions?"

I raise my hand tentatively. "Señor, what's that red binder on your desk?"

Now his eyes light up. "Ah, let me show you." He opens it to the first page, then hands it to me and asks me to read aloud.

So, I take a deep breath and begin: "*I am Marta Alvarado . . .*" I pause, and he makes a sign with his hand to tell me to continue. "*I am a teacher at Juana Ross School, and this is the story of what happened to me during the dictatorship.*" I stop and look up at my teacher in surprise.

"This binder is the beginning of a project I started soon after the general died," he says. "You see, as a history teacher, I'm passionate about collecting facts. I interviewed all the teachers and the staff here who were willing to speak with me. I'll be sharing their stories with you. . . . I hope that by hearing stories from people you already know, it will spark your compassion and help you to think about sharing your own stories."

I almost can't believe what he's saying. It meshes so well with what I want to do to remember my missing classmates.

"This brings me to a term-long project we will be doing. You will write about your own experiences during the dictatorship, no matter where you were. Then you will interview five other people from different walks of life and document *their* stories. Each story should be no less than two pages. While you are working on that, I will be teaching you the historical facts that were previously covered up. We now have access to more documents from that time, and can get a better sense of what occurred."

He takes back the binder, paces back and forth for a few moments, and then asks, "Do any of you know how many people were harmed or disappeared during the dictatorship?"

It's Gloria who raises her hand first. "Maybe a couple hundred? And, they didn't 'disappear.' They just left the country," she says in an authoritative tone.

"Well, during the dictatorship, that's exactly what was reported, señorita. So I understand why you think this. However, the Truth Commission has just come out with a different number. Does anyone else want to take a guess?" Gloria looks down, perturbed.

"Five thousand?" ventures Cristóbal.

"Ten thousand?" I say.

"No." Señor Molina shakes his head, whether at the number he's about to say, or at our ignorance, I'm not sure. "The latest figures are that . . . more than thirty-seven thousand Chileans were either tortured or disappeared during the dictatorship."

We all gasp, even Gloria.

"Your lack of knowledge—nearly *everyone's* lack of knowledge—about what happened is precisely why I'm having you do the term-long project. The collection of stories you'll contribute by the end of the term will serve as part of a living memory of what happened during the dictatorship. We can never allow this to happen again, and a huge part of changing things is understanding them."

PART 4
Maps to Remember

What a **Team!**

After our last class, we head to Café Iris, where my friends and I share an enormous slice of thousand-layer cake, some chirimoya (apple custard) ice cream, and a handful of cuchufli, which are tube-shaped cookies, each one filled with something different. It's Genevieve's first time trying cuchufli, which she proclaims are "Magnifiques!"

Once the plates are empty, Marisol says, "I think the history project is going to be really interesting. I'm going to interview my grandmother, but I don't know who else yet."

"I'm going to interview my mamá and you, Celeste," says Cristóbal.

"Me . . . ? Why me?" I ask.

"Your perspective is different. Plus, I'd like to hear more about what things were like for you on Juliette Cove during that time. You know . . . what it felt like to be in exile."

"But I've already told you," I remind him.

"You have, but not everything. You've told me about the things you did and how much you missed your family, but you've never really told me what it was like not to be *here*. So, I think your story will be different from all the others."

I hadn't thought of it like that before.

"Well, I want to interview *you*, Cristóbal, and you, too, Marisol. Principal Cisneros told me some stories this morning about what happened at our school while I was away. I sort of wondered why you didn't tell me about what it was like." I swipe up some spilled filling on one of the plates with my index finger, avoiding their eyes.

Marisol and Cristóbal glance at each other. Then Marisol says, "Well—you never asked. . . . And we didn't really want to talk about it either. To tell you the truth, when you returned, it was kind of nice to pick up where we'd left off . . . to get a bit of normal back."

Cristóbal adds, "Exactly. There was a lot we wanted to forget, like the sound of the soldiers' boots and the way they held their machine guns with their fingers on the triggers. Sometimes they would shoot into the air just to scare us . . . and they *did* scare us—the sound was deafening, like nothing we'd ever heard before. We became as silent as stones, afraid to utter a word." He pauses, tilts his head. "Actually, it was as though there was a blanket of silence over everything back then. But I guess Señor Molina is right. It's time we began thinking about those things again. . . ."

With fresh resolve I say, "I'm thinking there must be a way to combine whatever we do to remember our missing schoolmates with Señor Molina's project. Don't you think?"

Genevieve suddenly sits forward, excited. "He wants us to interview people, right? So, what if we interview the people who know the missing students, to find out more about them?"

"That's a great idea! And . . . and . . . what else can we do? Something more . . ."

"Well, once we know who the children are, maybe we could start by drawing a map of the city and finding out where they all lived . . . where they were from," suggests Marisol. "You know, make a map of the missing."

I look at my friend and feel an idea bubbling up.

"You're brilliant, Marisol. That's it! We need a map. No, not a map, *lots* of maps. Let's create memory maps!" I exclaim.

Marisol gives me a curious look. "What do you mean by 'memory maps'?"

"I'm not exactly sure, but . . . what you said gave me a vision . . . a vision of us . . . placing markers around the city that tell us something about each person's life. Each map could show the places where that person liked to go, the things they liked to do. It would be like a map of their lives, bits all over the place, and people would see the markers everywhere! Do you get what I mean? It would be a way of—"

"Of bringing who they were into the present," Cristóbal interrupts, and starts to grin. "I think I get what you're saying. We could find that stuff out through our interviews." I nod. Yes, yes!

"What kind of markers would we leave, and how would we tell the different children apart?" Genevieve asks.

"We need something permanent," I muse.

"Right," Marisol agrees. "Posters will eventually get ruined by the weather. . . ."

We sit looking at one another for a while, and then I cry out, "Stones!" My friends look at me like I'm nuts. "Really! On the beach . . . all those flat stones." I turn to Cristóbal. "Come on, you know—the ones we skim over the water?" Cristóbal starts to nod.

"But what would we do with them? Genevieve is right. We need to be able to tell them apart," says Cristóbal.

"We could paint the children's names on them in different colors," suggests Marisol.

We look at one another again, and give a group high five. We pay for our desserts and practically run back to school. Señor Molina is still there, hooray! And as we tell him our idea, we can't believe it, he actually smiles!

So Many
Names!

After school we gather stones, so many stones. You wouldn't believe how heavy a bucket of stones can be! On Wednesday afternoon, the principal calls us to his office. True to his word, he has the list of names. He hands us an envelope and also tells us that at an assembly tomorrow, he's going to tell the school about our project! Señor Molina must have told him about it.

We quickly adjourn to Plaza Aníbal Pinto, where we sit under the shade of a big araucaria tree.

"Who wants to open it?" I ask, glancing at the envelope in Cristóbal's hands.

"You do it, Celeste," says Marisol. "I'm too nervous."

"Okay . . ." I take it from Cristóbal, slip my finger under the flap, and, ever so gently, ease it open. There are only two sheets of paper inside, but they seem to weigh a ton.

"There are so many names," Marisol gasps, reaching toward the list and then drawing her hand back as though afraid of it. Cristóbal begins counting over my shoulder.

"Forty one? . . . Just from our school?" he cries out, shocked.

"How many schools are there in Valparaíso? Twenty? More?" I ask.

Marisol bites at her lower lip. "And Juana Ross is small compared to most other schools. . . . If every school in Chile is like ours, then . . . then thousands of kids disappeared!"

We sit in silence, stunned by the enormity of what we've just discovered.

Cristóbal takes the list from me at last and reads it a bit more carefully. "I only recognize the names of the people we were in class with, and a few of their siblings."

"Why don't we read them out loud—see who we recognize?" I suggest. Marisol nods, and though her hands are trembling, she takes the list.

"Okay . . ." She takes a deep breath. "Martina Andrade, grade six." She looks up at us, but Cristóbal and I shake our heads.

Then, out of the blue, Cristóbal exclaims, "Wait! I *do* recognize that last name. I think I met another Andrade, a boy in the grade below ours. His name is . . ." He looks up at the sky, trying to remember. "Gonzalo! He was in one of the magic classes I took with el mago a few years ago." Marisol looks back at the list and then at Cristóbal.

"His is the next name on the list," she says solemnly.

"Did you know him well, Cristóbal?" Genevieve asks.

"Not really, but he seemed like a nice kid. I guess he and Martina are brother and sister."

Marisol continues reading. "Cristina Chávez . . . Dani Echeverría . . ." We all shake our heads again. "Patricio Farmiga . . ." Cristóbal, Marisol, and I nod.

Genevieve looks at us expectantly. Marisol's eyes tear up. "He's one of the four missing students from our class," she explains. "He wasn't one of our best friends, but he was really sweet. He mostly kept to himself. I really hope he went into exile like Sergio. . . ." She looks down at the list again and then rapidly looks up, her eyes glistening. "Lucila López . . . ," she says, and lets the papers fall to her lap. Cristóbal puts his arm around her.

"I'm sorry, amiga," he says.

I stare at the ground, because I know if I look at Marisol, I'll lose it. Hearing Lucila's name is like being hit by a bolt of lightning. It makes her being gone some-how . . . *more* real. My arms break out in goose bumps. I need to hold it together for Marisol. Genevieve squeezes my hand. Then she takes the list from Marisol's lap and continues reading.

We know some of the remaining names, but most we don't.

"How could we not know these kids?" Cristóbal asks as Genevieve gets to the bottom of the second page. "We should have tried harder to get to know the other people in our school."

"I know what you mean," I say. "I feel bad, not just because they're gone but because I made no effort to get to know them when they *were* there."

"What gets me the most—apart from seeing Lucila's name on the list—are the three first-grade students. They were only, what? Six years old?" says Marisol, outraged.

It's terrible enough to think of any kid in the hands of the dictator's men, but *six*-year-olds?! "Sometimes in class last year," Marisol says, "I would look at where Lucila used to sit and think of her, but I wonder how many other people have thought about her." Then she takes the pages from Genevieve and shakes them in the air. "Each of these names has a story, and we're going to find out what it is!"

Natalia Paz

The next morning at the assembly, Principal Cisneros explains the memory maps project to the rest of the student body. He and the other teachers have decided it will be part of our history grade for the term. He explains that we will be divided into small groups and that each group—composed of kids from a variety of grades—will interview people who knew the missing children. Once we find out about our people, we will place memory stones around the city. He tells everyone to return to the auditorium at three to find out which group they're in and who their disappeared person is.

When the clock strikes three, we make our way back to the auditorium, where the principal's assistant taped the list of groups to the wall. When I get to the front of one of the lines, I see that Genevieve is in my group and that we, along with three other students, will be finding out about a student named Natalia Paz. I run my finger down the list of groups again to see who will be working on Lucila. Echeverría . . . Farmiga . . . López . . . Oh good! Cristóbal's in that group. Then I return to Natalia's name and read that I'm supposed to meet my group in classroom number two. Her name is not at all familiar to me, so I'm hoping someone else in my group might know something about her.

In classroom number two, I find Genevieve along with Jorge Ramírez, Carmen Buendía, and Alfonso Fuentes. I know Carmen a little bit—she's a few grades below me, in sixth. I don't know Jorge and Alfonso at all. They're in seventh grade. After we introduce ourselves, Señorita Alvarado stops by and gives us an envelope with some information about Natalia: She was seven when she disappeared, which would make her about ten now. Her address before the dictatorship was over on Barón Hill. Also in the envelope is an outdated photograph of a beautiful little girl with shiny brown hair and blue eyes. "Do any of you know her?" I ask, showing my classmates the photo.

"She looks familiar," says Carmen, taking a closer look at the photo and tapping her finger against her lips. "Hmmm . . . Wait . . . I remember now! We played together at recess a few times. She was very quiet . . . but . . . ummm . . . she had a brother—she used to talk about him a lot."

"Do you remember his name? Did he go to our school?" I ask quickly, not remembering another Paz on the list of missing children.

"No, I'm sorry, I don't. I'm not sure she ever said it, but I'm pretty sure he went to a different school."

"Well, it's a start," I say. "Let's see if we can find other students who were in Natalia's class and ask them. Does someone want to do that?" I ask.

"I'll do it," says Alfonso. "My sister, Soledad, is in fifth grade now. She or her friends might know something."

"I'll go with Alfonso to talk to some of the younger kids," says Jorge.

"Great. Carmen, do you want to come with Genevieve and me to see if anyone lives at the address Señorita Alvarado gave us, or maybe we can talk to some neighbors who might have known the family?" She nods in agreement. "Great. We can meet back here tomorrow after our last class to compare notes."

Carmen, Genevieve, and I have fun getting to know one another more on our way to Barón Hill—it's quite a hike! Even though Carmen's only eleven, she fits right in—she seems grown-up for her age, much more mature than I remember being!

We reach the address, but it's clear the house is abandoned. The windows are boarded up and the garden is completely overgrown. Next door is a small secondhand bookshop called Libros Queridos—Cherished Books. We all nod at the same time—we're going in. A bell above the front door chimes as we enter. I'm met with one of my favorite smells in the whole world. I inhale deeply, savoring the woodsy, papery scent, and then let out a satisfied sigh. Carmen and Genevieve look at me, amused.

"Um . . . I like books," I explain sheepishly. "A lot."

"No! Really?!" they say in unison, and laugh.

The shop is small, but there are so many books. Books on old wooden shelves painted a deep forest green, books in stacks on the tiled floor, books propped up in the front window. . . . There are big books, small books, comic books, cookbooks, you name it! But it's also really dusty, and Genevieve has a sneezing fit.

"Can I help you?" comes a frail voice from somewhere in the back of the shop. An old man is hobbling toward us, clutching a cane with a beautifully carved butterfly on top.

"Good afternoon, sir, and yes," I say. "We're doing a project for school. . . . We're trying to find out about the people who used to live in the abandoned house next door. Their family name was Paz. You wouldn't happen to know them, would you?"

"Oh, come in, come in. I'm Señor Barbablanca, and to answer your question, no, I never met them, but this used to be their store. The government took it over when the family disappeared. A year later, I was told I could have this place at a steal as long as I only sold certain books that were approved by the regime. I agreed. Although, I must confess I kept all of the forbidden books that Señor Paz had in stock in the far back."

"What forbidden books?" Carmen asks.

"Well, books on Communism and the Cuban Revolution, as well as books of poetry by authors like Pablo Neruda. . . . I assumed the reason why Señor Paz and his family disappeared was because he was secretly selling those books." My mind flits to Abuela Frida. How lucky her secret stash was never found!

Genevieve asks, "Did Señor Paz happen to leave anything behind? Anything that might help us find out more about his family?"

Señor Barbablanca scratches his head. "Now that you mention it, I think there's a box of Señor Paz's things in the back room. Let me go and look for it."

While the old man goes in search of the box, Carmen, Genevieve, and I begin looking around. He has a wonderful collection, including a great selection of children's books. I call Genevieve over. "Wouldn't this book"—I hold out an animal alphabet book—"and these"—I point to several others—"be great for the kids at the top of Butterfly Hill? I still have some of the money my aunt sent. Should we buy a few?"

"Great idea! Let's do it!" Genevieve readily agrees.

We pick five picture books, along with an early reader about a boy detective we think Paco might like, and stack them next to the cash register just as Señor Barbablanca returns with a shoebox under one arm.

"Here. You're welcome to whatever's in this box. No one has ever come to claim it." Then he notices the books. "Ah, you've chosen some nice ones," he says, tapping the one on top. "Are they gifts?"

"Actually, we're going to take them to the children at the top of Butterfly Hill," Genevieve tells him. "Celeste started a program up there to help the children, and even some adults, learn to read and write."

He peers at me as though trying to place me. After a moment, he asks, "Are you Celeste Marconi?"

"I . . . I am. . . . How do you . . . ?"

"I know your abuela Frida. She's a fellow lover of books," he says. "I heard about your classes. Please, take these as my gift to your program. I would have donated them sooner, but I was in the hospital recovering from hip surgery until this week. . . . Here, take some more," he says, pointing to the shelves. "Some of these books have been here since I took over this place. I would really like for someone to enjoy them." He selects ten or so others.

"Thank you, Señor Barbablanca!" Genevieve and I exclaim happily.

"It's my pleasure, young ladies. And please come back and visit me soon."

We assure him that we will and then head outside with our treasure trove of information on the Paz family and a big old stack of books.

Uncovering
Treasures

We decide to head down to Muelle Barón to open the box, although what I *really* want to do is open it right this minute!

When we reach the beach, we take off our socks and shoes and sit on the sand, still warm, even though the sun is low on the horizon.

"Shall I open it?" asks Carmen.

"Yes! I'm dying to know what's inside," Genevieve practically gasps, and I realize she's as excited as I am to discover its contents.

Carmen removes the lid, sets it carefully on the sand, and then pulls out a small stack of photographs.

"That looks a little like the photo of Natalia from school," says Genevieve, pointing at the one on top. "Does it say anything on the back?"

"Ummm . . . yeah. '*Nati, age five, Santiago.*'"

"I wonder if that's where they're from. What are the other photos of?" I ask.

Carmen picks up the next one and shows it to us.

"This one's of a wedding. Natalia's parents?" Carmen asks, holding the photo out to us.

"Probably. I can't see their faces too well, but the lady and Natalia look alike," says Genevieve, pointing.

"Let's see. . . . On the back, this one says . . . '*Eusebio and Clementina, Santiago,*' and the date is . . . ummm . . . twenty years ago," says Carmen. Then she holds up another photo of the same adults, Natalia, and an older boy. My mouth drops open.

"Hey, wait a minute. . . . Isn't that the guy who helped us on Butterfly Hill that first day?" Genevieve exclaims.

I hold the picture up, then manage to stammer, "Y-yes. . . . I think you're right." Can this be true? I stare some more. He's what? . . . Natalia's brother? "Wow, what a coincidence."

Carmen reads, "'*Eusebio, Clementina, Natalia, and Sebastián, Valparaíso,*' and the date is three years ago. This must have been taken just before Natalia disappeared."

Sebastián. . . . His name is Sebastián. But at that moment, it hits me like a ton of bricks. Sebastián's parents and sister are probably dead. Suddenly I'm fighting back tears. But . . . but then I think again about the rumor, the rumor about some of the children being saved. Is it possible Natalia might be one of them? It's not *impossible*. . . . We have to talk to Sebastián right away! I share my thoughts with Genevieve and Carmen, and they both agree.

We sift through the remaining items: the original deed to Libros Queridos with Eusebio and Clementina Paz listed as the owners; a will and testament in their names; and four passports—although the last name listed is not "Paz." Interesting. The sun's about to set and we can hardly see to read anymore.

Even though we should probably be getting home, we sit on the sand a while longer and listen to the waves lap at the shore, and to the caws of the pelicans flying overhead. Genevieve finds a buried Coke bottle, and as she digs it out of the sand, my imagination takes flight. I envision a message inside with handwriting I recognize . . . Lucila's. It says, *Come find me, amiga*. When Genevieve stands to search for a trash can, I come back to earth and shake my head, dispelling the vivid vision. Then I pick up a flat stone, hop to my feet, and skim it into the water like my papá taught me when I was little. One, two, three, four, five, six! Six skims! I've only ever been able to do five before.

It seems like a good omen.

Confessions in a Whisper of **Time**

Later that night after feeding and brushing Milui—I'm going to miss her so much when she goes home to Señor Martín after his house is finished—I'm doing my literature homework while listening to a French singer called Édith Piaf. Genevieve recommended her to me. She has quickly become one of my favorites. I especially like "Non, je ne regrette rien" ("No, I Don't Regret a Thing") and "La vie en rose" ("Life through Rose-Colored Glasses").

Señor Castellanos has assigned us five of Pablo Neruda's poems to read and write about for tomorrow's class. Today he told us about a rumor that the dictator hated Señor Neruda so much that he had the poet poisoned, though we'll never know that for sure.

I'm finishing writing a paragraph on Señor Neruda's "Tonight I Can Write (the Saddest Lines)" in green ink— Señor Castellanos told us that the poet wrote in green to symbolize hope and desire—when I hear a tap on my window and almost jump out of my skin. It's Cristóbal! He's perched outside my window right next to Olivia.

They're both staring in at me. Creepy! "What are you doing out there?" I ask, opening the window.

"I thought I'd surprise you," he says with a grin.

"It worked!" I give him a playful slap. "You scared me."

"Sorry about that. El mago has been teaching me some acrobatic moves," he tells me as he tumbles expertly into my room. Olivia gives a little wing flap and returns to looking out at the sea. "But I'm here for something serious. . . . How did your group meeting go? Do you know the person you've been assigned?"

"My person is Natalia Paz. I don't know her. Do you?" He shakes his head. "We found out a lot already, but we still have a ton of work to do. How about you?" I ask.

"My meeting went okay," he says, but then he pauses, his brow furrowing. "We've been assigned Lucila. . . . Did you know?" I nod, an ache creeping up in my throat. Cristóbal looks at me, his eyes soft.

"I interviewed Marisol just now, but I want to interview you, too, Celeste. Of course, I already know quite a bit about Lucila, but I want to know her through *your* eyes. Do you have time now?" He takes a notepad and pencil from his backpack.

Just then, Nana Delfina knocks at the door. "Niña Celeste, open up. Nana has snacks for you and Señor Williams." How does she know Cristóbal is even here?

Nana sees everything! In she sweeps, carrying a tray with hot chocolate and cookies. She's wearing the most interesting outfit: a wool poncho in a beautiful scarlet, her Wellingtons, and a strange little hat with a string that's tied under her chin. I dare not ask. Nana is eccentric sometimes.

"Gracias, Nana Delfina," we say, and she strides out of the room humming along to Édith Piaf's "Les mots d'amour."

Cristóbal and I settle on the floor of my room; I lean against my bed and Cristóbal sits opposite me with his legs stretched out in front of him. He begins asking me questions while fiddling with my conch shell. "Let's start with small things. . . . What's Lucila's favorite color?"

"Green," I say, without hesitation. "She loves anything green: leaves, mint ice cream, chimichurri, broccoli, avocados. . . . If it's green, she likes it."

"I remember! She always wore green earrings, right?" asks Cristóbal, putting the shell down and jotting some notes.

"Yes, her mamá gave her peridot earrings for her tenth birthday. She wore them every day."

"Okay, now. . . . Where did you two like to hang out?"

"Well, Café Iris, of course. Sometimes we'd dress up and even put on a little lip gloss; not much, because we weren't allowed. We'd order tea and pastries . . ."

"And?" asks Cristóbal.

"Huh?" I ask, forgetting the question, still thinking about those special days.

"What would you talk about?"

"Well . . . like, Señorita Alvarado's high heels. She seemed to have a new pair every week, and they were always spectacular. I remember when she came to school wearing a pair of forest-green pumps and Lucila's eyes nearly bugged out of her head. She wanted those shoes!" I say, laughing. Then I stop short, remembering something else. "She was reading *Anne of Green Gables* right before she disappeared. She'd read me her favorite parts while we sipped our tea, pretending to be elegant ladies." Cristóbal is writing everything down. "We also talked about boys." He stops writing abruptly.

"Who did you talk about?" he asks, interested.

"Back then, I had a crush on Sergio, but Lucila liked . . . well, she really liked you, Cristóbal."

My friend turns beet red. "Me? . . . No. . . . Really?"

"Well—she used to talk about you all the time."

"I'm not writing that part down," he says, a sad look clouding his face. "Celeste . . . I . . . uh . . . liked Lucila too. But I never told her." He looks away.

"I know," I say casually.

"You know? How? What do you mean?"

169

"The two of you—you were so obvious! You both thought you were being supercool, but nope!" I say.

Cristóbal suddenly stands and begins pacing the room. He has picked up my shell and is passing it from one hand to the other. "I'm an idiot. Why didn't I say something? Why didn't I ever tell her? And now I can't. Now it's too late." His fists clench around my shell, and I worry it may break. I reach up and ease it away from him.

"There are lots of things I wish I'd told Lucila too. She was my best friend and I loved her so much, but I never told her," I say, my voice catching in my throat.

"She knew, Celeste. She did," Cristóbal says, sitting down beside me.

"Where else would you and Lucila go together? I know the hangouts we all went to . . ."

I frown. "Well . . . we used to like to go down to the port and look at the *Esmeralda*. . . ."

"Have you spoken more with your mamá about what happened?" Cristóbal asks.

I take a moment, then say in a strangled voice, "Yes. . . . Actually, she's told me a lot . . . things I never could have imagined. The people who were taken on that ship . . . Cristóbal, they suffered so much." I swipe at my face with the sleeve of my sweater, angry at the tears that have sprung to my eyes. Then I blow my nose.

"You sound like an elephant," Cristóbal teases.

"Shut up! I do not!"

"Yes, you do." So I blow my nose again, and realize I *do* sound like an elephant. I begin to laugh. I laugh so hard that I fall against Cristóbal, who is laughing so hard, he snorts. And we laugh even harder.

"Thank you," I say, giving him a punch on the arm. "I really needed that."

"Let's stop for today. I can ask the rest later."

He puts his backpack on and goes onto the roof. Then, as nimble as a squirrel, he jumps onto one of the limbs of the tree and scurries down the trunk. And right before he gets to the bottom, he does a magnificent flip and lands squarely on his feet. "Ta-da!" he says. I clap and he bows. "See you tomorrow, Celeste Marconi! Bye, Milui!" he says, taking off at a run.

Olivia comes closer, and the two of us look out at the Pacific Ocean together. Olivia seems to be looking for Lucila too.

Stones
of Memory

The next day, my group meets again in classroom number two. Alfonso starts us off. "My sister remembers Natalia a little, although she said Natalia wasn't at Juana Ross very long. All my sister remembers is that Natalia once told her she liked to go down to the beach to look for pretty shells with her mamá."

Then Jorge says, "We also found out more about her brother. His name is Sebastián. He went to one of the other high schools. A few kids mentioned they used to see Natalia walking with him down by the ocean, eating flavored ice."

"We found out about Sebastián too!" Genevieve shows the guys the box Señor Barbablanca gave us. Alfonso picks up the family photo and Carmen points out Sebastián. Alfonso shakes his head. He doesn't recognize him.

"Before I knew who he was, I'd seen him a couple of times down by Muelle Pratt," I tell them. "Perhaps we should go down there every afternoon, see if we can find him?"

Everyone agrees. Jorge says, "Who else should we interview? Maybe Natalia's teacher?" We agree that this, too, is a good idea, and Alfonso volunteers for that task. Then Carmen spies a long table in the back of the room. It holds a bucket filled with stones, several bottles of acrylic paint in different colors—green, blue, yellow, purple, and fuchsia—and several fine-tipped paintbrushes.

"I think we should start putting Natalia's name on these stones," Genevieve suggests, striding to the table. We follow her lead and pick brushes and separate shades of paint.

"This isn't as easy as I thought it was going to be," says Jorge after a while. He's right; it's hard to write with a paintbrush on a small stone.

"Why don't we put her first name on one side and her last name on the other," suggests Alfonso. "That will give us more room."

Soon we have enough memory stones ready to start placing them at the few places we've found out about so far.

"I'll take two over to Barón Hill on my way home," offers Carmen. "One for Señor Barbablanca's shop, and one for Natalia's old house."

"I can take one down to the beach," says Jorge. "In fact, I should probably take a couple . . . put them in different places."

"I'll go with you," says Alfonso, picking up a few more stones.

"I can go to Señora Nieve's frozen ice and ice cream shop. Want to come, Genevieve?" I ask.

"Oui. Formidable!" she says, picking up another of the stones. This one has a little fuchsia heart painted above Natalia's name—Carmen's handiwork. Nice touch.

Las Animitas

Two weeks have gone by and it's another Saturday, and the reading tent is finally finished! Today Don Alejandro drives Señor Barbablanca up the hill with the taxi *full* of books! It's a bumpy ride, but enough of the road has been cleared that vehicles can now reach the top. Marisol, Genevieve, Cristóbal, and I eagerly unpack the books and neatly line them on the bookshelves—we have three now!—while Don Alejandro and Señor Barbablanca get to know Señor Martín and the other pupils. Milui is now back home and is so happy. She comes to class too!

At the end of our lesson, Señor Barbablanca takes me to one side. "Celeste, would you mind if I work with Don Alejandro and Señor Martín?"

"That would be wonderful. Thanks for your help," I say with genuine appreciation.

"No, thank *you*. I've been rather lonely. . . . Old age is no fun. I've been waiting for something to do so I can feel a bit more alive, and this is it!"

I know exactly what he means.

I arrive back home later in the afternoon to find Mamá and Papá weeding. Abuela Frida is sitting on a beach chair, taking a nap. Mamá has a smear of dirt on her face, and the front of Papá's pants are filthy.

"Hola, Celeste. Ever since Milui left, we've had to start weeding again. Want to help us?" asks Papá.

"Sure," I say, planting a soft kiss on my grandmother's cheek as I head to the shed to find a trowel. Abuela Frida lets out the most adorable little whistle in her sleep.

As I begin to loosen weeds with my trowel, I tell Mamá and Papá about the tent and all the books Señor Barbablanca brought. Then Papá says, "We noticed some memory stones around the city while we were doing our rounds yesterday. It seems like things are off to a good start."

"Oh, yay! It's going so well! I couldn't have hoped for better. My group has learned quite a bit about Natalia Paz already. Did I tell you her brother was the one who helped us with Milui's straps on the first day we went up the hill to help the fire victims?" Mamá and Papá glance at each other.

"Only about ten times," says Papá, trying to hide a grin.

Mamá puts down her trowel to add, "Maybe more like twenty!" And she can't hide her grin at all.

I ignore them and begin pulling weeds like I've

177

entered a weed-pulling competition. I'm glad my head is down, because I know my face is as red as a tomato!

Thankfully, Papá changes the subject while wrestling with a particularly stubborn dandelion. "Mamá and I were talking just last night about how creative the memory maps are—and the idea of them reminded us of the animitas."

I've heard that word before, but I can't place it. "Animitas? What are they again?"

"You don't remember?" says Papá. "When you were little, you were bewitched by them—they're the tiny houses built on the sides of roads, with open fronts, like grottoes. You would ask over and over again if fairies lived there. I was never quite sure how to answer, because how did I know for certain they didn't? You, on the other hand, were *very* certain they did."

I smile. . . . Now I remember. I imagined fairies with gossamer wings living in those tiny houses. "They were lit by candles, right?"

"They were, indeed. . . ." Papá wipes his forehead with the back of his gardening glove, leaving a smear of dirt behind. Now he and Mamá match. "I'm not sure I ever told you the real purpose of the animitas."

I shake my head and say with some sass, "Well, I know that fairies *don't* live there, Papá. I stopped believing in fairies a long time ago."

"No, you didn't," says Mamá, catching me in my fib. "You'll always believe in fairies, because they *do* exist." Mamá also believes in magical things. I probably get that from her.

Papá looks at us now, shaking his head. "Well, whether or not fairies exist, they don't live in the animitas."

"So, what are they, then?" I ask.

"They're memorials . . . for people who died violently, like victims of shootings or car accidents. Family and friends build them where their loved ones died. Over time, many people have come to believe that those dead people—who become, well, like unofficial saints—have magical powers and can perform miracles," he says. "The point is that the animitas are meant to help loved ones remember the person who died."

"Are there ones for the people who disappeared during the dictatorship?"

"No, hija," Mamá says, "because no one knows what happened to them for sure. You can't build memorials in the place where they died if you don't even know for certain they're dead, or, if they are, where it happened."

"That's what we like so much about the memory maps," Papá adds. "You and your classmates are remembering the disappeared as though they're still alive. The people who build the animitas are thinking of the dead."

"Huh . . . So, the memory maps are a kind of memorial to life, not death."

"Exactly."

"But I still think the animitas sound neat. I don't think I've really looked at one up close since I was a little kid."

"Why don't we go look at some now," Papá suggests. "It's almost nightfall, and that's the best time."

"How come?"

"You'll see," he says mysteriously.

After we get Abuela Frida settled inside and we wash up, we put on our jackets and scarves and head out into the chilly fall evening. We make our way over to Avenida Errázuriz, one of the busiest roads in the city. I hardly ever come down here, because it's dangerous, with all the cars whizzing by. I suppose that's why there are lots of animitas here—lots of car accidents.

We pass by a restaurant-bar called La Piedra Feliz—the Happy Stone—and hear someone playing a guitar. The sound seems to accompany us, and as it fades on the wind, we come across our first animita.

"Look!" Mamá says, crouching down. "It's beautiful."

I squat in front of the little house, which is painted red. Inside there's a kind of altar on which sit candles, figurines, and photos.

"The candles make you feel like you're in church,

don't they?" Papá says. "And they make the animitas look especially pretty at twilight. See the little saint in there holding a plaque that says 'Rodrigo'? And look, there's a small soccer ball in the back, and a cassette tape."

I take a closer look. "It's one of your favorites, Papá—Violeta Parra's *Cantos Campesinos*." Papá nods pensively.

Then I examine the other contents of the animita. Tucked in the back is a stack of letters tied together with a velvet ribbon. These are pieces of this person's life, I realize. The photo of a smiling young man set up in the center of the shrine says *Rodrigo Valencia, 1955–1970* at the bottom. Wow, this person was pretty young, just one year older than I am! I wonder what happened to him, and how long the animita has been here.

"Who looks after the animitas?" I ask, standing back up.

"The family, usually," says Mamá," but anyone can help make sure they're taken care of. If you ever come across one and you see a candle burned out, or that something's been knocked over, you should fix those things; that way you're doing your part in helping the family keep their loved ones alive in people's memories."

"I'll remember that," I say, wondering how many

of these little shrines I've probably walked right by in my haste to get to this place or that.

We walk a little farther and come across a totally different kind of animita.

"This one's *really* unique," says Papá, pointing not to a small house but to a bicycle painted white. It has delicate pink flowers threaded through the spokes, along with long strands of greenery that wrap around the base of the seat and twist up the tree to which the bike is chained. Hanging from the crossbar by slender ribbons

is a small fairy with lilac hair wearing a white tulle skirt. There's also an ivory rosary draped over the handlebars. The cross dangles just above the front tire, and there are toy ladybugs nestled here and there that look up at whoever might be regarding the bike. On the handlebars rests a laminated photo of a beautiful woman, and at the bottom it says, *María José Pizarro, 20, was murdered here by an irresponsible driver who hit her while she was riding her bike home*. The contrast between the fanciful fairy, the whiteness of the bike, the whimsical ladybugs, and the word "murdered" is shocking, and I actually take a step back.

Watching me, Mamá says, "I have the same reaction every time I see this one. The contrasting messages are . . . striking." We spend the next few minutes straightening the flowers, and thinking about María José, even though none of us ever met her. I'm probably too old to be holding Mamá's hand, but I grasp it nonetheless. I lean into her and whisper, "I'm so glad you're here, Mamá." She came so close to being killed. Where would I have built an animita for her had she died in the ocean? She would have just faded away like all the other disappeared people who never returned, and I would have always wondered where she was, like I wonder about Lucila. Papá comes over to us and the three of us embrace. I think we must all be thinking the same thing. We walk home hand in hand in hand, and I realize I no longer feel upset with my parents for sending me away. I guess time and patience really do heal all wounds. Abuela Frida, as usual, was right.

A **Letter**
Brought by a
Gentle Wind

Just as I'm finishing my homework on Monday night, Mamá and Papá arrive home looking exhausted. Mamá plops down at the kitchen table, and Abuela Frida comes into the room at a clip. . . . Well, a clip for someone her age, that is.

"Mamá, what is it?" My mom looks astonished and somewhat alarmed.

"I may be old, but I can still get from one place to another in a hurry when I need to," my determined abuela huffs. "Here, this came in the mail for you today, hija." She hands over an envelope that looks old and crumpled.

"What's this?" Mamá asks, looking for a return address.

"I don't know, but when the mailman handed it to me, I knew it was important. When I touched it, it was warm," Abuela replies enigmatically, a look of excitement in her eyes. "Open it, open it!" she says impatiently, which is *exactly* what I'm saying in my head.

The envelope looks like it's been in a war zone;

a corner's been torn off, and something's been spilled down the center, smudging the letters that spell out Mamá's name.

"Who's it from, Mamá?" I ask.

"It doesn't say, hija, but . . ." She's peering at the postmark.

"What is it, Esmeralda?" asks Papá, noticing the confusion on Mamá's face.

"Hmmm. . . . Look at this," she says, pointing.

"That's really weird," says Papá. "This was sent more than a year ago! The mail can be slow, but this is ridiculous."

Mamá slides her finger under the flap and pulls out a single sheet of paper with writing on both sides. As she turns it over to see who it's from, her hand flies to her mouth.

"What is it, Mamá?" I ask, alarmed. She's gone as white as a ghost.

"Esmeralda, who's it from?" asks Papá.

"It's . . . It's . . . This can't be. . . . It's from . . . María Fernanda," she says, her voice suddenly small.

"But, but, I . . . We . . . we . . ." Papá fumbles for words.

"Andrés, shhhh. Let me read." Mamá skims the letter and goes even paler.

Papá touches her arm. "Esmeralda?"

My mother shakes her head hard. Then she begins to read aloud.

Dear Esmeralda,

I don't really know why I'm writing this letter, because people don't survive the general's torture camps. But I have to tell you . . . in case . . . in case of a miracle. I was there the day they took you. I was on my way home when I saw them drag you out of my house. I was so scared . . . I didn't know what to do. I guess I'm writing to apologize to you, wherever you are, for not helping you . . . for being too scared. I have nightmares about that day, and I wish I could go back and do something, anything, to help you.

If you're not reading this letter, then I hope someone in your family survived the dictatorship and is reading it now. I just wanted someone to know how brave you were. You probably, inadvertently, saved my life, because I was able to run away after I saw the soldiers take you. Had I arrived home half an hour earlier, I would have been taken away with you. . . .

Mamá pauses, one lonely tear spilling down her cheek. "Andrés, María Fernanda survived."

"Does she say where she is?" Papá asks, his hand now around Mamá's wrist, as if to keep her steady.

"Celeste, will you finish reading, please? I can't see," says Mamá, wiping at her tears. I take the letter from her and find where she left off.

I fled to the docks to see if I could find someone to get me out of Valparaíso by boat. Flying was too risky. My name was surely on the general's list by then. The problem was that I didn't know who to trust. I hid behind wooden crates and fishing boats for two days, until I saw an old man dressed in the full uniform of the naval officers of twenty years ago. He was muttering to himself. I realized he must be Captain Pratt. Most people believed he had lost his mind, and the general's men must have thought the same thing, because they had obviously left him alone. It was a huge risk, but I followed him to his houseboat. He took one look at me and whisked me inside. All traces of madness disappeared and his eyes became sharp and alert.

I stop reading for a moment. "I think I know who Captain Pratt is. I've seen him down by the pier. I've always been kind of scared of him. . . ."

"Yes. That's him. Mamá and I always say hello to him, and he's polite, but he never seems to want to talk," Papá says. "What does the rest of the letter say?"

I tried to tell him my name, but he wouldn't let me, insisting on calling me Isabel instead. He gave me a blanket and something warm to drink. Then he asked how he could help. I explained what I needed, and a light came into his eyes. He told me he would take me to a safe place. It was like a miracle! During the three days we were at sea, we talked about everything under the sun, except who we really were. He left me in Castro, the capital of Chiloé Island, and I never saw him again. Truly, he was my guardian angel.

I've been on Chiloé ever since and have built a nice life. I love the people, and I met my husband, Esteban, here. He's a fisherman and a good man. I'm writing this letter now because the general just died, and people are saying it's safe to write letters again. I don't plan on returning to Valparaíso. There are too many bad memories there. I hope . . . I dream that you, or someone in your family, receive this letter. I am sorry, so very sorry, for not keeping you safer, Esmeralda. I

*will always be haunted by the image of you being
taken away.*

Your friend always,
María Fernanda Santiago

Mamá goes to the kitchen window, looks out at the
sea. Then she swings back around. "María Fernanda
should not feel bad for what happened to me. She risked
so much just to keep me in her house. I'm so glad she got
away!" she says fiercely.

I look at the postmark again. "Why did it take so
long for the letter to get here, though?" I ask.

"I don't know," Papá says, "but I'm going to find
out. Esmeralda, where does Señor Pascual live?" he asks,
referring to our postman.

"On Happiness Hill, a couple of houses down from
where Celeste told us Genevieve and her father are staying," she answers.

"I'm going to see if he knows anything. Want to
come, Celeste?" When I nod, he turns to Mamá. "Esmeralda, are you okay?"

"Yes, I'll be fine. . . . But, Andrés . . . I have to find
her." She looks at Papá, and the two of them seem to
reach an unspoken agreement.

Wayward **Mail**

Señor Pascual answers the door wearing blue plaid pajamas. His reading glasses are perched on the end of his nose, and he peers at us over them.

"Señor Marconi, Señorita Celeste," he says, surprised. "What's wrong? Did I mix up the mail?"

"No, not at all," Papá assures him. "It's just that we received a letter today that was postmarked more than a year ago. Do you know why it's just now getting delivered?"

"It's interesting you ask," Señor Pascual says, waving us into his house, which smells of cinnamon and vanilla. His little dog, Coco, wags her tail furiously and comes over to say hello. I crouch down to scratch her ears. Señor Pascual continues, "All of us postmen had more mail to deliver today than usual, and when we asked our supervisor about it, he said that a hundred or so undelivered letters had been found hidden in an abandoned shipping container down by the pier. Some fishermen were moving the container when they found them.

I'm sorry for the delay. I hope you didn't get bad news."

"No, nothing like that. We were just curious," says Papá. "Thank you, Señor Pascual. Sorry for disturbing you."

"Adiós, Señor Pascual. Adiós, Coco," I say, giving the dog one last pat on her head.

As we walk back toward home, crossing from one hill to another, I ask, "Why would someone have hidden the mail?"

"I'm not sure, but judging by the date on María Fernanda's letter, I would guess it has something to do with the transition from the dictatorship to democracy. Right after the general died, his men still tried to maintain control over the radio and television stations, and the phone companies, in order to manage what was communicated. They were also still censoring letters. I'm wondering if María Fernanda's letter was intercepted by the general's men during the transition and was perhaps lost in the shuffle."

"But . . . I got Abuela Frida's letters on Juliette Cove around that time," I say.

"I don't know how to explain it, hija. But Señor Pascual said there were about a *hundred* letters. I wonder what other kinds of news people received today." Papá sounds uneasy.

As we reach Butterfly Hill, I see someone running toward us. It's Marisol.

"Celeste!" she yells. "Celeste, Lucila's alive! She's alive!" When she reaches me, she hugs me so tight, I can't breathe.

"Lucila's alive?" I parrot back, stunned. "LUCILA'S ALIVE?" I scream.

"Yes! Come quickly. I have to show you something." Then she grabs my arm and starts tugging me in the direction of my house. Papá, Marisol, and I take off at a run.

Another Letter?

When we burst through the front door, Marisol's abuela is sitting at the kitchen table with Mamá, Abuela Frida, and Nana Delfina. Doña Estela is dressed, as always, in black. Marisol's grandmother seems to be in shock, and Nana Delfina is trying to get her to sip some brandy.

"Look, Celeste!" Marisol hands me a letter. I recognize the handwriting immediately. Lucila!

I stare at Marisol, my heart thudding. Marisol is nodding, nodding, nodding . . . yes, yes, yes, almost to the beat of my heart.

"Read it, Celeste. Read it. . . . I . . . It's . . . Your

mamá's already read it, but read it out loud so your papá can hear too." I do just that.

> Dear Abuela,
>   The people I'm staying with told me this morning that the general is dead, so I think it's okay to write you. Still, I'm scared to write. I don't even know if you're still alive, or if Marisol is, or Celeste. I'm okay, Abuela, but I'm still scared. Did you know Mamá, Papá, and I were held prisoner on the Esmeralda? Were you taken somewhere too?

No way! I glance over at Mamá. She's deathly pale. I quickly turn back to the letter.

> I never want to see that ship again. Terrible things happened there. The guards . . . they killed Mamá and Papá. They killed them! . . . Just killed them. Abuela, I know it's true because they made me watch! I fought against the guards, but there was nothing I could do. They just threw Mamá and Papá overboard wrapped in chains. . . .

Tears fill my eyes. Oh, Lucila, how awful. How AWFUL! I lower the letter and stare unbelieving at everyone. Doña Estela drinks the brandy in a single gulp, her eyes closed.

"Señora Estela, Marisol, I . . . I don't know what to say. I'm so sorry," I whisper.

The old lady gives me a sad smile. "I think I knew my Patricio and his Elena were dead. When I talk to them at night, as I have done every night since they disappeared, they never answer me, and I cannot see them clearly in my mind anymore. But whenever I talk to Lucila, I see her face as clear as day, almost as though she's still here with me." She taps the letter. "Celeste, please read the rest. Then Marisol and I have a great favor to ask."

I feel cold all over. *Pull yourself together, Celeste*, I tell myself. Lucila's alive. Lucila! That's all that matters. I turn back to the letter.

> *The guards locked me in a cell. I was there with a girl who was only seven. The guards told her they did the same thing to her parents and her brother. We cried and cried. Each time the door opened, we were so scared the guards were going to throw us overboard too.*
>
> *One day, a guard did come for us. But he didn't hurt us or throw us off the ship. Instead he hid*

Natalia and me in a laundry cart. He told us to be really quiet. . . .

Natalia? *Natalia?!* Could that be *my* Natalia? And now Marisol says, "Celeste, do you think . . . Is it possible Lucila's talking about the same girl you were assigned to—for the memory map project? 'Natalia' isn't a very common name."

I manage to nod. Could it be? Then I skim the rest of the letter, desperate to know more. "She says the guard smuggled them off the ship and took them to his fishing boat. Apparently, he'd seen Lucila forced to watch her parents . . ." I gulp. "He decided, at that moment, that he was going to defect and take them to Chiloé, where he thought they'd be safe." Marisol and I lock eyes. Then I continue skimming the letter.

"She says she's staying with three sisters who are basket weavers and that . . . she has terrible nightmares . . . all the time." I can't hold back the sob that has risen in my throat. Papá takes the letter from me and continues to read.

I miss Mamá and Papá so much . . . all the time. But the sisters take good care of Natalia and me, and I try to take good care of Natalia too. She has worse nightmares than I do.

Abuela, are you still alive? I talk to you, Marisol, Mamá, and Papá every night before I go to sleep. I hope that maybe, wherever you all are, you can hear me.

Your loving granddaughter,
Lucila

"Where's the envelope?" I ask desperately.

"Here," says Marisol, handing it to me. The post-mark, just like on María Fernanda's letter, is from more than a year ago. Lucila doesn't know that her grand-mother and cousin are still alive, or that I am! She must feel so alone.

"We have to go and get her!" I exclaim, standing up as though I'm ready to set off for Chiloé Island this very minute.

"Hija, sit down," says Mamá. "Señora Estela has something she wants to ask us."

Señora Estela grasps my hand and I sit. "Celeste, the moment we received Lucila's letter, we contacted the authorities. They said they will send someone to look at it in the next few weeks. After that, they will begin to investigate."

"The next few *weeks*?!" I cry out.

Mamá clicks her tongue. "Hija, let her finish!"

Doña Estela nods and continues. "They said they got numerous calls today from other people who received old letters from disappeared people. They said it could take months to go through all the requests. They did give us the number of the police station in Castro. The police there said they will see if they can find Lucila, but they are not at all hopeful. Apparently, many children were taken in by the residents of Chiloé, but no official documentation was ever filed." Doña Estela pauses to catch her breath, and it takes all my self-control not to ask a billion questions, to let her continue.

"When we asked them what we should do, they said it might be best if someone from the family could travel there and help look for her." Lucila's grandmother grasps one shaky hand with the other. "Delfina, can I have a little more brandy? I need to calm my nerves." She takes another healthy gulp. "I want to travel to Chiloé, to look for Lucila. So does Marisol. But . . ." Tears spring to her eyes. "I'm too old, and Marisol insists she needs to stay to take care of me. I know this is a lot to ask, but you found your papá with Cristóbal Williams. Do you think you could find Lucila, too?" Hope fills her eyes.

Mamá comes over to me. "While you were at Señor Pascual's, Señora Estela asked me if we could help. I told her I'm not letting you go anywhere without me. I want to find María Fernanda, too. We're going to go to Chiloé together to find them," she says. We both glance over at Papá. He looks pensive, then worried, then fierce, all in a matter of seconds.

"Well . . . I can stay here and look after our patients." Sensing what I'm going to say next, he adds, "I'm sure we can ask Principal Cisneros for an extended absence—this is much more important than school."

My heart is thudding again, but in an excited way now. "Okay, so when can we leave?" I hop up again, ready to pack in a heartbeat. "Tomorrow?"

"Slow down, Celeste," Mamá laughs. "There's a lot we have to figure out. First, we have to get there, and we barely have enough money for one plane ticket, let alone two. If we find Lucila and Natalia, we will be four people coming back. That's going to be really expensive."

"Would it be cheaper to go by boat?" I ask, thinking I've come up with a great solution.

All the color drains from Mamá's face. "I . . . I can't go on a boat, Celeste. I'm sorry, but I can't." I'm such a dolt! *So stupid!*

"I'm sorry, Mamá. I wasn't thinking! Please forgive me," I apologize.

"No, no, you were thinking of solutions. That's good!" She pauses, and an intense look, not dissimilar to the one on Papá's face a moment ago, crosses her face. "You know, at some point I must face my fears. Why not now?" Mamá brightens, but then her brows knit together and she turns even paler. She's definitely not ready for a long boat ride yet. She takes a deep breath. "But you're right, Celeste, we will probably have to bring the girls back by boat, and who are we going to get to help us do that for next to nothing?"

Just then Mamá and I look at each other and, almost at the same time, say, "Captain Pratt!"

"María Fernanda said he helped her. Perhaps he will help us, too!" I say excitedly.

Then I glance at Marisol. "Are *you* okay with this plan, amiga?" I ask, worried she might be miffed that I'm going and she's not. Lucila is, after all, her cousin.

But Marisol nods. "It was my idea, Celeste. I want you to go. You're much braver than I am—I can wait a few extra days to see Lucila." Then she leans in toward me and whispers, "Anyway, with Abuela learning that my aunt and uncle are . . . gone forever—it's been a huge shock for her. I can't leave her." Once again, I think how grown-up Marisol sounds. We're not little girls anymore. We no longer fly kites, or spin tops, or play emboque. She was much better at flipping that wooden egg up into the air and catching it on a stick than Lucila and I ever were. So much is so different in just three years. . . . I wonder how Lucila has changed. I pray I will soon find out.

"Gracias, Marisol. Mamá and I will do everything we possibly can to find Lucila and bring her home."

Doña Estela grasps my hand again. "Thank you, Celeste. Thank you, Esmeralda. Now, if you will excuse me, I think I need to go home and lie down. The worst of news and the best of news, all at once. It has been quite a day."

It has indeed. Once Marisol and her abuela leave in Don Alejandro's taxi, the Marconi family has a meeting. We need to figure out a plan for bringing Lucila home.

A **Surprise**
Encounter

We have a plan! Mamá and I will fly to Chiloé at the end of the week. That way, Mamá won't have to worry about going on a boat. Besides, she'll need to come back sooner than I will because she can't miss too much work. Now all we need to do is persuade Captain Pratt to make the trip to Chiloé with his boat so he can bring me, and hopefully Lucila and Natalia, back.

When I tell Cristóbal and Genevieve the news about Lucila, they're as crazy excited as I am, and want to know what they can do to help. I talk to Carmen, Alfonso, and Jorge as well.

"We really need to find Sebastián Paz," Jorge says. "If Natalia *is* his sister, we have to tell him." We all agree to redouble our efforts to find him—we don't have much time. The next thing to do is talk to Captain Pratt.

After school, despite a heavy fog setting in, Nana and I walk down Butterfly Hill toward the water. Nana is wearing potato peels on her temples again today. Perhaps they will help her ward off any evil spirits hiding in the fog.

"This is a good sign," Nana Delfina is saying.

"What is?" I ask.

"The fog. It will protect us. . . . If you look at it with your heart instead of your eyes, you will find answers. It's like a guide if you know how to read it and follow it. I think the fog is telling us Captain Pratt will help us."

"Where do you see *that*?" I ask, as all *I* see is a whole lot of gray.

"There." She points, but I can only see more fog. "Pay attention, Celeste!"

I look again, and out of nowhere, I see a boat. But no sooner does it come into view than it fades away.

"Aha! You saw it, didn't you?" asks Nana gleefully.

"I . . . I *did*, but how . . . ? I can't see more than a foot in front of me."

"You're seeing what's going to happen, because you believe in it," she says mysteriously.

"But all I saw was a boat. What does *that* mean?"

"It can mean what you want it to mean, but to me it means Captain Pratt is going to travel to Chiloé to get Lucila. . . . And I'm going with him," she declares in no uncertain terms.

I stop short. "What? Do you know him?" I ask, concerned that Nana's losing it.

"No, but I think I'm supposed to go with him," she says without any further clarification, and that's the end of that conversation. I know better than to push once Nana has made up her mind.

At the water's edge, we make out the hazy shapes of a line of houseboats. How are we going to find Captain Pratt's? We don't know which one is his. They're all secured to the dock with heavy ropes tied to metal cleats. While some can be reached by ramps, most are flush with the dock and look pretty easy to board. We decide to knock on a few doors, see if someone can point us in Captain Pratt's direction.

Nana approaches the first boat, which is two stories tall, but narrow. It has windows that look like portholes, and the deck seems to go all the way around the first story. It's a pontoon boat. They have flat bottoms and are great for fishing. People also like to live in them because they're really stable on the water, as long as you stay fairly close to shore. While there's a clear entrance onto the back of it from the dock, Nana doesn't want to step onto the person's property without permission, so she cups her hands and calls out, "Hola! Is anyone home?" When no one responds, she grows bolder, steps onto the deck, and heads for the door. I follow behind timidly. As she's about to knock, the door swings open. On the other side is a man in his sixties wearing fishing gear. He doesn't look happy.

"What do you want?" he asks tersely. When we

explain who we're looking for, he spits out, "That crazy loon? He's four houseboats down. It's a good thing that grandson of his moved in with him, or someone would have had him committed by now." And then, without so much as a good-bye, he slams the door in our faces. How rude!

I glance at Nana. Maybe we've made a mistake looking for Captain Pratt, especially if he's a "crazy loon." As we leave the pontoon houseboat, Nana says to me, "Don't listen to that old grouch, Celeste. I can tell he has bad intentions." Nana's read of people is usually right on, so I decide to make up my own mind about the captain once I meet him.

When we get to the fourth boat, we stand admiring it before setting foot on board. It's different from the others. It's not a pontoon boat like the first one, but a larger vessel, like the kind that can go far out on the ocean. The hull is painted teal, almost the color of the water. Windows run all along the side, but we can't see in because the curtains are drawn. There's also a rooftop deck, piled with fishing gear, a rowboat, and a few chairs. The wooden decks gleam. Someone has taken very good care of this boat. As we walk around to the bow, we see something unusual. . . . The captain has a masthead attached to the side of the door, instead of on the front of the boat, where one usually is. It's a beautifully carved mermaid. I run my fingers along her tail and can feel the scales. She seems like she's about to come alive.

Nana knocks on the door, and we hear heavy footsteps approaching. A man Nana Delfina's age opens the door, dressed head to toe in red. I smile because he looks like a giant poppy. He has so many medals on his uniform that I can't even begin to count them!

"Who's knocking on my door?" he demands, his voice gruff, looking first at me and then at Nana Delfina with squinty eyes. I take a step back, but Nana Delfina moves forward. "I'm Delfina Nahuenhual Marquén, and this is Celeste Marconi. Are you Captain Pratt? We need to talk to you," she announces, and walks right in without an invitation!

The old captain steps aside, clearly unsure what to do. "Ummm . . . Well, now, ummmm. Would you like some tea?" he mutters, which is the absolute last thing I thought he would say! He seems almost hypnotized; he's staring at Nana Delfina intently. Nana seems equally spellbound as she reaches up to remove the potato peels from her temples and tame her hair into place.

"Thank you. That would be very nice," says Nana. "Celeste, why don't you help the captain."

"O-okay," I say tentatively, and follow him to a small galley kitchen that has butcher-block counters, lower cabinets made of the same wood as Principal Cisneros's desk, a metal sink, a small stove, and a tiny fridge. Where some people have a tiled backsplash, there's a painted seascape with white-capped waves and seagulls in flight. As Captain Pratt fills the kettle and directs me to the cups and saucers, I hear a door creak open in the back of the houseboat, and a voice calls out.

"Who's there, Captain Pratt?" I recognize that voice, I think, just as a young man appears in the corridor. Wait a minute. . . . It's the boy . . . the boy . . . It can't be! But it *is*. . . . It's Sebastián Paz! He's taller than I remember. His hair, the color of coal, is shaggier than it was the last time I saw him, and he has deep-blue eyes. He's skinny and hunches over a bit when he walks, like he's shy, or is trying to protect himself from something.

"It's you!" I exclaim, blinking hard. Has the fog scrambled my vision? But when I look at him again, he's still there. He seems less surprised. "You're Celeste Marconi," he says, telling me my own name. "I met you up on Butterfly Hill."

"I, um, I know," I say. "I remember you." Dang. I can tell my face is turning red! "My classmates and I—we've actually been looking for you. I can't believe you're . . . here! Do you live here?"

I'm blabbering questions, and can't seem to stop. Then I remember the mean man saying the captain had a grandson living with him. But Natalia and Sebastián don't have grandparents, do they? What's going on?

Sebastián seems amused by all my questions. "Well, I've been staying with Captain Pratt for a long time now, and—"

"Is he your grandfather?" I interrupt.

"No! That's just something we tell people so they won't ask too many questions—it's a long story. But you said you were looking for me—why?"

Wow, where do I start? I need to talk to Captain Pratt, and I need to talk to Sebastián. And I sort of need to talk to them separately, but now they're here together! Argh! So, I start by introducing Nana Delfina to Sebastián.

Then I say, "Can we sit down so Nana Delfina and I can tell you why we're here?" I need to gather my thoughts. I wish I had Lucila's letter with me, but I don't, so Nana and I will just have to do our best to explain everything.

As Captain Pratt pours tea into fine china cups—so unexpected!—Nana tells him how we know about him and asks if he remembers helping a young woman he called Isabel—really María Fernanda—get to Chiloé during the dictatorship. He puts down the teapot, scratches his chin. "I took several people there. Each time I went on one of my 'excursions'"—he uses air quotes—"I told the authorities I was going on a fishing trip. They bought that excuse every time." He slaps his knee and laughs. "When I took people to Chiloé, I *never* asked their names, to keep them, and me, safe. So I'm sorry. I don't know the exact person you're talking about. What else can you tell me about her?"

"Well, she was a seamstress," I say. "I wish I could describe her to you, but I've never met her; she's an old friend of my mamá's, Esmeralda Marconi." The old man taps a finger to his head, and then his eyes light up. "I remember now! She must be the lady who repaired my uniform. . . . She was a lovely one. And I think I know your mamá, as well. She's a doctor, yes?" He slurps his tea loudly.

I nod and ask, my heart suddenly feeling like it's in my throat, "I'm just curious, Captain Pratt. . . . Did you take any children to Chiloé?" He looks at me curiously.

"Children? No. Why do you ask?"

I decide to jump right into the reason why we're here. Now, though, I also have to let Sebastián know about Natalia and the reason why my classmates and I were trying to find him. And . . . what if I get his hopes up and it turns out it's not his sister?

When I get to the part of the story about Lucila

being a prisoner on the *Esmeralda*, Sebastián goes rigid, his teacup halfway between the saucer and his lips. Captain Pratt places a gnarled hand on Sebastián's arm and guides his cup down. "It's okay, my boy," he murmurs.

"I'm sorry," says Sebastián, clearly embarrassed. "It's just that . . . I was on that ship too, and . . . well, my whole family . . ." At that, he excuses himself and hurries to the back of the boat.

"Should we go after him?" I ask Captain Pratt anxiously.

"No. He just needs a moment to himself. He lost his entire family on that ship." Nana and I look at each other again. Sebastián does not know about Natalia—if Natalia is his sister, that is.

"We may have some good news for him," Nana Delfina says.

The old captain gazes at her. "And what might that be? None of us has had much good news since the dictator came to power."

So, we tell him about Natalia and Lucila and their escape from the *Esmeralda*. And that the Natalia with Lucila is the same age Sebastián's sister would have been. Now the captain's arm is stuck with his teacup halfway to his lips and Nana Delfina has to lower his arm. When he recovers from the initial shock, the captain, who must be in his seventies, trots down the hallway like a man half his age. "Sebastián!" We hear a door fling open. "Come quickly," the captain tells him, and a moment later, he returns with Sebastián, who looks gutted.

"What is it, Captain?" he asks despondently.

"You need to hear this." Captain Pratt guides him back to the table, signaling for me to repeat what I just told him. Sebastián sinks down in his chair; he won't look at any of us.

I begin by telling him about the memory map for a Natalia Paz that I'm doing at school. Then I shift to our recent discovery about a young girl named Natalia who was rescued from the *Esmeralda*.

Sebastián is now shaking his head, shaking his head. "No . . . No, that's impossible. She . . . she and my p-parents were killed on that ship." His voice is hardly louder than a whisper.

"I'm sorry to push, but are you certain?" I feel horrible for having to ask; he seems almost at a breaking point.

"Yes, I'm quite sure," he says shortly.

"Can you tell Delfina and Celeste what happened?" asks Nana Delfina gently. "Because we really think this Natalia might be your sister."

Sebastián blinks rapidly, looks around almost like he's hunting for an escape hatch. Then he shrugs and seems to make up his mind. "Okay . . . I'll tell you. I'll tell you for my sister . . ." His voice breaks, but he swallows hard and then continues. "My family was taken at the beginning of the dictatorship. Papá was the head of the workers' union under President Alarcón in Santiago. . . ."

I remember that the first photo we found in Señor Paz's box was taken in Santiago. It makes sense now.

"A few months before the president was murdered, he told Papá to take us and leave Santiago, that it was no longer safe in the capital. That's how we came to live in Valparaíso. Papá managed to buy us new identities—he had friends in the government who helped him. My first name has always been Sebastián, but we had a different last name before. We settled here, Papá and Mamá bought a secondhand bookshop, and things were going well for a few months. . . ."

I'm nodding my head, gradually piecing together the things my group learned about the Paz family.

"But someone from the capital must have tracked us down, because one night, a group of men broke down our door, tied our hands behind our backs, put gags into our mouths, forced us into a panel van, and took us to the *Esmeralda*." Sebastián's jaw clenches as he works it back and forth. "As soon as we boarded, they separated us. Natalia . . . she was hysterical." He looks away, then back again. "Instead of locking *me* up, though, the guards decided I would make a good deckhand. They made me work up to twenty hours a day. My main job was to . . . to clean up after their torture sessions. . . ."

Sebastián pauses again. Captain Pratt gets up and pours him a short glass of what looks like whiskey or brandy. "Here, this will help," he says, putting the glass into Sebastián's hand. Sebastián takes a sip, coughs. "Take your time, boy. You haven't talked about this in a long while." The captain, who I realize is neither senile nor crazy, calms him.

Sebastián's eyes are focused somewhere in the past. "I didn't realize before then how . . . how strong the smell of blood is. . . . It's metallic. And then there's the vomit . . . and urine . . ." He trails off again. "I saw the most horrible things. . . . Teeth . . . and fingernails . . ." My hand flies to my mouth. Nana grabs my arm and squeezes.

"Sorry," says Sebastián. "Do you want me to stop?"

After a moment and a couple of swallows, I say, "No, please go on. It's just that . . . I guess I didn't know all the things that happened there." I look him in the eye. "My mamá was a prisoner on that ship too. She's told me some things, but not everything. . . ."

"Your mamá survived?" he asks, his voice suddenly soft, tender . . . hesitant.

"She did. She was really lucky," I say.

He takes this in and mutters, to himself more than to us, "She survived. . . . So, maybe others did too. . . ."

But, perhaps not wanting to think about something so improbable, he shakes his head rigorously and plunges back into his story.

"One day while I was cleaning one of the rooms, the most vicious guard on board came in and said, as though it meant nothing at all, 'Your little sister didn't even scream when I pushed her into the water this afternoon.' Then he laughed in my face and told me to get up on deck and scrub everything until it shone. Otherwise he would do the same to me as he had done to Natalia. When I started to cry, he kicked me, hard.

"It turned out that the guard had timed my trip up on deck to coincide with the other dreadful thing that happened that day. . . ." Sebastián reaches again for the glass, but his hand is shaking so badly that he has to put it down. "Just as I reached the deck, I saw that two chained prisoners had also been brought upstairs . . . my parents." He clears his throat. "Mamá saw me and shook her head ever so slightly as if to say, *Don't try to do anything, Sebastián.* The guard looked at me and said, 'Let's see if these fishes swim any better than your sister.' Mamá, when she realized he meant Natalia, screamed, 'Noooooooooo!' Then, with one brutal shove, he sent first my father and then my mother overboard. All I remember after that was screaming—I'm not sure if it was me or my parents, or both—and hurling myself over the side of the ship before the guards could stop me. I clutched at my mother as she began to sink, but the weight of the chains pulled her out of my grasp. I dove down deeper, trying to grab her or my father, but they sank so fast. I was running out of air."

I realize that *I'm* gasping for air. Everyone is looking at me. "I'm sorry. . . . It's just too . . ." I stop myself. "But you managed to get away?"

"At first, I thought about letting myself drown with my parents, but I found out it's not easy to drown yourself. My body wouldn't let me! Instinct kicked in, and suddenly I was swimming like crazy to the surface. I took in an enormous breath of air, only to be shot at by the guards. I quickly dove back under and swam until my lungs felt like they were going to burst. Luckily, it was dusk—I must not have been easy to see, because eventually the shooting stopped. Anyway, I imagine the guards probably thought I would drown before I made it to shore. I was nobody to them . . . just another political prisoner, and there were so many of us."

"May I have some of that brandy?" Nana Delfina now asks, *her* hands shaking.

Captain Pratt gives her a snifter and pats her awkwardly on the back. I almost ask for one myself. I'm aching, aching for Sebastián and his family.

"How . . . How did you go on?" I have to ask. "I

217

don't think I could have survived what you did."

"I had a lot of help," he says, looking over at the old man. "The captain found me on the beach. He brought me here."

"At first, the boy needed space," the captain explains. "He barely spoke the first three months he was with me. We made up the story that he was my grandson who had come to look after me because I was beginning to lose my mind. I've been putting on a good show of it for a long time now," he adds with a sly smile. "Even now I pretend to be a bit crazy, just to annoy my horrible neighbor."

"Well, the captain has always been a bit . . . eccentric," says Sebastián, his voice layered with affection, "so it wasn't a stretch to say that he was becoming senile and needed some extra help. . . . Anyway, Captain Pratt and I have been careful not to say too much about who I am. I didn't return to school and I didn't go back to the bookstore or my old home either. I still avoid those places," he admits.

"But why? Isn't it safe for you to return now?"

"Probably," he says, "but why would I go back? Those places just remind me of my family. . . ."

"Oh! Of course. Sorry," I say quickly. How do I manage always to ask the wrong questions?

"No worries, Celeste. I know you didn't mean anything by that." He takes a moment and then says, "Do you see now why the Natalia your friend is talking about can't be my sister?"

Captain Pratt looks at Sebastián thoughtfully. "I don't want to upset you or get your hopes up, but isn't it possible that the guard was just trying to hurt you and your parents when he told you what he had supposedly done to Natalia? What if it *wasn't* true?"

"But if *this* Natalia is not *my* Natalia, I don't know if I can take it." Now he's punching at his thighs.

"But what if it *is* her? What if your sister's still alive?" the captain counters.

Sebastián looks from me to Nana, then back to the captain. "Do you really think there may be a chance?"

"I do. There are too many similarities, and we'll never know unless we go find out." The captain turns to us. "Ladies, what exactly were you hoping I could do for you? It's why you're here, after all."

"My mother and I are going to fly to Chiloé on Friday, but we don't have enough money to fly back with the two girls, if they're there. So we were hoping . . ." I pause, and Nana continues, "We could pay for your services and provide all the food you would need and some money for gas, and you could meet Celeste and her mother there."

Captain Pratt looks at Sebastián, and the two of

them make a decision. "It's a deal," says the captain. "Except for one thing." Nana and I glance at each other nervously. But then he grins. "You're not permitted to pay me. But some home-cooked meals, I will accept." And just like that, we have a plan for getting everyone back to Valparaíso from Chiloé. . . . If we can find Natalia and Lucila, that is.

The captain now looks at Nana Delfina. "Will you be coming with us?" he asks hopefully.

"Of course," she says as if there was never any doubt. "Who else will prepare those home-cooked meals?"

"I'm delighted," says the old sea captain, taking Nana's hand and planting a loud kiss on it. For the first time in the fourteen years I've known Nana Delfina, she blushes.

As we prepare to leave, I extend my hand toward Sebastián to give him one of the memory stones that I had with me with Natalia's name on it. "I was going to drop this down by the water where I saw you a few weeks ago looking at the *Esmeralda*. Here, take it. I hope it helps you to remember the happy things you used to do with Natalia, and not the awful things that happened to your family."

"Thank you, Celeste," Sebastián says, holding on to my hand for a fraction longer than necessary.

PART 5
Chiloé, the Island of Orange Parrots

Magic
Carpetbags

Nana Delfina, Captain Pratt, and Sebastián have decided they will leave right away, as it will take them at least three days to get to Chiloé by boat. I wish we could all go together, but this will be better for Mamá.

I'm helping Nana put everything she needs for the trip into two large carpetbags. In the first, she packs food items, because she intends to keep Captain Pratt and Sebastián well fed. A bag of flour, a bag of sugar, a string of garlic, her secret spices, a few avocados, and lots of potatoes. As she packs the potatoes, she tells me that potato peels not only keep headaches away; they also scare away the witches that live where we are going. She stuffs in even more potatoes, and then a big bag of salt. "Witches don't like salt, either!" she declares.

Next we head to her room to pack her clothes. I love Nana's room—it's like going back in time. It's always dimly lit in there, but not in a depressing way. She keeps a few candles burning all day long, preferring their light to the lamp that sits on her bedside table. A small altar sits on a table in one corner, where she prays to the ancient gods and spirits of the Mapuche, her native people. She lets me pray with her sometimes, and has taught me several words in Mapudungun. There are no rules for that mysterious language; Nana says it creates itself as you speak it. What's extra great is that many people on Chiloé speak a variation of it, we've discovered, so Nana will be a huge help!

Nana takes a few items from her altar, kissing them before placing them carefully into her bag. Then she puts in her favorite brown shawl, which she tells me is the color of the soil in her native Araucanía in the south, close to where we're heading.

After packing a few clothes, she picks up an old, old photograph of her mamá and caresses it with her thumb. Nana speaks to her every night before she goes to bed. She calls her Mamita Susana.

"How's your mamá?" I ask now.

"Last night in my dreams she told me everything I need to take with me on this trip," Nana tells me. In her religion, people who have died stay around, as if they're still alive, for as long as they're remembered. They only fade back into the universe when loved ones stop thinking about them. Nana communicates with a number of her relatives who have left this world but who still inhabit the world of her imagination. Sometimes she lets me listen in on their conversations.

Now she's folding my favorite dress of hers. "Nana, why are you taking your pretty blue dress?" I ask with mock innocence.

"None of Celeste's business. Nosy girl." And Nana blushes for the second time in two days.

"I'm sure Captain Pratt will like it," I say, grinning.

Ignoring my teasing, she says, "That old man needs a few good meals in him. I plan to fatten him up. Nana doesn't like skinny men, and that captain looks like . . . like he's made of straw." She tosses a jar of face cream—which she makes herself in the kitchen—into the bag.

"Do you mean a scarecrow?" I ask, still trying to egg her on about the captain.

She ignores me and soon declares, "Nana's ready! I saw Lucila's face in my tea leaves this morning, and she looked very sad. She needs us." With that, she picks up her bags and heads to the front door.

Sometimes
It's Hard to
Come Home

It's finally Friday, and Mamá and I are nearly ready for our trip to Chiloé. We're both a bit nervous, but excited as well. As I'm packing, it hits me again that I haven't seen Lucila in *three years*. Such a long time. What if she's changed so much that I won't recognize her? What if she's forgotten about me? Why hasn't she tried to call anyone? What if she doesn't want to come back? Mamá walks into my room and, seeing the look on my face, asks what's wrong.

"I was just thinking that it's possible Lucila won't remember me, and that she may not even want to come back."

"The two of you were as thick as thieves, and you've been best friends since you were in diapers," says Mamá. "Of course she'll remember you. . . . But you're right. It *may* be hard for Lucila to come back, especially without her parents. I wonder if that's why she hasn't tried to reach out more," Mamá says more pensively, echoing my own previous question. "We don't know how she's doing mentally. She's been through something so awful."

I consider this, then ask Mamá in a quiet voice, "Why didn't *you* call or come back home right away after the general died? I would think . . . I would have thought you'd want . . . well, to come back to me and Papá and Abuela Frida just as soon as you could." I try not to sound hurt, even though the hurt never seems to go completely away.

She sighs. "Ay, Celeste. You and Papá were the only reason I survived! I always had you with me in my heart and my mind. But . . . some of the things that happened to me were unspeakable, and the burden of those memories was so heavy that I couldn't come home right away. I was ashamed . . . and embarrassed, and frightened. And also this—when I read in the papers that the general was dead, I didn't fully believe it. I thought it was just another trick he was playing to get people to come out in the open so he could take us prisoner again. It took quite some time before I felt safe enough to come home."

"Is that why Papá stayed on the ghost ship for so long?" I ask.

"I think so, Celeste. *That* ship was rumored to be the only truly safe place in all of Chile."

"So, how did you decide it was time to come home?" I ask.

She looks at me thoughtfully and says, "Abuela Frida told me."

"What?! Abuela Frida knew where you were and didn't tell me?!" A flash of outrage sizzles through me.

"No! No, nothing like that! She had no idea. I just heard her voice one day in my head, and it brought me such peace. She said, 'Come home, hija. It's time.' And that very day I began to make my way back to Butterfly Hill."

I let out a deep breath. "I feel so lucky that you did," I say, thinking of Sebastián, forgetting all my hurt, and hugging Mamá tight. "I don't ever want to be apart from you again."

Up, Up,
and Away

Our first flight is on a big plane that reminds me of the one I flew on to Portland, Maine. We can see the Andes Mountains out the window on one side of the plane, and the Pacific Ocean out the other. As we fly along the long coast of Chile, I notice that Mamá's face is ashy and clammy.

"Are you okay?" I ask, nudging her arm.

"Yes. . . . I was just thinking about some of the stories . . . the stories I've heard about, well, about . . . how the general got rid of some of his enemies by dropping them out of helicopters into the ocean, wrapped in chains. . . ."

I catch my breath as my mother gazes out the window. Then she continues: "I know those are terrible things to think about, but what's worse is how many of our fellow citizens pretend nothing happened. I guess it's easier than to admit that their own friends or family members could have been such monsters."

I nod at that, thinking about how complicated people

are, and how it's possible for people to see things so differently. I used to think that everyone thought like I did, that I was always right. I don't believe that anymore. Sometimes I'm not sure what to believe.

Out of nowhere, I ask Mamá, "Do you think any other people on this plane are going to look for the disappeared? What if they received letters like we did?"

"Anything's possible, Celeste. I know many others have gone looking for their loved ones before us—like you did to find Papá—and many more will follow after us, especially now that the rumors of people surviving have surfaced. . . . Did Papá ever tell you the story of his friend Señora Violeta?" I shake my head. "Her brother, Newton, disappeared during the dictatorship, but Violeta received an anonymous phone call telling her he was alive. Unfortunately, the person on the phone disguised his voice and didn't give her any other information."

"That's awful. Why would someone do that? It's like giving someone hope and then taking it away!" I say, cross.

"Well, we don't know the circumstances, Celeste, so we can't jump to conclusions about the person's intentions. All I know is that Violeta took it as a good sign. She set out with a small suitcase full of photographs to search for Newton. She traveled all over Chile, from the Atacama Desert in the north to the icebergs in Patagonia, in the south. She visited hospitals, morgues, anywhere she could think to look. She showed everyone she met photos of Newton. She hasn't found him yet, but she's never given up hope."

"That's such a sad story, Mamá. I hope we're not as unlucky."

"I have a feeling we'll be more fortunate. For one thing, we have a bit more information to go on."

I hope, so very, very much, that she's right. For the remainder of the flight, Mamá tells me what she has learned about the people of Chiloé from Papá, who did part of his residency on the island. "Celeste, they are very private people who will likely be suspicious of us. We'll need to be patient and make sure they trust us so that they'll help us find María Fernanda, Lucila, and Natalia."

It's not long before the pilot announces we're about to arrive in Puerto Montt.

Another
World

Mamá and I climb down the airplane stairs and are greeted by air that's cool and humid at the same time. Our next flight will be on a seaplane that will take us over to Castro. I've never flown in a seaplane before—Wow! It's really small! There are only six of us and a pilot! It's also a bumpier ride, but the view is amazing. We're not as high, so I can see fishing boats below us, and forests off in the distance. It's a short flight—only about twenty minutes— and we touch down right on the water. Very cool! Mamá grasps the arms of her seat as we land. At least we're only on the water a short while. As we glide toward the dock, she releases her grip and begins to relax. I see sea lions on some rocks nearby—we get close enough to see their whiskers and shiny brown coats.

When the seaplane reaches the long wooden dock, everyone disembarks. The other passengers hurry in the direction of the city center, but Mamá and I take a minute to look around us. It's as though we've entered another world. Whereas Valparaíso seems like a city of hills that

point toward the sky, in Castro everything points to the sea. The houses along the coast, which are built on enormous stilts submerged in the water, are painted every imaginable color—cinnamon red, canary yellow, sky blue—and they're all squished together, straddling land and sea. I hope I get to go in one while I'm here to see what it feels like to walk on water . . . sort of.

Just then, we're hit with a gust of wind, and I realize it's everywhere, coming at us from several directions at once. Everything's in motion! The ferns on the shore are swaying this way and that, fishing boats are bobbing up and down, and people's hats are being lifted right off their heads. One man is chasing his down the dock, but the gusts keep changing direction and sending him running to and fro, as though playing with him. The wind's loud, too; it moans and wails. Nana Delfina would say it's letting me know it will be accompanying me on my quest to find Lucila. I hope it blows me in the right direction.

We make our way slowly down the dock. On the shore, we see a line of women gazing out at the receding sea with forlorn looks on their faces. I wonder what they are waiting for—a boat full of colorful fish? A husband? A child? Someone who disappeared? Someone who was lost at sea? Nana Delfina always says that waiting is good, even though the person you're waiting for may never return. At least you're remembering while you're waiting, and the person is still alive in your memory.

As we pass the fishermen loading nets into their boats, they eye us warily. At the end of the dock, street vendors are selling all sorts of things: shells, ponchos. . . . One lady is selling cookbooks. Her accent is lilting. She sounds like a bird when she says, "A hundred potato recipes. Only six hundred pesos!" I move closer and see that the cookbooks are written by hand in an old-fashioned script. The pages are also handmade and are tied together with reeds. Six hundred pesos is nothing! Back in Valparaíso that wouldn't even buy a cup of coffee at Café Iris. "Mamá, I have to get one of these for Nana Delfina." I dig in the front pocket of my jeans. "Here, señora," I say, handing her the money.

"Gracias, señorita," she says. "The women of Chiloé created these recipes over hundreds of years. When you make one of our dishes, think of us here on the island." Then she hands me a perfectly formed peach-toned shell. "Here's another small gift for you. If you listen, you will always hear the waves on Chiloé Island, a different sound from all the other waves in the world."

I take it happily. "Gracias, señora." I can't wait to see if it sounds different from my conch shell at home.

"Now, Celeste, don't get too distracted," Mamá reminds me. "We have work to do. There will be time enough for us to explore." We look around for a news-paper kiosk where we can buy a map of the city. Papá has made us a reservation at a small hotel right off the Plaza de Armas, but we need to know how to get there.

With our map in hand, we head down Avenida San Martín, which will take us to the main plaza. There are cars whizzing along the streets, but there's not nearly as much traffic here as back home. As we walk, Mamá and I can feel people staring. Papá said the Chiloéans would be wary of us. Boy, was he right!

We arrive at the plaza, where there's an impressive yellow building. "What's that, Mamá? A church?" She looks at the map.

"Let's see. . . . Yes, that's the cathedral, and so our inn should be over in that direction." She points ahead and to the right. As we walk, we pass more vendors. An indigenous woman holds out a guitar to us and begins to speak, but we can't understand her. We shake our heads. She quickly switches from her native language to Span-ish and says in a heavy accent, "I'm selling this guitar for very little. Some of its strings are missing, but there's a bird's nest inside," as though that will make it more attractive to buyers. When I look more closely, though, I realize there really is a bird's nest in it and there are two baby birds chirping away. All of a sudden, the mamá bird lands on the neck of the guitar, hops down to the middle, and feeds her babies through the hole in the center. The woman looks at me and laughs happily. "Señorita, you don't need all the strings, because this instrument comes with music built in." Then she turns from me and begins to call out to other potential buyers.

Everything's really different here! We reach the hotel, which is run by a woman named Doña Eduvijes Cáceres. She's an "interesting character," as Papá would say. She starts talking to us in what seems to be the same language the street vendor used. Seeing the confused look on our faces, she switches to Spanish, but still with a smattering of what sounds like Mapudungun thrown in. Doña Cáceres leads us to our room, which is tiny but has a window that looks out onto the plaza.

"Breakfast is at eight, onces are at five, and supper is at ten," she tells us. "I make everything fresh here. Onces are always sopaipillas, because it rains here every day. I will also be happy to make you some traditional Chilote meals if you don't make other plans." She hands Mamá an enormous metal key. "Just leave the key at the front desk when you go out." I think, *Of course we will. That key is way too heavy to cart all over town!* After we wash up and go downstairs for onces—the most delicious sopaipillas I've ever tasted; don't tell Nana Delfina—Mamá and I decide to start asking some questions.

Mamá goes first. "Doña Cáceres, do you happen

to know a seamstress named María Fernanda Santiago who lives in Castro? She's an old friend of mine from Valparaíso."

The innkeeper looks at Mamá suspiciously. "Why are you asking?"

"I ummm . . . I lost touch with her a few years ago, but I recently got a letter from her telling me she lives here now. So, I've come to visit," says Mamá, smiling her warmest *Trust me* smile, the one she uses with her most nervous patients.

Doña Cáceres stares at Mamá and says curtly, "No, I don't believe I know anyone by that name." Then she turns abruptly and leaves us to finish our onces. My mother and I gape at each other, as it's obvious she's not telling the truth.

"We must have patience," Mamá reminds me. Patience, I think, is not always easy, and I begin fidgeting. But then, not fifteen minutes later, the innkeeper comes back followed by a woman I don't know. She looks to be about Mamá's age. She has long curly brown hair that's tied back in a ponytail, chocolate-brown eyes, and a spray of freckles across her nose. She's tall and slender, and . . . what's that on her wrist? A pincushion? I look over at Mamá, who's staring at the new arrival, eyes wide. Her coffee cup clatters onto its saucer.

"María Fernanda?" Mamá cries out, standing.

"It's me, Esmeralda!" the woman responds in a wobbly voice. "When Eduvijes came into my shop telling me there was an Esmeralda Marconi here, I didn't believe her. I had to come and see with my own two eyes. ¡Dios mío! It's true. . . . You're here! You're alive! Oh, I've dreamed of this so many times," she says, and pulls Mamá into an embrace. Then she begins to sob. "I'm so sorry, Esmeralda. . . . I'm so very sorry."

The two of them stay there hugging and crying for a long time. When they finally pull apart, Mamá touches her friend's cheek, her hair, as if she still needs convincing that this truly is her. "Part of the reason I've come to find you is to tell you, in person, that you have nothing to be sorry for. You helped me so much, at great risk to your own life, and I've always been so grateful—"

"Grateful?! But I didn't stop them from taking you away!" María Fernanda moans, gulping down fresh sobs.

"How could you have stopped them? They would have taken you, too. It's a miracle I survived. Had we both been taken, it's unlikely either of us would have made it out," Mamá argues.

"Please, tell me what happened. I thought you mustn't have made it, because I didn't hear from you after I sent my letter—"

"I will tell you everything, but first you must meet my daughter. Celeste, this is María Fernanda."

"I've heard a lot about you, Señora Santiago," I say politely. "Thank you for hiding Mamá. I'm glad you managed to get away from the general."

"I met you when you were just a toddler," says María Fernanda. "You probably don't remember. You've grown up so much. How old are you now?"

"Fourteen," I say.

"Well, it's nice to see you again after all these years . . . *both* of you," she says, still clutching Mamá's hand as though afraid to let go.

"Do you have time to talk now?" Mamá asks. "Celeste and I also want to ask for your help with something."

"Of course. Can you stop by my shop for a minute? I'll close up for the night, and you can come to my house and meet my husband, Esteban. We can talk for as long as we can stay awake!" And she pulls Mamá toward the door.

"Thank you, Doña Cáceres," Mamá and I say in unison as we pass the reception desk, and the old lady gives us just a hint of a smile.

We walk a few blocks to a street called Eusebio Lillo, lined with small shops and boutiques. María Fernanda stops outside Fernanda's Fanciful Fabrics. In the window, I see the most beautiful garments. There's a wedding gown that sparkles as though it's lit up from within, and then

239

there's an embroidered poncho that reminds me of the one Nana Delfina often wears. There's also a baby outfit covered in appliqued animals, some of which I've seen before—sea lions and penguins—and others I have not.

"Señora, what are those animals on the onesie?" I ask.

"Ah, they are some of the magical creatures of Chiloé. Let me show you." She ushers us into the store, then reaches into the display window for the small garment. "This gold figure is part fish and part man. He's called Millalobo, the golden wolf. He controls all the creatures of the sea. And this one," she says, pointing to another strange figure, "is Pincoya. She's Millalobo's daughter and she helps the fishermen of Chiloé fill their nets."

I'm already wondering what other creatures there are in Chiloé when I notice hanks of multicolored wool that smell of rain and smoke hanging from the ceiling. María Fernanda explains that all the people on Chiloé hang their wool like that. She shuts off the lights and puts the closed sign in the window of the front door, then leads us back toward the water. It turns out her house is one of those on stilts! I can hardly believe it.

María Fernanda and Esteban's house is small but cozy. It's one of the cinnamon-red ones and has a long braid of garlic hung on the front door to keep away evil spirits. María Fernanda explains that the walls of the house are made of soil mixed with different substances to make it as waterproof and durable as cement. The roof is made of shingles. We go up five steps and then enter. I expect the house to sway, but it doesn't. It's as rooted in the ocean as a tree is in the ground.

María Fernanda has run to her husband, Esteban—a man in his thirties with a handsome, weathered face—and is quickly explaining who we are. His mouth drops open in surprise. He comes over to Mamá and says, "Esmeralda? I can't believe it's you. María Fernanda has told me so much about you. She thought you were . . . well . . ." He grasps one of Mamá's hands with both of his. "It's such a pleasure to meet you. You don't know how happy you've made my wife." Then he turns and greets me. "Welcome." From a room to the left we hear cooing. María Fernanda takes Mamá's hand again and leads her into a small bedroom, a nursery.

"And . . . this is Clara Esmeralda," she says, lifting a baby from the crib and placing her into Mamá's arms.

"Oh, oh . . . ," says Mamá as fresh tears stream down her cheeks.

"She's five months old," says María Fernanda. Mamá touches the baby's delicately arched eyebrows and her nose, and turns to María Fernanda in wonder. "A daughter! She will bring you such joy!"

María Fernanda beams. "I know you said you have something to ask me, but I'd like to ask you something first."

"Of course," my mother says, eyes back on the baby, who's now reaching for my mom's earrings.

"Will you do us the honor of being her godmother?" she asks. "Esteban wants this too. Right, cariño?" Esteban nods and smiles.

"I . . . I . . . Well, of course. I would be delighted. Hello there, Clarita," Mamá says, tickling the baby under her chin. "Thank you both. Are you sure?"

Esteban laughs. "I can't imagine anything that would make my wife happier."

"Celeste," says Mamá, "come and say hello to the baby. She's adorable!" I look at the baby who's staring at Mamá. Then she grasps my finger with her little fist and gives it a squeeze. I giggle and tickle one of her feet. She's wearing one of the cute onesies that María Fernanda makes in her shop. I recognize Millalobo and Pincoya right away.

María Fernanda asks Esteban to give the baby a bottle so we can talk. We walk to the back of the house, where there's a small deck overlooking the ocean.

I love sitting over the waves like this. At first, María Fernanda seems uncomfortable discussing what happened during the dictatorship in front of me, but Mamá reassures her that I've already heard quite a lot and am doing a good job of processing it all.

After Mamá tells her what happened on the *Esmeralda*, María Fernanda buries her face in her hands. Mamá takes her by the shoulders. "María, I was *so* lucky! Look, I'm back with my daughter. I'm here with my dear friend. I'm alive!" Mamá says with fervor.

We tell her about Captain Pratt, that he'll be here tomorrow. María Fernanda can't believe it. Then we tell her about the lost mail, the letters, about Lucila, and Natalia.

"And that leads to my question," Mamá says at last. "Would you and Esteban help us find the girls?"

"Oh, those poor, poor children! I can't imagine what I would do if something happened to my Clarita. Of course! Of course we'll help you. Esteban is from here—he knows half the island. Here's the thing—if you two go around asking, it's unlikely anyone will even answer you. The people here protect one another, as you saw with Eduvijes earlier today." She goes inside and comes out with Esteban and the baby.

After we tell him the story, he rubs at his upper lip and says, "So we know the girls were taken in by three sisters and that they make their living weaving baskets?" Mamá and I nod. "There are a number of women who make baskets on the main plaza, and more down by the pier where they sell to tourists, but they're only there in the mornings. In the afternoons they're usually out gathering the reeds they use to make their baskets and the fungi they use to dye them." He pauses, then adds, "Tomorrow morning, when I go to set my nets, I'll ask my buddies if they know the sisters. I'll let you know what I find out. Where are you staying?"

"They're over at Eduvijes's place," María Fernanda tells him.

"Perfect. I'll find you there once I have some information," says Esteban. "Now, when you arrived, I was preparing a fish stew with what I caught today, and I just took a fresh loaf of bread out of the oven. Will you join us for dinner?"

After a delicious meal of salty and succulent fish, potatoes, celery, and carrots, along with crusty bread with homemade butter, I play with Clarita while Mamá and María Fernanda talk. At eleven, Mamá and I head back to the inn, tired but happy. We fall into bed and say our prayers together. Then I write in my notebook about Millalobo and Pincoya and guitars with birds inside, until I can't keep my eyes open any longer. I put up the journal and switch out the light. "Good night, Mamá," I say, and then I whisper, "Good night, Lucila. See you soon."

A Most
Precious Find

The church clock has just bonged eight times—Chiloé's clocks seem to keep better time than those in Valparaíso! The churches aren't made of mortar and brick here, but of wood painted unexpectedly vibrant colors, especially purples and yellows. *Everything* here is different, and there's an air of magic about it. Nana Delfina is going to love it.

Mamá and I are having toast and coffee on the patio of the hotel when we see Esteban strolling toward us. He greets us warmly with kisses on our cheeks and joins us, ordering his own coffee in the strange mix of Mapudungun and Spanish they use here.

"I asked around the dock first thing, and one of my friends said he thinks his wife once purchased baskets from some women she thought were sisters. Although he doesn't know exactly where to find them, he said the last time he saw them, they were set up on the other side of the plaza. The vendors usually start selling around nine o'clock. I hope that helps."

"It helps a lot, Esteban," Mamá says. "Thank you." He drinks his coffee in two gulps, wishes us a good day, and invites us to stop by the house again later. Then he sets off for the docks.

Now that I think I may actually get to see Lucila again soon, I'm getting really nervous, and I can't stop folding and unfolding my napkin. Mamá smiles. "Settle down, Celeste. Fidgeting won't make anything happen any faster."

"I can't. I feel like I'm going to bust out of myself! In less than an hour—"

Mamá cuts me off. "I know, but don't get ahead of yourself. We don't know for sure that we'll find Lucila today."

"I know," I reply, slouching down in my chair.

"Niña Celeste! Esmeralda!" I look up, and there's Nana Delfina. She's here! Right behind her are Captain Pratt, who's carrying one of Nana's bags, and Sebastián. Mamá and I hug Nana, and then I impulsively hug Captain Pratt and Sebastián as well.

Mamá asks the men if they want to stay at the inn with us and Nana Delfina, or if they are going to stay on the boat.

"The boy and I will stay on the boat. It's our home, after all," says Captain Pratt, decked out, as usual, in full uniform. "But, of course, we plan to spend the day here with you looking for the girls."

"María Fernanda . . . I mean Isabel . . . is eager to see you again, Captain Pratt. I'm sure you'll remember her when you see her," I gush, and we fill them in on what we've already learned.

We decide to split up to begin searching for the sisters. At nine on the dot, Sebastián and I head to the other side of the plaza where Esteban's friend saw the sisters previously, while Nana Delfina, Mamá, and Captain Pratt go down by the water to see if the sisters are working there today.

"How are you?" I ask Sebastián hesitantly as we begin to walk across the square, both of us trying hard not to call attention to ourselves by walking crazy fast.

"Nervous," he replies, not looking at me, shoulders hunched, hands in his pockets. "I'm not sure what I'll do if we can't find Natalia, or if the girl we find isn't her." I give him a sidelong glance. If we don't find his sister, won't it be like he's losing her all over again? I'm filled with a horrible ache for what he must be feeling right now.

On this side of the plaza there are woodworkers, fruit vendors, women selling baked goods, and yes, basket weavers. It turns out that Chiloé is famous for its baskets. People use them for everything from carrying things to and from the market, to storing things over the long winter months. The weavers don't have stalls or stands; they set up on the ground and work in a circle. The first group we see has five women. All have their heads bowed, concentrating on their work. Each of them is working on her own basket. One of them is just starting; she's weaving brightly colored reeds—reds, greens, blues—together in a crisscross pattern that looks like it will be the base of the basket. Another is working on a circular design that looks like a coiled snake. An older woman is expertly weaving a wavelike pattern around the side of a basket. No matter their age, their hands work at lightning speed.

Sebastián and I decide we'll go down the line and talk to each group of basket weavers in the hopes of finding the sisters. We don't know if they work alone or with others.

I feel badly for interrupting the first group's work because they're clearly on a roll, but I gather my courage and ask, "Buenos días, señoras. Do you speak Spanish?" They're all wearing large-brimmed hats, so I can't see their faces clearly. They make no attempt to look up at me. "I . . . ummm . . . I was wondering if you can help me. I'm looking for my friend. Her name is Lucila López. She's from Valparaíso and I've come to find her." The women shake their heads. I wait awhile to see if they'll say anything at all, but they just continue weaving. Sebastián and I walk away, dejected.

We try to talk to four more groups, but no one wants to help us; some of them don't even *acknowledge* us! I've never come across anything like it. Sebastián has his hands thrust even deeper into his pockets, and that hollow look is coming over him again.

"We can't give up, Sebastián," I say encouragingly, although I'm beginning to lose hope too.

We come across a final group, this one with six weavers, right at the end of the plaza. We use both Lucila's and Natalia's names to try to get their attention, but once again we're rewarded only with head shakes. As we begin to pull back, Sebastián, scowling, blurts out, "I told you it wasn't true, Celeste. My sister . . . Oh, forget it! Why did I let you and Captain Pratt convince me this was a good idea?"

"Sebastián!" I start, but he jerks his arm away from me. Before I can say anything else, I notice that one of the women in the group has lifted her head ever so slightly. I feel certain she has heard our conversation. Just as quickly, she ducks her head back down and begins muttering to the two women on either side of her in hushed tones, in what sounds like Mapudungun.

Sebastián has turned in the direction of the inn, or Captain Pratt's boat, or . . . anywhere but here, when one of the women calls out in a thick accent, "Wait!" She's heavyset and is wearing a red floral housecoat and bright yellow espadrilles. She has taken off her hat. Her hair is the silver of the moon, and her eyes have the same silvery glint. Her skin is weathered, like most people's on this island, where the wind relentlessly whips off the sea. The two other women she was talking to before are now looking up at us as well. They, too, are wearing similar clothes and shoes, just in different colors. When I look at their faces, I can tell they're related, and a wave of excitement flows through me.

"Come back here, young man," the first woman says. Though Sebastián has his back to her, he stops

walking. "We would like to ask you something." Sebastián whips around. His eyes are red, his cheeks flushed.

"What?" he says rather rudely, and I can't blame him. He's had enough. I nudge him, but he bats me away.

"Natalia doesn't have any family," says the woman. Sebastián freezes. "Her family died while the general was in power," she continues. "We don't know you. Who are you?"

Sebastián stares at her for a long while, but then finds his voice at last. "I'm . . . I'm her brother!" His voice cracks; his eyes are desperate. "Where's my sister? Please! Please, where is she?"

"It's true, señoras. This is Sebastián Paz," I add. "He escaped. . . . He didn't die. . . .

His sister is Natalia. She's only ten." Then I can't stop myself. "And . . . And Lucila . . . Do you know Lucila? She's my dearest best friend. Maybe she has talked about me? My name is Celeste. Celeste Marconi."

The three ladies confer again, and then the spokeswoman for the three nods. "Yes, Lucila has mentioned someone named Celeste many times, and Natalia speaks of Sebastián every day."

My heart is going to burst. Lucila! "Can you . . . ? Can we . . . ?" I can't even finish my sentence. My hands are trembling.

The sisters look at one another again and come to a decision without ever saying a word. "The girls have been staying with us. Are you really who you say you are?" the woman with the yellow espadrilles demands, scrutinizing us both.

"I give you my word, señora. Por favor, please, tell us where Natalia and Lucila are," I plead, noticing that Sebastián has gone quiet.

The sister wearing the blue espadrilles says, "They're in school."

"Where is it? How do we get there?" I'd break into a run, but I don't know where I'm going.

"It's about a kilometer down Avenida San Martín on the right side. I will take you," says Yellow Espadrilles. The third sister, who hasn't spoken, looks down at the ground. I wonder what she's thinking. I nudge Sebastián again, but this time he doesn't respond at all. I think he's in shock.

"Thank you, señora! Let me tell my mother where we're going first," I say, looking around to see if I can spot Mamá. Just then I spy her, Nana, and Captain Pratt entering the plaza. "Please, wait here for just a minute. I'll be right back." I run as fast as I can. I reach them, out of breath, and pant out, "Mamá . . . Nana . . . we've found them! I . . . I think we've found them!"

Mamá grips my arm. "You've found them! Oh my! Thank the stars. Where are they?"

"At school. Let's go!" I say, pulling Mamá.

The four of us trot back to Sebastián and the sisters, weaving in and out of the crowds of people who have stopped to look at the crafts.

I realize I don't know the sisters' names and introduce them awkwardly as the women who've been taking care of Lucila and Natalia.

"I'm Sol, and these are my sisters, Luna and Sonia," says the sister in the yellow espadrilles.

Mamá, Nana Delfina, and Captain Pratt introduce themselves. Then Sol, who is clearly the leader of the three sisters, says: "We can talk later. If you are who you say you are, we must go to the school right away."

Everyone eagerly agrees, except Sebastián. His eyes

are guarded, and he has stepped back. Captain Pratt takes one look at him and says, "Come on, son. You have to take a chance. I have a feeling this is going to work out much better than you're imagining."

Sebastián nods solemnly. He seems to be thinking something over, for then he says to Sol, "I . . . I'm really sorry if I was rude, señora. I . . . I . . ." His head hangs low.

Sol rests her hand on his arm. "Don't say anything else, young man. I can see in your eyes the pain you feel. And now that I look at you, I can see the resemblance between you and Natalia . . . something in the eyes. Come." Her voice is soothing, but it quavers, too.

Nana Delfina grasps Mamá's arm. "You go, Esmeralda. Captain Pratt and I will wait here with Sol's sisters." Mamá nods.

Captain Pratt gives Sebastián an encouraging pat on the back. "Go and get Natalia," he says. "I'll be right here when you get back. We don't want to overwhelm the girls."

The walk, which probably only takes ten minutes, seems to take hours. No one speaks. No one really knows what to say. Finally we arrive at the school, an old brick building with lots of big windows. It's two stories tall and has a fenced-in yard off to one side where some younger kids are playing hopscotch and spinning tops.

Sol tells us this is one of the few schools on Chiloé—

children of all ages go here. She opens the big wooden front door, and we walk down a blue-and-white-tiled hall to the principal's office. Sol explains briefly who we are, and the principal stands up slowly. "Can you get Lucila and Natalia, please?" she asks him. I'm guessing by the look on the principal's face that this sort of thing has not happened often, if ever.

The principal goes one way and asks his secretary to go the other; the girls are in different classrooms. I'm shifting from one foot to the other. Mamá is twirling her wedding band. Sebastián stares at the floor. He hasn't said a word since we left the plaza.

The first to come down the hall is a girl of about ten—the very girl from the old photo I had of her—Natalia! I nudge Sebastián, but still he won't look up. "Sebastián!" I say more forcefully and nudge him again, hard this time. "Look!" He slowly lifts his head and blinks multiple times, as though not believing what he's seeing.

"Natalia? NATALIA!" he screams, and starts off at a run in her direction.

When the girl hears Sebastián's voice, she too looks up and stops short. "S-Sebastián?" Then, to our astonishment, she crumbles to the ground. The principal manages to catch her before her head hits the tiles. She's fainted! Sebastián falls to his knees in front of her and leans over her so his face is directly above hers. Gently he pats her cheek. "Nati! Nati! Wake up. . . . *Please* wake up," he says desperately.

Mamá and I rush over to see if we can help. Natalia's eyes flutter open. At first, she looks scared and confused. She lets out a whimper. Sebastián says, "Shhhhh, Nati, shhhh. It's okay. It's me. It's Sebastián." Natalia sits up unsteadily. She looks her brother in the eye, and slowly, slowly touches his face.

"Sebastián? But you're dead. Am I in one of my nightmares?"

"No, Nati. It's really me," he says, choking back a sob. "I've missed you so much."

Natalia grasps his shirt with both hands and then burrows her face in his chest. "I thought you were with Mamá and Papá in heaven," she cries. "On the boat—they told me . . . The mean guard told me he had thrown you all into the ocean." And she begins to sob. But then, suddenly, she looks up at her brother. "Does this mean Mamá and Papá are alive too?" she asks, her eyes going bright.

Sebastián lets out a moan. "Ay . . . No, Nati. Mamá and Papá . . . they *are* in heaven."

"But maybe the guards lied to you, too—"

"I . . . I . . . saw what happened to them, Nati. They're . . . they're gone." The two siblings grab on to each other and quietly sob.

We step back to give them privacy. I can hardly believe this is real. I put my arm around Mamá's waist, and she pulls me close. I'm so thankful we've found Natalia.

Just then, we hear a sound behind us, and Mamá and I spin around. The principal's secretary is coming toward us with a tall, skinny girl wearing the same uniform as Nati: a pleated gray skirt, a white blouse, a navy-blue vest with the school's crest, high socks, and brown shoes.

My heart sinks. This girl is as tall as the secretary, and Lucila's as short as I am. Just as I'm fearing my reunion today will not be happy like Sebastián's, the girl draws closer, I realize she *is* Lucila. She's just grown *really* tall in three years. Oh, it's her! It's her!

"Lucila?" I say at the exact same time she says, "Celeste?" And we run to each other. I hug her and keep squeezing her, trying to convince myself she's real.

"Celeste, I can't breathe!" Lucila finally manages to say.

"Oh, sorry!" I loosen my grip on her, but I don't let go. Mamá comes up and pulls us both in for a hug.

When we do step apart, Lucila looks . . . well, I can't really tell. She looks confused? Scared? Happy? Sad? All of those emotions are crisscrossing her face at the same time. She clearly doesn't know what to say. Mamá leads

Lucila over to one of the benches that line the hallway. We sit on either side of her.

"First of all," Mamá says, touching her chin, "your grandmother and Marisol are alive." Lucila lets out a breath, and her shoulders slump with relief.

"Where are they? Are they here? Can I see them?" Questions suddenly tumble from Lucila's lips.

Mamá laughs happily. "No, hija. They're back in Valparaíso, waiting for you. The travel would have been too hard on your grandmother, and Marisol is looking after her. They asked us to come and find you when they got your letter."

Lucila nods, then pauses, her face growing dark. "But I never heard back from them! Why not? All this time I thought they were *dead!*" Her voice is angry, hurt.

Mamá rubs Lucila's arm. "Your abuela only received your letter last week! A whole bunch of undelivered mail was discovered—it had been hidden by the general's men. You need to know—your grandmother never stopped looking for you, Lucila. Never. . . . She marched every week with the other grandmothers in front of the government building, demanding to know what happened to you and the other disappeared families," Mamá explains.

Lucila takes that in, then turns to me. "What . . . What about everyone else? Did . . . ? Is your papá okay?

What about Abuela Frida and Nana Delfina? Are Cristóbal and Señora Williams okay? Is Señorita Alvarado? I . . . No, don't tell me. . . . No, tell me . . . ," she says all at once.

"Señorita Alvarado is fine," I say. "So is everyone in the Marconi household. There's a lot to tell you, but they're all okay. Cristóbal and his mamá are fine too. He's grown up a lot. You won't believe it!" I say, trying to make her smile, but she doesn't.

"I'm . . . I'm so glad. You can't imagine the terrible things I've thought about what might have happened to all of you. . . . Like what happened to us . . ." She trails off and glances down at her lap. I notice her fingernails are bitten down to the quick. I begin to say something, but Mamá shakes her head. I close my mouth and sit looking at my friend, who's somewhere else in her mind.

Just then Natalia bounds over. "Luci?" she says, tapping Lucila on the shoulder.

"Nati, what are you doing out of class?" asks Lucila, confused.

"The principal came and got me because . . ." Sebastián comes up behind his sister. "Because my brother's here." She's grinning from ear to ear. "Luci, this is Sebastián."

"But . . . I thought . . ." Lucila looks from Sebastián

to Natalia, from Mamá to me. "What's going on? Nati, you told me . . ."

"I know, I know. . . . But listen, the guards lied to me. This *is* my brother. He's come to take me home," Natalia states. She's positively glowing.

Lucila stands and shakes Sebastián's hand. "It's nice to meet you. I've heard a *lot* about you. I'm glad you're okay."

"Thank *you* for taking care of Nati. She's already told me a lot about how you helped her. Gracias," he says again, and hugs Lucila.

"She's helped me a lot too," says Lucila as she pulls away and looks fondly at Natalia, who beams at the compliment. Then Lucila sits back down on the bench. "I . . . I can't believe it," she says, and stares off into space again.

"Lucila?" I ask gently. "Are you okay?"

"It's just . . . I just got used to the idea that this was where Nati and I were going to finish growing up . . ." She trails off again.

"But now you can come home to Valparaíso!"

"Celeste," warns Mamá, and then it dawns on me— Lucila's struggling. . . . She's really struggling.

"What is it, Lucila?"

"*My* parents aren't in Valparaíso, Celeste," she says, her voice laced with anger. "I don't know if I *want* to go back." And she covers her face with her hands.

I feel like I've been punched in the gut, but then I realize what Lucila has just said. . . . *Celeste, you idiot. Why don't you think before you speak!*

"I'm sorry, amiga. I wasn't thinking. . . . It's just . . . I'm *sooo* happy to see you. I've missed you so much." I tentatively wrap my arm around her shoulders.

Mamá says, "Lucila, of course you need time to think about what all this means and what you want to do. You've probably only just gotten used to your life here, and now we've arrived, and in five minutes everything's been turned upside down. Talk to the sisters. Take the time you need. We'll be here when you're ready to talk."

Lucila glances down again. "Thank you, Señora Marconi." Mamá kisses her on both cheeks. Sol, who has been patiently observing everything from a respectful distance, comes over. "Lucila, let's go home so you can rest. We can talk about everything later and you can decide what you want to do." Lucila nods and stands up.

"Mamá Sol, would it be okay if I go with my brother? He's staying on a houseboat down by the docks," Natalia asks. She's gripping Sebastián's hand with both of hers.

"Of course, my girl." Then Sol turns to Mamá and me. "Why don't you come to our house in the morning? If you continue down this road for another kilometer and turn right by the big Canelo tree, you will see it in the distance. It sits in the middle of a field of blue mushrooms."

"Thank you," Mamá and I say.

Before leaving, Lucila hugs me. "I missed you, too, Celeste." Then she turns to Nati. "I'll look after Toñi for you."

"That's my pet turtle!" she tells Sebastián happily.

"See ya, kiddo," Lucila tells Nati in an upbeat tone that I can tell is forced. "Have fun with your brother." As she leaves with Sol, her face is unreadable, as though she's trying to figure out the most difficult puzzle in the world, and I notice she hasn't asked if she can call her grandmother or cousin.

I watch after her, my heart breaking. *She may not come home with us*, is what I'm thinking as Sebastián taps me on the shoulder. "Celeste, you've already figured out that this is Nati, but I wanted to introduce you properly. . . . Nati, Celeste and her classmates are the reason I was able to come and look for you."

"I know who Celeste is, silly," says Natalia. "She's Lucila's best friend. I know all about her." She looks up at me and says, "I know your favorite color is blue and your favorite food is cuchufli . . ." Natalia spouts off a whole list of things that Lucila has obviously said about me, and I realize how silly I'm being—Lucila didn't forget about me at all. . . . She still loves me.

Scary
Captain Pratt

On the walk back to the plaza, Natalia is pulling on Sebastián's arm, skipping—she's so happy, she might just start floating! As for Sebastián, he can't take his eyes off her. I, on the other hand, waver between glee for them and worry for Lucila. Her reaction threw me for a loop. I guess I never realized, or fully considered, all she's been through. Mamá, who misses nothing, says, "Give Lucila a little time, hija. Think about this from her perspective. She's had an enormous shock today. I have a feeling if we're patient with her and give her some space, she'll come around." I nod. Mamá's probably right, but I stupidly thought that—okay, selfishly thought that—the minute Lucila saw us, things could be like they used to be when we didn't have a care in the world.

A stray leaf blows in the air, and I catch it midflight. It's very pretty, but I don't recognize its patterning. It must be from a plant native to Chiloé. I consider putting it in my pocket to ask Esteban about later, but then I toss it back into the wind, which instantly snatches it back up.

I watch as the flutter of green takes its own path, and spy Captain Pratt and Nana Delfina sitting outside the inn. The other sisters are nowhere in sight. They must have gone home.

When Natalia first sees the captain, she shrinks behind Sebastián. Maybe it's the uniform. Sebastián leans down and whispers, "Don't be scared, Nati. This is Captain Pratt. He's been looking after me all this time, just like Sol and her sisters have been looking after you."

The old captain comes over to Nati and very formally holds out his hand, as if meeting a grand lady. "It's a pleasure to meet you, Señorita Natalia. Sebastián has told me so much about you. I can't wait to show you where we live. Would you like that?" She looks at him, uncertainly at first, but then shakes his hand. In a polite and grown-up voice, she says, "I would, Captain Pratt." And I notice for the first time that Nati has a unique accent when she speaks Spanish. I guess that's from being here on Chiloé for so long.

After Nana Delfina meets Nati, we sit down and order more coffee, a Fanta limón soft drink for Nati, and some bite-size empanadas stuffed with potato and onion. Nana is so excited when she hears the news about Lucila that she keeps grabbing Captain Pratt's arm. He smiles at her, clearly amused by her excitement. "When can Delfina see Lucila?" she asks.

Mamá explains that we'll go over to the sisters' house in the morning. "How is she?" Nana whispers. Mamá gives a quick head shake. Whether that means *Not good* or *Not now*, I'm not sure.

"Can we go and see your houseboat now, Captain?" Natalia asks, shoving the last empanada into her mouth. Mamá and I worried that Natalia and Lucila might not want to go on a boat again after the *Esmeralda*, but it doesn't seem to be a problem. I remember then that the guard brought them to Chiloé on a boat, so they're probably not as scared of the water as Mamá is.

"Of course, young lady!"

To my surprise, Sebastián reaches under the table and grasps my hand. In a low voice, he murmurs, "Thank you, Celeste. None of this would have happened if you and Nana Delfina hadn't found me." My arm is tingling where he's touching me.

"Ummm . . . but it was really pure luck."

"Even so, I'm really grateful." I squeeze his hand and then let go, my eyes looking everywhere except at him. "See you later," he says, jogging to catch up with Nati and the captain. I watch them until they're out of sight. So does Nana, I notice.

"Celeste, I need to call Doña Estela, Marisol, and Papá and tell them the good news. Do you want to go with me to tell María Fernanda after that?" Mamá asks, breaking me out of my trance.

"I . . . I think I'll stay here with Nana. A lot has happened, and I need to think . . ." I trail off.

"Okay, hija. I'll see you in a while," she says, and gives Nana Delfina a look I can't interpret, as she heads inside.

As soon as my mother is out of earshot, Nana leans in close. "Okay, niña Celeste, what's wrong? Nana can tell something's not right."

At first, I don't answer. Nana raises an eyebrow. Soon, out tumbles, "I just thought it would be different, you know? I thought Lucila would be, well, like she used to be. But she's not the same, not the same at all—I can't even tell if she's happy to see us!"

"You're not the same either, Celeste," Nana reminds me. "You just don't realize it because you're in your own skin. You've changed a lot since you came back from Maine. But just because you're both different doesn't mean you can't still be best friends. Some things never change. You trust Nana. She knows what she's talking about." She says this with such conviction that I feel instantly better. "Now, stop moping and let's get something else to eat. Nana's still hungry," she says, signaling to Doña Cáceres for some sopaipillas, even though it's not the traditional time for them.

"What a morning!" I murmur a short while later.

"What a wonderful morning!" says Nana as she digs into Doña Cáceres's sopaipillas. "Mmmm . . . these are almost as good as mine." I look at her and grin.

"So, Nana, how was the trip here with Captain Pratt?" I ask, raising *my* eyebrows a couple of times.

She reaches for her coffee.

"What is Celeste implying?" She takes a sip.

"Me? Nothing! I just wondered . . ." I put on my sweetest, most innocent face. "He's kind of cute . . . for an old man."

Nana Delfina chokes on her coffee. "Celeste Marconi! I didn't notice anything about that man except that he's too skinny for Nana!"

"I'm sure you can fix that," I full-out tease. "What did you do while you were sailing?"

"I cooked," says Nana, and then she crosses her arms across her chest. "And I taught them some words in Mapudungun."

"That's all? What did you talk about?"

"Well, I found out your Sebastián is a nice young man."

"*My* Sebastián? He's not *my* Sebastián," I say, flustered.

"Hmmmm . . ."

"What about the captain? He's kind of . . . eccentric."

Nana laughs. "He's what Nana would call . . .

colorful." She adjusts her poncho. "All he told me was that he spent many years training young sailors and that he retired before the dictator came to power. That man will not speak of his family. When I asked, he changed the subject and asked me to dance."

I practically jump up out of my chair. "He asked you to *dance*?!"

"Yes. Nana likes to dance, and the captain knows the tango." Nana likes to *dance*? I try to imagine her twirling around the houseboat with Captain Pratt.

"Did Sebastián dance too?" I ask incredulously.

"No, he was too shy. But the captain, he's not shy," she says, a coy smile on her lips.

"Nana, you're in trouble," I declare.

"I hope so!" she replies, and we both burst out laughing.

A Heart
Split in Two

The next morning, Mamá, Nana Delfina, and I make our way to the sisters' house, which is tiny—one level—with a tin roof. It sits smack in the middle of a vast field of blue mushrooms—bluer than the bluest sky, bluer than a periwinkle. As we wade through them, I keep bending down to touch them. It's like I'm in a fairy tale. Just as I'm wondering how the mushrooms might taste, the front door opens.

"Buenos días," Sol greets us, her smile wide. "Come in." I suddenly feel nervous, especially when Lucila steps into the doorway, the fringe of the cream poncho she's wearing—so pretty with rust-colored stripes running horizontally through it—brushing her elbows. She's also wearing jeans and a pair of green espadrilles.

"Hola, Celeste. Hola, Señora Marconi," she says, kissing us on the cheeks. Then she sees Nana Delfina. She squeals and hurls herself into Nana's arms.

"Ay, niña Lucila, you've made Nana Delfina so happy," Nana says, squeezing Lucila tight.

After the two have had a moment to hug and squeal and hug and squeal some more, Sol says, "Lucila was about to go collect some reeds for our baskets. Why don't you go with her, Celeste? After the long walk, I expect your mamá and Delfina could use a rest and some tea."

Lucila and I glance at each other—we know we've just been set up, and we laugh at the same time.

As we step outside into the clusters of mushrooms, I hook my arm through Lucila's, just as I used to on our way to Café Iris after school. Usually I was complaining to Lucila about math. I didn't understand numbers. Those pesky things used to dance across the page and wouldn't let me catch them or work them out. It's not like that with words. I can lasso words and put them in order and make them say pretty things. Numbers . . . they just run away. Lucila was good with numbers, and she would give me pep talks, tell me that if I stopped daydreaming about dancing numbers, they might make more sense. I shake my head at the memory and, pointing down, ask, "How do they taste?"

"The mushrooms? Hmmm—it's impossible to explain. . . . They . . . well, they taste like . . . magic. They're not soft, or hard, or bitter, or sweet. They're delicious. You'll have to try them while you're here. I'll ask Sol to cook some for us." I tell her I'd like that, but then an awkward silence falls between us. I feel . . . nervous.

Nervous that I might say the wrong thing . . . ask the wrong thing.

Then, out of the blue, Lucila asks where *I* was during the dictatorship. "All these years I worried you had disappeared too."

I give her the short version of being in exile in the United States. Then I tell her about how Cristóbal and I found Papá. She listens so carefully that I feel I can finally ask the question that's been bothering me the most. "Lucila, why didn't you . . . Well, why didn't you try harder to find us after the general died? I know you sent a letter, but why wouldn't you have called . . . I don't know . . . You could have called the Valparaíso police, or . . . or your abuela and Marisol, or me even! I realize things here are not as advanced as back home, but I know there are telephones."

Lucila doesn't answer for the longest time. Finally she says, "It's so hard to explain. . . . When I didn't receive an answer to my letter, I decided it was a sign that I was meant to stay here and take care of Natalia. She had lost her entire family, or so we thought. And I had lost . . ." She presses her lips together, hard.

"But . . . so you never tried to call?" I ask, still confused.

"No, I never did! Does that make me a bad person?" A tinge of anger flares in her question.

"Uhhhh . . . no, but . . . but why? It's just—we were mad with grief, thinking you—"

"I don't expect you, or anyone else, to understand, Celeste," Lucila interrupts, unhooking her arm from mine and striding away.

"Try me," I call after her. She pauses, then walks back toward me.

"Okay. Okay, Celeste. This is going to sound really awful, but, I was sort of glad Abuela Estela didn't write back."

I gasp inwardly. Of course I want to ask her why, but I know I need to hold my tongue and give Lucila a chance to explain. After a moment, she does. "I . . . I . . . can't tell you what it was like after Mamá and Papá were murdered. It . . . it changed me, Celeste. That day, a coldness entered my heart and it won't ever go away. I felt numb, completely numb. Natalia, on the other hand, was hysterical. She needed me, and I'm so grateful, because that gave me something to do, to focus on, other than thinking about my parents. . . ." I squeeze her arm, encouraging her to continue. "At first, when I thought about reaching out to Abuela Estela and Marisol, I couldn't bring myself to do it; I'd convinced myself they were dead, and that made it easier for me in some ways. . . ."

"Easier?"

"I know it sounds weird, but I just wanted to continue feeling numb. Because, if you're numb, you don't feel *anything*, which was a million times better that feeling that . . . that . . . Anyway, finally the sisters practically forced me to write that letter. They kept saying, 'Lucila, what if your abuela and your cousin are alive?' They nagged me so much that I broke down and wrote. When I got no response, like I said, I took it as a sign, and vowed not to try to contact anyone else." She pauses one more time, then adds, "I didn't want to go back to Valparaíso anyway."

"But Valparaíso . . . is your *home*. And there's your abuela, and Marisol, and Cristóbal—he'll be so excited."

Lucila shakes her head in a way that makes it clear I don't understand her. "It *was* my home, Celeste," she says. "Here's the truth. That's where Mamá, Papá, and I lived together. We were so happy. I can't imagine going back there without them." Then her anger turns to something else. "Celeste, my parents . . ." And she trails off.

"I know. . . . I read your letter. I'm so sorry, Lucila," I say, realizing my words are inadequate. Then, in a very quiet voice, I tell her, "Mamá was on the *Esmeralda* too."

"What? No!" she cries. "*I'm* sorry, Celeste. How . . . How is she?"

"It's been hard, but she's doing much better. She's only just started talking about what happened to her."

"I can't believe we used to watch that ship sail into the harbor, like it was part of some wonderful nautical parade. I hate it now. I never want to see it again!" Lucila spits out angrily.

"If you come back to Valparaíso, you'll *have* to see it," I say cautiously. "President Espinoza has decided it will be turned into a museum, to help remember the people who were held prisoner there . . . and . . . and . . . those who died there. Mamá says that one day she wants to visit the ship with me." Lucila takes two quick steps away from me again, horrified. "I'm sorry!" I say, afraid I've really set her off. "I . . . I . . . didn't mean to upset you." I reach for her arm again. She lets me take it.

An orange parrot alights in the tree beside us. Its color is stunning. Lucila watches it preen, then says at last, "Celeste, in order not to lose my mind, I had to throw away the key to my past. It's not that I didn't talk about my family and friends—I did! I still do!—but I just knew I couldn't go back. Nothing is the same. I have so much . . . hatred in my heart." She kicks hard at a cluster of mushrooms. They explode into pieces, like the sky shattering.

I rack my brain for the right thing to say. "Look, I wanted to hate the men who hurt Mamá and Papá—I *did* hate them—but Abuela Frida . . . she's helped me understand that hatred doesn't help. By hating them, I'm letting them continue to, well, hurt me. But, yeah, it's hard not to. I'd never tell Abuela, but I must confess—I still write horrible things about the dictator in my note-book of dreams, and then when I shut the cover, it's like . . . it's like I'm writing him into a coffin. And is it horrible to say that it makes me feel . . . better?"

"You don't!" says Lucila, a spark of light coming back to her eyes.

"Oh, yes I do!" I exclaim.

"I still have the worst nightmares," Lucila admits. "So does Natalia. The sisters take turns calming us down. I'm scared that . . . I'm scared those bad dreams will never go away."

"I can't imagine how bad your nightmares are, Lucila. I've been having some as well since Mamá told me what happened to her. Some nights I dream I'm on the *Esmeralda* with Mamá and I see all the terrible things the guards are doing to her, but I'm frozen, like a statue, and I can't do anything to help her." I shiver. "Nana has always told me that my dreams—the good ones and the bad ones—are important, because they're telling me something. She told me that my bad dreams show me how much I wanted to help, but couldn't, and that I should take that as a sign that I should find other ways of helping . . . other ways of changing things."

"Like what?" asks Lucila, her eyes going flat again. "Teenagers can't change anything."

"Sure we can, Lucila. President Espinoza is making sure all Chilean children learn about the dictatorship. If we *know* how it happened, *we* can keep it from ever happening again. We started right after the summer vacation. Are your teachers doing the same here?"

Lucila thrusts her chin out. "No, things on Chiloé work differently. We're behind the times here, and we like it that way." She pulls away from me once more and turns her back.

"But, Lucila, we have to do something—"

"Why?" she interrupts, turning to face me again. "Why do *I* have to do something?" She's yelling now, and *I* take a step back.

She glares at me, and then her face crumples. "I . . . I just don't know what I want anymore. . . . Well, I *do*: I want Mamá and Papá back. All I want is Mamá and Papá back! It's *all* I want. But they're dead. They're DEAD!" She falls to the ground, surrounded by flecks of blue. She puts her head between her knees, crying so hard, her shoulders heave.

I approach her slowly, carefully, and crouch down. I don't know what to do, what to say, so I rub her back and let her cry. After a while, she reaches for me and hugs me tight.

A strange cry erupts high above, drowning out Lucila's sobs. She pulls away, looking up at the enormous Canelo tree, her cheeks streaked with tears.

"What was *that*?" I exclaim, alarmed.

"The—" Her breath hitches. "The parrot. We have huge ones here. Their call can wake you up out of the deepest sleep." The bird lets out one more screech, then launches itself from the tree, displaying its vibrant feathers. I can't stop staring—I've never seen a bird so orange.

Lucila wipes her eyes and looks at me. "Do you remember the legend Señorita Alvarado taught us, about the lady who lived in the underworld?"

I think for a minute, then say, "Hmmm . . . Wasn't her name 'Persephone'?"

"Yes! Well, that's who I feel like—that woman. Every time I start to think things are getting better, like Persephone did when she was allowed to come back to the earth in the springtime, I feel guilty. . . . Guilty for being happy playing with Natalia or for feeling happy helping the sisters weave their baskets, and I'm thrust once again belowground, where everything is dark and I can't breathe. I want to be aboveground all the time, Celeste, but I don't know how. I want to be happy, and I don't want to feel guilty anymore."

"Let us help you. Your abuela and Marisol, they will help you. I will too! All of your friends . . . you can't imagine how much we've missed you, and we're all here for you! Please, please come home," I say, trying hard not to cry myself.

"I need some time to think. Do you understand? I want to talk to Sol, Luna, and Sonia, and I want to weave a basket. I never really understood your need to write before, but now, when I weave, I think I do. . . . Sometimes I just *need* to weave. I can think clearly while I'm working the reeds."

"I get it! I can't believe you can actually make those baskets! Maybe one day . . . would you teach *me*?" Lucila looks up, nods shyly.

"Listen, Mamá is flying home the day after tomorrow. She can't be away from her patients for longer than that, but Nana Delfina and I, we're staying here for a few more days. You'll have all the time you need. Captain Pratt will bring whoever is going back to Valparaíso. I hope . . . I hope so, so much that you'll come too. I'm betting Natalia is coming—I don't think she'll leave Sebastián's side."

Lucila considers this. "Nati . . . she's truly who kept me sane." She thinks for another moment. "And if she leaves and I stay, then she's losing someone *again*. . . . Oh, Celeste. I need time to think this all through. But I will. . . . I promise I'll think about everything."

On the way back to the house, Lucila asks me what

Valparaíso is like now, and I remember again that she's been away for *three years*. I tell her about the things that haven't changed: Café Iris, the north and the south winds, the brilliant blue and yellow houses, the ever-present pelicans. And we talk about the things that *have* changed: the American businesses everywhere, how the mom and pop kiosks have closed down, the people who are much quieter than they used to be. I tell her about Señor Molina, Señorita Alvarado, and about the memory maps. "Oh! I almost forgot," I exclaim, reaching into my pocket and handing Lucila a memory stone with her name on it. "Cristóbal gave it to me, because I was one of the people who was important in your life, but I want you to have it. You should have a piece of your own map."

Lucila looks at her name on the stone and smiles. "What *else* have you been up to since you got back from Maine?" she asks.

"Oh, this and that," I say nonchalantly.

"Celeste Marconi, you're always up to something. What have you been doing? I'm sure your 'this and that' is quite something."

I tell her about the traveling library and the reading and writing classes. I tell her about Milui and Olivia, about Señor Martín and Señor Barbablanca. My friend listens as I draw a picture for her with my words so that she can imagine life back in Valparaíso. I wonder if she can see herself in these stories. I hope so. I really hope so. Then I launch into yet another story to lure Lucila back into a world where I think she can be happy again, with me, with Marisol, with her abuela, and with everyone else who loves her.

Help
on the Horizon

Up ahead Natalia is running through the blue mushrooms, half dragging Captain Pratt with her.

"Luci, Luci! This is Captain Pratt. He taught me to tango last night!" she exclaims, her eyes sparkling.

"He did? That sounds like fun," Lucila says, shaking the captain's hand. "What else did you do?"

"Sebastián and I talked for a long time about Mamá and Papá." Nati frowns, then brightens. "We cried a lot, but then we started telling each other stories we remembered about them, like how Papá used to make funny faces at us to make us laugh, and how Mamá used to take us to the beach to search for shells. . . ."

Lucila strokes her hair. "And how did you sleep?"

"I had a nightmare, but Sebastián sat with me, and Captain Pratt made me hot chocolate," she says. She flashes a grin at the captain, who gives her a tiny salute. As Lucila and Natalia are chatting, Mamá and Nana Delfina look at me and ask, without asking, if things are okay. I nod. Then Mamá says, "We've just had the most delicious maté tea, but we must head back to town now. We promised to help my friends. They're preparing a traditional feast for us tonight. I think it's called curanto?"

"Yum!" Lucila and Natalia sing out in unison. "It's one of our favorites," Lucila adds.

"Good!" says Mamá. "Because you're all invited. Let's meet at María Fernanda's at eight o'clock. It's the red house on stilts to the right of the fish shop."

"We know which house you mean," says Sol. "We'd love to come."

Natalia tells Sebastián she'll see him later—she wants to stay and help Lucila collect reeds and tell her about the houseboat. I can tell Sebastián doesn't want to leave her, but he also doesn't want to make a big deal, so he heads back to town with us.

On the road to the plaza, Sebastián and I lag behind, each of us lost in our own thoughts. Just as I'm wondering what it must be like for him to have his sister back in his life, Sebastián takes hold of my hand. *Stay calm, stay calm, Celeste*, I tell myself. I glance up at him. For the first time since I met him, he looks . . . happy. I squeeze his hand, and we walk together like that until we reach the inn.

"How was it spending time with Nati after so long?" I ask him.

"Even though she's ten now, Nati's still sweet,"

Sebastián muses. "I thought she might have changed, but she's pretty much as I remember her . . . except for the nightmares, of course. I told her that I have bad dreams too, and that seemed to make her feel better. . . . There's still so much to process." He stops and looks at me. "She wants to come back with us, which is what I want more than anything else—but I don't know how to take care of a ten-year-old. I know how to be her brother, but . . ."

"What does Captain Pratt think?" I ask.

"He thinks everything's going to be fine. He told me last night that he's happy to look after both of us."

"That's so great, Sebastián. I'm sure he'll be terrific with Nati!"

"Yeah, he is, already. . . . He's like a grandfather to me, so I'm sure it will be the same with Nati. . . ."

Now he looks me right in the eye. "How are things with Lucila?"

I'm surprised at how easy it is to talk to Sebastián. "Lucila's . . . well, she's different. She was always happy, and now she's so angry and uncertain. And of course, why *wouldn't* she be?"

Sebastián nods. "I get that. I feel that way a lot too."

"How do you deal with it?"

"Sometimes I don't. . . . Poor Captain Pratt—he's seen me yelling and throwing things because I get so mad. He just gives me space until I calm down. He's always saying 'This storm will pass,' and you know, he's usually right. I read a lot as well. I let myself get lost in imaginary worlds, and then things don't hurt quite as much."

"I love to read too . . . and write," I confess. "I write about everything."

He swings our arms. "What will you write about today?"

"Hmmmm. . . . I think I'll write about finding my best friend, and about making new ones," I say, and BOOM, my cheeks flame.

At the hotel, I wave good-bye to Sebastián and watch him walk away with Captain Pratt. Nana Delfina sidles over to me. "You really like this boy, don't you?"

At first, I don't want to admit it, but then I say, "Yes, I do. I'm pretty sure I like him a lot."

"I like him too," she says, putting her arm around me.

In our room, Mamá asks me about my conversation with Lucila.

"I don't know if she'll come back with us," I admit, hardly daring to say it.

"I think she will, hija. The sisters said Lucila, well, she tries. . . . She puts on a good face, but Sol says she seems lost and deeply unhappy. We talked about what should happen next, and the sisters said they understand if Lucila and Natalia choose to go back with us. They knew from the beginning that the girls weren't theirs to keep. . . ." Mamá gazes out the window at the passersby on the plaza. "If the sisters are any indication, the people of Chiloé are wonderful. Apparently, many people hid here during the dictatorship, and the people of the island took them in with no questions and looked after them until they were ready to leave. Sol told me they encouraged Lucila to contact her family, but with the exception of the one letter, she didn't want to try. They even took her down to the telephone exchange once, but she refused to call anyone." The question in Mamá's voice is apparent.

"I asked her about that," I say. "She said it was just too hard. I still don't really understand, because it would have been so easy for her to call. . . . I mean, there's a phone in Lucila's house and in ours!"

"The dictator—he damaged people's minds, Celeste. He made everyone so very afraid. The physical torture was just one part of the damage. The psychological effects are something else entirely—and are a very different kind of damage to work through."

"Mamá, I think Lucila needs help, not just from us. . . . She's so angry and she has nightmares all the time."

"I agree," says Mamá. "I'm going to call Doña Estela

today to ask her permission to schedule an appointment with the counselor at our clinic, if Lucila agrees to come back with us. I see this counselor from time to time."

"You see a counselor?" I ask, surprised.

"Both Papá and I do. We have to. It helps us to work through what happened to us. Every day we feel a little bit more like our old selves. Perhaps with a little help, Lucila will begin to feel like her old self too. We can't expect her to act like nothing happened, though. Her whole world fell apart. Some parts of her may never be the same. But things can always get better than they are now."

Decision
Made

There are too many people to fit inside María Fernanda and Esteban's house, so we gather for dinner outside where the curanto is being cooked in the front yard . . . in a hole in the ground!

"There are rocks at the bottom of the hole that are super hot," Lucila explains. "We wrap all the food— mussels, clams, chorizo, potatoes, chicken, and pork—in nalca leaves, and put them on top of the rocks."

"Then we cover everything with soil," Nati adds excitedly.

"What are nalca leaves?" I ask.

"They come from a giant rhubarb plant and they're huge, like an elephant's ear," says Nati. "Look, you can see some poking out." She points.

"And . . . you cover them with *dirt*?" I ask.

My face must be scrunched up, because Lucila quickly reassures me: "The dirt never touches the food— that's why it's wrapped in leaves. It keeps everything warm. Just wait! It's going to be the best thing you've ever eaten!" A delicious scent—spicy chorizo and salty mussels—wafts up from the pit, and my mouth begins to water.

"It won't be long now," Lucila tells me. "Once you can smell it, it's nearly ready. Nati, why don't you go find Sebastián."

We watch her skip away. Captain Pratt and Nana Delfina are chatting with María Fernanda, Esteban is talking to the three sisters, and Mamá is holding Clara, tickling her feet. The baby giggles in delight. Lucila and I walk away from the group and sit on the grass, looking out at the water.

Lucila is the first to speak. "Celeste, I know I've been . . . acting strangely, and I'm sorry for that. But I hope you know how much I've missed you."

"I've missed you, too," I say. "I've written to you, or about you, every single day. I hoped that maybe my words could reach you somehow. Dumb, huh?"

"No, it's not dumb at all! It makes me feel so good that I wasn't forgotten." She plucks a blade of grass as she drifts to another place in her mind. I don't say anything, letting her gaze into nothingness until she's ready to speak again.

"I know it might sound crazy, but it's like I'm afraid of being happy. As if, as soon as I let myself feel happy, something else bad will happen. Now, I bet *that* sounds dumb!"

"No, it actually doesn't. Have you been happy here at all?" I ask.

Lucila thinks about that for a minute, then says, "Sometimes . . . like when I'm playing with Nati, but it's like I told you. I always remind myself that I shouldn't be feeling that way."

"But . . . don't you think your mamá and papá would *want* you to be happy?" I ask cautiously.

"But I *was* happy with *them*, and look what happened." She shreds the blade of grass, flicks it into the wind.

I reach for her hand. "Lucila, I don't know what to do or to say to help you, but you know I will always be your BFF."

Lucila smiles at that and then says, "The sisters and I were up late last night talking. They think I should go back with you. Nati definitely wants to be with Sebastián, and I want to stay close to her. So . . . this morning, I made up my mind. I'm going back to Valparaíso." She takes a deep breath, and I can tell she feels better for making a decision. I give her hand a squeeze, and she adds, "When I get back, I want to make memory maps . . . for Mamá and Papá."

"I'll help! We all will!" I tell her. After a few moments of silence, I ask carefully, "Would you maybe like to call your abuela tonight, so she can hear your voice?" Lucila slowly nods. . . . She's finally ready. I wrap my arm around her shoulders, and we sit quietly like that for a while, listening to the waves, the waves that will take us home.

Saying
Good-bye

Mamá is tucking the last few things into her suitcase when she says, "Celeste, this is the first time we'll be apart since we were reunited after the dictatorship. I'm feeling a little nervous about it—how about you?"

"Me too," I admit. "But Nana Delfina will take good care of me. Don't worry, Mamá."

"You're so grown-up, Celeste. I'm really proud of you," she says, and hugs me.

"Will *you* be okay on that little seaplane? I know you don't like being on the water. . . ."

"I'll be fine. We made it over here, so I can make it back. Perhaps this is the beginning of me being ready to go on a boat again," she says, despite the color already draining from her face.

"Mmmmm. I think we should wait a while before you try that. What is it you tell me when I have a big problem? 'Take baby steps, Celeste.'"

Mamá chuckles. "You're right, my bright girl. Now let's go downstairs. I think everyone's waiting to say good-bye." In fact, the small lobby of the hotel is crammed with people. María Fernanda and Esteban promise to visit soon. Sol, Luna, and Sonia ask Mamá to watch over Lucila and Natalia. She promises we will send them updates regularly. Captain Pratt promises Mamá that he'll have me, Nana Delfina, Lucila, Sebastián, and Nati back home, safe and sound, in five days.

"I know you will, Captain. You're a good man." Mamá kisses him on the cheek.

At the dock, I watch until I see Mamá's plane disappear into the clouds. "Adiós, Mamá. Te quiero mucho. I love you," I call into the wind.

Life on
Chiloé

Nana Delfina and I have moved back to the houseboat with Sebastián and Captain Pratt while Lucila and Nati do what they need to do to get ready for the trip. They have already said good-bye to their few friends at school, and in their spare time, they have been showing us the things they love on Chiloé and telling us about its strange legends and myths.

Lucila takes us to a forest, where we see more of the orange parrots that never stop talking. They don't sound like birds at all, but like people speaking a strange language. She also leads us down to the water, where we get to see two different types of penguins decked out in their tuxedos. She says they're called Humboldt and Magellanic penguins after famous explorers. I think my favorite birds here, though, are the red-legged cormorants, with their orange-red duck-like feet, their eyes that look like tiny suns, and their red-tinged faces.

I finally get to try those blue mushrooms. Lucila's right, the taste is impossible to describe. In fact, it changes as I'm eating. . . . They're bitter, then sweet, then bitter again! Weird! While we're eating, the sisters tell us about El Trauco, an ugly dwarf-like creature with no feet that lives deep in the forests. He attracts young and old women with his magnetism. Everyone is wary of El Trauco, because he's said to be able to impregnate young women just by looking at them, and he casts spells on men who get too close!

I snicker, but Sol gives me a hard look. "El Trauco's not funny, Celeste; he's dangerous. He's one of our most feared demons. You must beware!" Oops. I can tell she's completely serious, and I bow my head, sorry for giggling.

She also tells us about the witches that fly over the houses of Chiloé at night, and a giant sea creature called El Cuchivilu. And why not, on an island of orange parrots and blue mushrooms!

One afternoon when it's not raining cats and dogs, Sebastián, Nana Delfina, Captain Pratt, and I go to the bandstand on the Plaza de Armas to listen to a group of Mapuche musicians. They only use small wooden flutes, a type of circular horn that I learn is called a *trutruka*, and drums called *kultruns*. I've never heard anything like it, but I recognize some of the tunes—Nana has hummed them around our house. Now she listens with her eyes closed, swaying, and I wonder what she's thinking.

After the concert, Nati wants to show Sebastián and me the sea lions diving into the water from their rocky perches. I never realized how loud sea lions are! They sound like they're moaning and barking at the same time. They also sound a bit like Frankenstein's monster!

I can see why Lucila and Natalia have liked living here so much. It's almost as though the modern world hasn't reached Chiloé yet. Part of me hopes it never does.

La Minga

At dinner with the sisters, Sol can't stop smiling. Lucila glances between them and finally demands to know what's going on. Sol's smile grows even wider. . . . "Just in time—tomorrow morning—a most wonderful event is taking place, and I've gotten permission for you all to participate: *La Minga!*"

Lucila and Nati clap excitedly.

"What's a 'Minga'?" I ask the sisters. We're all squeezed around a small table with a pretty, woven table-cloth, eating shrimp ceviche. Delicioso!

"It's something very special. It's when people help their neighbors move their house from one part of the island to another, across the water," explains Luna, as though it's as easy as pie.

Sebastián's jaw drops. "Across the *water*? Is that even possible?"

"It sure is," Lucila replies. "Nati and I have helped with three or four of them. It's neat."

"The ceremony starts with something called

ofrendas," says Sol, saying the word in Mapudungun, and passing a basket of bread around the table.

Lucila sees our confusion and says, "It means 'offerings.'"

Sol doesn't tell us much more, because she wants us to be surprised. We spend the rest of the meal talking about everything under the Chiloé sun.

The next morning, immediately after breakfast, we head to a house that sits about a half a kilometer from the shore. It's not a huge house, but it's not small, either. It's one story and has scalloped wooden siding and scalloped shingles on the pitched roof. The front door is bright red, and there's a Chilean flag attached to the side of the house that's blowing gently in the wind. I wonder how on earth that house is going to sail across the water! It can't be light.

About fifty people gather to help see the house on its way. The owners—an elderly couple with gray hair and wearing ponchos and woolen scarves—welcome the crowd and thank everyone for coming. They have laid out a spread of food—including fresh bread, sopaipillas, and other delicious treats—for helpers to eat before they begin the work of moving the house. The woman, whose name Sol tells me is Valentina, begins the ceremony with the offering. She's speaking Spanish, thank goodness! Everyone falls quiet.

"The hour has come, the sacred hour, when the journey of this house across the water begins. All our friends and neighbors gathered here offer this house droplets of morning sun, the wings of swallows to watch over her always, the celestial objects that rule the island sky, and a mirror to see herself and all of us inside her like an open sea. We give you the green of this island, the foam on the sea, and the most brilliant of smiles as we begin the journey from this place to the next."

Then a group of about ten men hitch twelve oxen together in four rows of three. The ropes attached to their yokes are then secured to several points on the front of the house. One of the men slaps the rump of the first ox. The animal bellows, but then the tethered group begins ever so slowly to move forward, almost as though the first ox has given them an order "Forward march!" The house is literally being dragged across the ground! People take turns encouraging the oxen forward. Lucila and Nati show us how to help, and Sebastián and I join in. The lows of the oxen combine with the happy voices of the crowd. I can't believe it! This house is really moving!

Everyone follows the house on its leisurely journey to the water's edge. There, the men lead the oxen into the water, where giant, black, sausage-shaped buoys await. Sebastián and I wade into the water with Nati and Lucila to help secure the buoys to the sides of the house, so it will float.

"This is crazy!" Sebastián says, amazed.

"I know!" I feel like I'm in a most unusual dream.

Once the house is afloat, everyone climbs into small boats to accompany it down the canals that lead to different parts of the island. The front of the house is hitched to two larger boats that pull it through the water. We can hear people singing on the lead boats, and soon everyone is joining in. Sebastián leans over to Sol. "But how is this possible? I still can't believe it even though I can see it with my own two eyes."

"The people here believe that the kind and generous spirits of the island give us incredible strength to move the houses," she says, as though it's the most normal thing.

The whole island, and every person on it, is kind and generous, I think, smiling at Sol, Luna, and Sonia in awe. I'm going to miss it here.

PART 6

New Beginnings

All **Aboard!**

It's the day of our departure. Lucila's and Nati's few possessions are in four beautiful baskets the sisters made for them. It's hard to watch them say good-bye to Sol, Luna, and Sonia. Natalia is crying. Sebastián comforts her by saying, "Nati, as soon as school finishes, we'll come and visit." He looks at the three sisters, who, likewise, have tears streaming down their cheeks. They nod at him gratefully.

"Do you promise?" asks Nati, hiccuping.

"Absolutely. Lucila can come, and you, too, Celeste," he says, casting a glance my way. *You bet I'm coming back*, I think. After final hugs, Captain Pratt starts the engine, and we're off.

Everyone is waving white handkerchiefs at us from the shore. We watch until they become little specks on the horizon. Lucila and Natalia are wrapped in each other's arms. Soon Nana Delfina calls from inside the cabin.

"Celeste, Lucila, Natalia . . . Nana needs help shelling beans and peeling potatoes."

Nana knows exactly what to do, I realize. She's distracting the girls by giving them something useful to do. Pretty soon we're shelling beans and peeling the most amazing potatoes that Nana Delfina bought yesterday at a market. Some are huge and yellow, and others are small and deep purple, almost black. As we work, the sounds of Carlos Gardel, an Argentine tango singer, waft out from the captain's old record player. We sway with the beat, and sway with the boat, and I can't believe, I simply can't believe, we're *all* going home.

Isla **Mocha**

The next morning, the seas are calm, the winds quiet, and Captain Pratt has an idea he wants to share with us. He and Sebastián talked the night before about possibly stopping in a place called Isla Mocha that we'll be sailing past today. Sebastián says, "We don't have to go if you don't want to, but Captain Pratt told me it's where . . ." He pauses. Captain Pratt gives him a pat on the back, encouraging him to go on. "Well, it's where many of the disappeared who were dropped into the ocean washed up," he says. Lucila gasps. "I want to go," Sebastián quickly adds. "I know I won't find our parents there, but I feel like I need to see what it's like." He looks to each of us, that yearning look back in his eyes. "Would you mind if we stop?"

Captain Pratt adds, "I've never been, but there are rumors that the government sent barges to these shores and left the dead here. A friend, who's a fisherman, told me that one of the residents of the island decided to build a cemetery so those unknown people could at least have a resting place. We can go and pay our respects . . . if that's what everyone wants to do."

No one speaks for a moment, but then Lucila, brave Lucila, says, "I want to go." Relief floods Sebastián's face.

Natalia chimes in, "Me too," and Nana and I also agree. We don't know what exactly we'll find there, but we'll discover it together.

As we dock, a sandy landscape with barren mountains appears before us. There's no green anywhere. We don't have to walk far before we come across the cemetery. An old man sits under a leafless tree at the entrance, half-asleep. Captain Pratt approaches him. "Are you the caretaker, señor?" he asks. "We would like to pay our respects, if that's okay."

Curiously, the man doesn't seem at all surprised to see us, despite there being nothing else around as far as the eye can see. He nods and, without saying a word, signals for us to follow him. We enter the enormous cemetery. There's not a single headstone . . . simply row after row after row of mounds of earth, beneath which the disappeared must be buried. The rows seem to go on forever. Tears prick at my eyes.

As we walk around the graves, we come upon an elderly woman sitting on the ground, dressed in a frayed dress the color of the soil. Her hair is braided and hangs almost to the base of her back. The mound she's sitting next to has a wooden cross with a name on it. When she sees us, she waves us over. "Have you come to find someone in particular?" she asks.

Captain Pratt gathers Lucila, Nati, and Sebastián to him. "These three children lost their parents during the dictatorship. We don't know if they're here; we've just come to pay our respects. . . . Is this the grave of someone you knew?" he asks gently.

The woman's face is etched with deep lines. Some old people have wrinkles that show they've had happy lives, but not this lady. The pain of her loss is all over her face.

"Yes," she says smoothing the earth atop the grave. "This is my daughter, María Granados, who was returned here by the sea."

"We're sorry for your loss, señora," says the captain, taking off his cap and bowing his head.

"How . . . How did you find her?" asks Lucila tentatively.

"After many months of searching after she disappeared, and after the government telling me they had no record of her, I heard a rumor about the dictator's enemies being disposed of here. I came not expecting to find her, but . . . well, I did. I just happened to arrive on a day when several bodies washed ashore." I rub my arms as a wave of coldness comes over me. "I found my María on the beach, wrapped . . . wrapped in barbed wire," she says, her voice catching. Lucila covers her mouth with both hands, and Sebastián puts his arm around Natalia. His lower lip is quivering.

"I'm so, so sorry, Señora Granados," I say, not knowing what else to say.

Then Nana Delphina asks, "Will you tell us about María?"

"Of course. . . . I talk about her to everyone who comes here. She was forty-two years old when she disappeared. She was a popular teacher at a school in the capital that served children from underprivileged families, and she was also a member of the Socialist Party. She wasn't a militant, but she did have ideas and dreams about how to change our country for the better. One morning, she was having breakfast before heading to work, when, according to her neighbors, a car without license plates pulled up outside her house. Two men entered and brought her out blindfolded, with her hands tied behind her back. She was never seen again—until she arrived here."

Lucila is now trembling. "That . . . That sounds a lot like what happened to my family," she says. "We were taken at night, and no one knew where we were . . ." She trails off.

"Ours too," Sebastián chimes in.

"I'm sorry, niños. . . . The captain said you lost your parents, but . . . you are here. How did you escape?"

"It's a long story," says Sebastián.

"I have all the time in the world." Sebastián nods, and we all sit around María Granados's grave. My three friends tell their tales, haltingly at first, but then, when they feel more comfortable, the words and emotions spill forth like a river. When they've finished, Señora Granados pulls them close and says: "Your parents are always with you, as long as you remember them."

Captain Pratt has a distraught look on his face. "Can we do anything for you, señora? Do you . . . Would you like to come to Valparaíso with us?" he asks.

"Thank you for that kind offer, Captain, but the day I found María, I made the decision to stay here and keep my daughter company. I talk to her and to anyone else who comes to the cemetery and is willing to listen to her story." She glances around at the other graves. "These people deserve our attention and our respect. They must never be forgotten."

As we stand to leave, I assure her that I will never forget her or María. "I promise I'll keep looking for and remembering the disappeared."

"I think you will," she says. "The fire in your eyes reminds me of my daughter. If you come across others who have lost loved ones, tell them they're always welcome to come here and pray. Even if they don't find the people they're searching for, at least they'll have a place to go. Someday, perhaps the government will come and help identify these remains—and bring them home to their families. . . ."

We bid Señora Granados farewell, and when we reach the entrance to the cemetery, I stop.

"Amigos, would you like to leave some memory stones here?" I ask. "I know they won't have your parents' names on them or anything—"

"I think that's a great idea, Celeste." Sebastián says it so quickly that I don't even need to finish my sentence. Lucila finds two flat stones, as do Sebastián and Natalia. They kiss them and place them under the tree where the caretaker sits. Nati looks at the grizzled old man. "Excuse me, señor. Would you please take care of my mamá and papá, if they're here?" The old man's face softens as he looks at her sad, earnest little face. He nods twice—it would be his honor—then watches as we walk away.

The Night Sky, Like a Blue **Dream**

Traveling by sea is a bit disorienting, especially at night, because it's hard to tell where you are and where you're going. I used to be afraid of that kind of uncertainty, of not knowing things, like where my parents were during the dictatorship and why everything was changing. I'm not afraid anymore, though, and I kind of like being carried along by the waves toward an uncertain future. This trip has taught me so much. I no longer feel alone, because I realize I never truly was, and I never will be. I will always have my family, my friends, the sea, the moon, and the stars.

Tonight I'm sitting under the stars that seem so close that I might be able to reach up and pluck them right out of the sky. I am writing by the light of a lantern that Captain Pratt loaned me. Nana Delfina comes out wrapped in her favorite shawl. She sits beside me and sighs deeply. "What is it, Nana? Are you okay?"

"Sí, Celeste. Nana is just realizing you're no longer a little girl. You're nearly all grown-up. You don't need Nana so much anymore."

"I'll always need you!" I exclaim. "What are you talking about?"

"You used to ask me so many things, but you don't ask much anymore. Yet there's still a lot I wish to tell you," she says.

"You can tell me anything, Nana."

"Do you know how important this trip is?" she asks. "It's the end of something and the beginning of something else. When I look out at the sea, I imagine the past when Abuela Frida sailed to Chile more than fifty years ago, and I imagine your mamá on the *Esmeralda*. But I also see the future in these waves. They're taking us toward something new, something magical. I can feel it."

"You can see all that in the water?"

"Yes, and in the sky. If you look long enough, you will see things there too. Just look at how beautiful the stars are. There's Orion's belt, and there's his sword. And over there's Canis Major, the giant dog. Even in the darkness we have the light of the stars to guide us home."

"Nana, how do you know so much about the stars?"

"When I was a child, I lived in the forests of Araucanía. There was no electricity, so at night the sky was as black as coal. We could see all the stars. My brothers and sisters and I found all the shapes in the sky before anyone ever taught us the fancy names for them. My sister would say, 'Look, Delfina, there's a dog!' And one of my brothers would say, 'Look at the Mapuche warrior in the sky with his spear!' Later I found out that the group of stars is called Orion and that he's carrying a sword, and that the dog is Canis. We even made up stories about the stars."

"I do that too. Sometimes when I look at the stars for long enough, they start moving and I can create stories in my mind about the adventures of the dancing lights."

"Now, that sounds like my Celeste," she says affectionately, and kisses me on the forehead.

"I'll always be your Celeste! But perhaps we should talk about more grown-up things like . . ." And I look around as though searching for a topic. "What do the stars tell you about, say . . . Captain Pratt?"

"Cheeky girl!" Nana playfully swats my hand, but then she says, "I like that strange old man. My heart flutters when he looks at me, and he's a *very* good dancer." She looks away dreamily. "He's like your papá; he doesn't speak much, but he's good and brave. He's looked after Sebastián all this time because it was the right thing to do, and Nana likes a man like that."

"I like the captain too, Nana." Then I dare to ask, "Do you think you love him?"

"Maybe," she whispers, her cheeks dimpling.

Just then the captain appears. "Delfina, shall we

have a dance before bedtime? I found one of my favorite Gardel records, and I've made a fresh pot of tea. I think young Natalia wants to dance too."

"Go on, Nana. I'm going to finish writing. I'll be in soon," I say, and I give her a kiss.

As I watch her go inside with Captain Pratt, I think about what she said. I wonder where these stars and this sea will take me next.

Homecoming

It's almost dusk and the sun is sending streaks across the sky as we enter the bay of Valparaíso. Men in fishing boats yell "Hola" to the captain as we motor past them. In the hills, we see the twinkling lights of the houses and the streetlamps. It looks like a city of stars.

I'm used to looking down at the sea from up high, but it's just as beautiful looking up at the hills from the water. All the colors of the houses are visible in the distance, along with the steep, windy roads. As we sail closer, I have the feeling that the ocean is hugging these hills and protecting us as we enter the bay. This is the same bay into which Abuela Frida sailed on the Ship Called Hope, and the Spanish refugees sailed on the *Winnipeg*. It's also where Mamá was held captive. But the water isn't to blame for what happened on the *Esmeralda*. I like to think that the sea saved Mamá, by pushing her forward with its waves until she could reach the shore. The sea also helped save Lucila and Natalia, and now it's bringing us back home to where we're supposed to be.

Lucila and Natalia have been quiet all day, huddled together in what Captain Pratt says will be Nati's room once we get back to Valparaíso. I'm sure they're filled with doubts about how things are going to be when they return. As we reach the dock, Sebastián makes the odd point of steering the girls to the left side of the houseboat. I look to the right and realize he's keeping them from seeing the *Esmeralda*. It's too soon for that, for them. What a good brother and friend.

The sun is slowly sinking into the sea, but we can see rows of people on the dock waving white handkerchiefs. For a split second I think, *Oh no, they're waving at the* Esmeralda*!* But then I realize they're waving to us! Captain Pratt used his ship-to-shore radio this morning to let a few people know we are arriving this afternoon. Clearly word has spread!

As we get closer, I see that the people in front are holding up a huge banner that says, WELCOME HOME, LUCILA AND NATALIA! in massive green letters.

When the boat finally docks, Lucila spies her grandmother and Marisol in the crowd. "Abuela? Marisol?" she murmurs softly, but then she yells, "Abuela! Marisol!" and waves her hands wildly above her head. Doña Estela calls back, "Nieta Lucila, I'm here, I'm here!" Lucila is jumping up and down, blowing kisses to her grandmother and cousin. I hope she doesn't jump right off the boat!

"Look, Lucila. There's Cristóbal!" I say, waving. Lucila gives a squeal and waves and waves some more. Then I see Mamá, Papá, and Abuela Frida. Mamá yells, "Welcome home, Celeste!" her own white handkerchief swinging through the air. Señorita Alvarado and Señor Castellanos are there too, as are Señor Molina and Principal Cisneros and tons of students from Juana Ross School. Even Señor Martín is there with Milui! Lucila grabs my arm and asks, "Is this real, Celeste? *Real*-real?"

"Real-real. You're home, amiga."

"I'm home," she says with a sob.

Celebration

As soon as Captain Pratt has tied off the boat, he rushes off to bring Doña Estela and Marisol on board so they can greet Lucila in private. Then he quickly ushers the rest of us onto the dock, where we're swallowed by the crowd. Mamá gets to me first and hugs me. All the noise of the crowd falls away.

"Are you okay?" I ask her. "The *Esmeralda* . . . I was worried."

"I'm fine," she says. "I really am." And I believe her. "How are *you*? Was the trip okay?"

Before I can answer, Papá pushes through the crowd. "Celeste!" He picks me up and swings around. "I missed you."

"I missed you, too, Papá!" I say as I kiss his cheek. Just then I feel a tugging on the sleeve of my jacket. Abuela Frida is staring up at me, her eyes shining like two bright stars.

"I'm so glad you're back, Celeste of my soul. The house was lonely with you away."

"I missed you, too, Abuela. Did you behave yourself while I was gone?"

"I got up to as much mischief as I could, but Andrés . . . he has an eagle eye. Every time I tried to take out my lemon liqueur, he'd show up at my door. Finally I just said, 'Andrés, come and have a drink with me,' and he did!"

As my family greets Nana Delfina, I go in search of Cristóbal and Genevieve. "You did it, Celeste!" they say, cheering, laughing, hugging me, and then cheering again.

"I didn't do much," I say with a shrug, though I can't wipe the grin off my face. "Things just happened the way they were supposed to."

"You sound like Nana Delfina," says Cristóbal.

"I know!" Then I laugh.

Cristóbal lowers his voice. "How's Lucila?"

"She's . . . okay. Well, you'll see for yourself. She should be coming off the boat any second. What's been happening here since I left?"

"Well, everyone's been working on their memory maps, and there are stones all over the city already," Cristóbal tells me.

"And you won't believe it," Genevieve adds. "Principal Cisneros talked to a principal at another school, and they're going to do the same project. Pretty soon there will be memory stones everywhere."

"That's so great!" I say, impressed.

"We also have a history test tomorrow," Cristóbal says, and I groan.

"Don't worry. We'll help you catch up," Genevieve says, looping her arm through mine.

Just then, Lucila hesitantly comes off the boat. When she sees Cristóbal, she makes a beeline for him. She hugs him, and kisses on both cheeks follow. "I'm so glad you are back, amiga!" exclaims Cristóbal with glee. They look at each other for a long time, astonished. Then Cristóbal says, "Lucila, this is Genevieve. She's from France and has just started at our school."

"I'm happy to meet you. I have heard a lot about you from Cristóbal, Marisol, and Celeste," Genevieve says, giving her three kisses. Lucila's face is unreadable.

Nati comes over, and Lucila introduces her. Genevieve crouches down so she's at eye level with Nati. "Welcome back! I can't wait to get to know you." And she impulsively hugs Nati. Lucila's face softens.

We all turn when we hear a loud whistle. Papá has climbed up onto the seawall and is calling for quiet. He has an announcement.

"Amigos, Señora Colibrí asked me to invite everyone to Café Iris for pastries and coffee." A cheer rises up again.

When we get to the café, we find it decorated with

balloons and streamers. I've never seen so many balloons, and Nati claps in excitement. I would have clapped too . . . if I was still ten years old! El mago is there on a makeshift stage with . . . Cristóbal? Wait a minute. How did he get here so quickly and change into his magician's outfit so fast? He and el mago are dressed in matching costumes and are juggling bowling pins back and forth. Cristóbal has learned all kinds of magic. . . .

Each table has an assortment of pastries—cuchufli, raisin bread, croissants filled with almond and chocolate, and thousand-layer cake—and Miguel comes around to take our drink orders. People don't sit at the tables for long, though—everyone is weaving in and out to visit with Lucila and Natalia. The party goes on for two hours, during which time Cristóbal saws Genevieve in half, el mago makes Cristóbal disappear off the stage and then reappear in another part of the restaurant—a very cool trick—and Cristóbal pulls a scarf out of Milui's long ear!

After a while, Lucila comes to tell me she's exhausted and is heading home with her abuela.

"How are you doing?" I ask.

"I'm okay, I think. . . . Can I see you tomorrow?"

"Of course! I think I need to go to school, but we can meet back here afterward. It'll be just like old times. Will that work?"

"Perfect. Abuela Estela says I can go back to school

next week. Tomorrow I have an appointment to see Señora Artigas, the counselor. Your mom set it up for me."

"That's great, Lucila, don't you think? You can tell me how it goes, if you like, but you don't have to. . . ."

"No, I want to tell you everything. It just . . . it might take a little time." She hugs me and then goes to find Natalia to tell her good-bye. Those two are going to have to figure out a way to see each other every day, at least for the next little while. It will be weird for them to be apart.

A few minutes later, Nati, clearly on a sugar high, bounds over. "Celeste, Captain Pratt is going to take me to get a blue bedspread tomorrow. He says I can decorate my room however I like. Will you and Lucila come and help me this weekend?"

"Wild horses couldn't keep me away," I say, and Nati laughs. "Have you and Captain Pratt talked about when you will go back to school?"

"Yes, next Monday. I'm glad we're all in the same school. It's going to be so strange, but I'll be with you!"

"Let's all walk to school together that day. How does that sound?"

"Sounds great!" she says.

I turn to Sebastián. "What about you? When will you go back to school?"

"I'm going back on Monday too, to the same high

school where I went before the dictatorship." He pauses and then blurts out, "Do you think I can see you over the weekend too?" And then he promptly looks at his shoes.

"Ummm . . . I, ummm, yes. Do you want to come up to the top of Butterfly Hill and help with our classes? We leave from Pan de Magia at eight a.m."

"Yes. Then afterward, let's go for ice cream." He smiles at me, and BOOM, the julepe is back.

Mamá comes over and hugs Captain Pratt. "Thank you for bringing everyone back safe and sound. Why don't you and the children come for supper one day next week once you're settled! Nana Delfina wants to make you something special."

"Thank you, Señora Marconi. We accept. But she and I have a date before then, don't we, Delfina?" he says, his eyes smiling.

"If you behave yourself, Delfina will come over tomorrow for our daily dance," she says affectionately.

Breaking
the Ice

I'm in a daze at school, still tired, and everyone is asking me a *ton* of questions. I'm not sure anyone is getting much schoolwork done. At least I've been excused from taking the history test. At recess, Cristóbal, Genevieve, and I sit under one of the big Canelo trees in the yard.

"You look tired, Celeste," Genevieve says in her sweet French accent.

"I'm pooped! My parents told me I should wait until Monday to come back to school, but I really wanted to be here. Now I'm wondering if it was a mistake."

"Well, we're glad you're here," says Cristóbal. "How's Lucila? I talked to her last night at Café Iris, but she didn't say much."

"She's . . ." And, without warning, I burst into tears. My friends gather close so that the other students can't see me.

"Celeste, what is it?" Genevieve asks, rubbing my back.

"It's just . . . I'm so sad for her. No matter how

hard I try, I can't stop thinking about what happened to her parents, to Sebastián and Natalia's parents, to my mother. . . . I don't understand how people can be so evil. . . . I don't know what to do with *that*, and I don't know how to make things right!"

Cristóbal looks at me as if I'm nuts. "You're already doing a *lot*! You brought Lucila and Natalia back. And we've got the memory maps to finish . . . and the reading program . . ."

I sit with my head down for a minute and then take a shaky breath. "Thanks, Cristóbal. . . . I'm just so mad—and there's no way to punish that horrible, horrible man."

"He's gone, and that's all that matters. Now we have a say in how things are going to be in our country!" He says this with such conviction that I have to smile.

"You're turning into a revolutionary, Cristóbal," I tease.

"Why not? We can be anything we want now!"

I glance at my friend, who's looking at me with kind eyes. I take a shuddery breath and nod. "Okay, I'm going to get it together before I meet with Lucila this afternoon."

Genevieve thrusts a bag into my hands. "We figured you'd see her today, so we put this together for her." When I open it, I see a couple dozen stones, a few paintbrushes, and some paint. "Lucila might want to make memory maps for her parents. We've got some for Natalia and Sebastián, too."

"Thanks, guys. You're seriously the best. Lucila already told me she wants to make the stones. I just don't know if she's ready yet. I'll tell Lucila you sent these things and said hello."

After the last class, I make my way to Café Iris. Lucila's already waiting for me. I'm surprised once again at how different she looks. Not only is she much taller, but her face has changed, or perhaps it's just the look on her face that's changed. It's a hard look, like she's telling everyone to stay away. But she smiles as soon as she sees me, stands up, and kisses me on the cheek.

"How was school today?" she asks, sitting back down.

"I was tired, but the day went quickly. Cristóbal and Genevieve said to say hi."

Lucila pauses, then says, "I want to go back to school right away, Celeste. I love being back home with my abuela, but I have too much time to think. I mean . . . I've only been home for one day, and I'm already going nuts. I want to be busy. . . . I *need* to be busy."

"Then that's exactly what you should do! Let's meet in the morning and we can go to school together."

Lucila nods, then seems to lose focus. She's gazing

out the window. She hasn't ordered anything, so I ask for suspiros de monjas along with two cappuccinos. Once Miguel has gone to get our order, I ask cautiously, "Did . . . Did you go to see Señora Artigas today?"

She nods again. "I was there for a long time. She's a very kind lady. I didn't want to talk at first, but she's good at asking questions and giving me space at the same time. Abuela and I talked about it, and we decided I should see her twice a week, at least at first."

"Did I tell you that Mamá and Papá see her too? I think she's helping them as well." She nods yet again, and then there's more silence. After a while, I say, "Cristóbal and Genevieve gave me these supplies in case you'd like to start on the memory maps for your parents. You may not be ready, but . . ." I hold out the bag with the stones. "I can help you if you like . . . or would you prefer to do it by yourself? Or . . . you don't have to do it at all. . . ."

Tears fill my friend's eyes. "I am so glad you brought me these. I want to get started on the stones right away, and I want you to help me." Her voice is so quiet, so sad.

"You've got it. Let's finish our pastries and we can go to my house and start painting."

"I think it will help me to feel closer to my parents. Does that sound weird?" Lucila asks.

I assure her that it doesn't sound weird at all, and as

we walk up Butterfly Hill, Lucila begins to talk to me like she did before she went away. She asks me more about Juliette Cove, and I tell her about Tom, the Korean boy I liked while I was there.

"But what about Sebastián? It's obvious you like him."

"I *do* like Sebastián," I admit, and it feels good to say it out loud. "He's coming to help teach on Saturday. . . . Will you come too? We're going out for ice cream afterward."

"Yes, I'll come and help with the lessons, but I'm *not* going to ice cream with you and Sebastián." A mischievous smile plays on her lips. *There's* Lucila. It feels so good to be talking about normal things like crushes and dulce de leche ice cream again.

When we arrive at my house, Nana Delfina and Abuela Frida offer to help with the stones, and we all sit at the kitchen table and begin to paint.

"Where do you want to put these, Lucila?" asks Abuela Frida.

"So many places. I'll start at our house, and then at Papá's old office, and all the places I used to go with my parents. I want to leave one at Señora Williams's flower stand. Mamá used to buy fresh flowers there every week. Then I have to go to Rosita's Pizzeria, where we liked to go for dinner. Of course, I have to put one on the

Esmeralda." We all draw in a sharp breath.

"Are you sure?" I ask. "Won't that be hard?"

Her fists clench. "Probably, but I have to do it," she says resolutely. "It may sound odd, but I don't want that ship to forget my parents. I want people to know that's where they were murdered. It can't just sit prettily as though nothing ever happened there."

When we finish painting, I walk Lucila home, and she invites me in. After saying hello to Doña Estela, we head to Lucila's room. When she opens the door, I feel like I've stepped back in time.

"Is that the picture of us at the fair when we were nine?" I ask in wonder. "Oh, and there's the poem I wrote for you for your sixth birthday!" I look around and realize that Lucila's room is exactly as I remember it. Then I see her school uniform draped across the chest at the foot of her bed.

"Abuela left my room exactly as it was the day I disappeared," says Lucila. "My uniform doesn't fit—at all! We'll have to let it out and buy some new socks and shoes." She picks up a framed photo of her with her parents at the beach eating ice-cream cones. "When I first saw my room yesterday, I thought it would be hard to sleep here, but it actually wasn't. I don't know how to explain it, but it feels . . . safe. Marisol stayed in here with me last night, and I didn't even have a nightmare."

"That's progress, right?"

"Maybe. . . . I hope so." She looks at me with pleading eyes. "I don't want to feel bad anymore, Celeste."

"I know, amiga. I want to help you."

"You are. . . . Just by being with me, you are. Now let's go show Abuela Estela the memory stones. She'll want to paint some too."

Making New
Friends

On Saturday morning, we all meet at Pan de Magia to head up Butterfly Hill. It's early, but that's when fresh baked bread is at its best. In the bakeries on the hills in Valparaíso, bread seems to rise especially high, like it's levitating. There's an old wives' tale that says that at this early hour ghosts appear in our bakeries, attracted by the delicious aroma of bread. They say that sometimes the ghosts even stay and have a cup of coffee!

Sebastián and Natalia are here today, along with Lucila, Marisol, Cristóbal, and Genevieve. The sisters from Pan de Magia load us up with fresh loaves of bread to take with us. When we reach the top of the hill and the library tent comes into view, Lucila dashes over to it. "It's wonderful!" she exclaims, looking at the colorful canvas that our students have painted with letters of the alphabet, pictures, and their names.

Cristóbal waves at the two children who have become our star pupils, Paco and Luci. Paco's cousins are in the tent today too, as are Señor Martín and Milui.

Paco charges right over. "Hola, Celeste. Where were you last week? Who are these people?"

"This is my best friend, Lucila. She disappeared, but she's back now. I went to Chiloé Island with my mamá to find her. Do you know where that is?" He shakes his head. "It's an island off the southern coast of Chile where many magical things happen. And this is Sebastián and his sister, Natalia. Natalia disappeared too. Sebastián went with me to find her. Isn't that neat?"

"I thought that people who disappeared never came back," says Paco, wide-eyed. "How did you come back?" he asks Lucila.

"I was very lucky," says Lucila, "but my parents never came back. Neither did Nati and Sebastián's."

"Are they in heaven, where my mamá and papá are?" he asks easily, as if these kinds of questions are simply routine for a little kid.

Lucila glances at me. "Ummm, yes, they are. What happened to your parents?"

"My tía told me that my mamá died when she had me, and my papá was a fisherman. His boat crashed on some rocks in a storm and he never came home."

"I'm sorry," says Lucila. "How old were you?"

"I was four when Papá went away, so it's a long time ago, because now I'm eight. I wear his sweater when I miss him. It's way too big, but I like to wear it anyway." Lucila covers her mouth, blinking back tears.

Then Cristóbal introduces Luci.

"Hey, you have the same nickname I do," says Lucila, still swiping at stray tears. "Is your name 'Lucila' too?"

"No, mine's 'Lucinda.' I'm six," she declares proudly.

"Wow, you're six and you're already reading books?" Lucila says, impressed.

"Not whole books, but I can read thirty-seven words now. I keep count. Marisol taught me my numbers! Will you read with me today?" She has clearly taken an instant shine to Lucila.

Lucila looks delighted. "I'd love to! Nati can help too. She's a good reader. We read a lot together when we were on Chiloé Island."

Paco is tugging on my sweater. "I have to show you something. Sit down," he says with authority. He picks up *Platero and I* and begins to sound out the words on the first page.

We all applaud. "That's great," I say, giving him a high five. "Pretty soon you won't need us at all."

Surprise!

Nati is skipping ahead happily, as, done with lessons, we're now on our way to help her set up her room on the houseboat. Neither she nor Sebastián knows that the rest of us have a surprise—we began gathering things for her room right after she told us she was going to be decorating. Marisol and I collected books we used to read, as well as clothes and shoes that don't fit us anymore, and a few stuffed animals we don't think she's too old for. Nana has been making her curtains, a pretty new dress, and a shawl made from the gray-blue wool she brought back with her from Chiloé. Genevieve and I also wanted to do something special for Sebastián, so last night, we went to visit Señor Barbablanca, and when we told him about the return of the Paz children, he insisted on giving us an armful of books, and even more when we told him Sebastián loved to read. He refused any money, saying that if we brought Sebastián and Natalia to the store so he could meet them, it would be payment enough.

When we reach the houseboat, we find the captain and Nana Delfina sitting at the kitchen table doing a crossword puzzle. "Ah, there you are, niños," says Captain Pratt. "Welcome back. Are you here to decorate Nati's room?" he asks, feigning ignorance, as though he knows nothing about the surprises that my parents and Nana Delfina brought over a few hours ago. "Go get started. Nana and I just need to finish this clue." And they huddle together.

Trying not to show our excitement and give away the surprise, we follow Nati down the short hallway to her room. When she opens the door, she is speechless. She looks around, looks at us, looks around again, running from thing to thing. "Where did all this come from?!" she cries out, picking one thing up and putting another down. Then she gapes at the closet. "Where did all these pretty clothes come from?"

"Surprise!" we all say at the same time. "They're yours."

Sebastián looks at me, confused.

"But . . . ?" Nati's eyes couldn't be open any wider.

"They're things we used to love when we were your age," says Lucila. "They need someone to love them now—you! You're like our little sister, so we'll be giving you lots of things as you grow up."

"Really?" Natalia asks, picking up a stuffed bunny I used to sleep with when I was little.

"Really. And I like your blue bedspread," I say.

"The captain chose it because he said it reminded him of the sea. Blue is his favorite color. Mine too."

Nati's happiness radiates, and Sebastián gives my hand a squeeze. Now I ask him, "Have you changed your room at all since you got back?" He gives me that confused look again.

"Ummm, no. I've lived here for a while now, remember?" He must think I'm losing my mind.

"Well, can Marisol see?" I ask.

"I don't know why she'd—"

"Oh, I'd love to!" Marisol interrupts.

He shrugs, opens his door.

"Surprise!" we all say again, and it's Sebastián's turn to stand with mouth agape.

Mamá, Papá, Captain Pratt, and Nana Delfina have set up a bookcase and filled it with the books Señor Barbablanca gave us, along with some others that Abuela Frida still had in the room under the stairs.

"This is fantastic!" he says, taking one book and then another from the shelves. "Thank you. Thank you so much," he says. "Were you all in on this?"

"We were. My mamá and papá too," I reply.

"I don't know what to say. . . ."

"You don't have to say anything, my boy," says Captain Pratt, coming up behind us. Then he says, "Now let's all go to Señora Nieve's for ice cream," leading the way to the front door.

Sebastián looks at me and we both laugh.

A Letter of
Hope

I can't stop thinking about what Lucila said about wanting to leave a memory stone on the *Esmeralda*, and about President Espinoza's plan to turn the ship into a museum. I've asked Lucila to help me write a letter to Señora Parpadea, the lady I've found out is in charge of the project, to see if there might be a place not only for Lucila's stone but where others could put their stones on that ship.

Lucila and I sit on the roof of my house. Olivia the owl is with us in her usual spot just outside my window. I have a fresh sheet of paper, a book to rest it on, and my favorite pen. We spend a long time brainstorming what to say. Finally we settle on telling her we're excited about the idea to turn the ship into a museum. Then we tell her about the memory maps; about Lucila's, Natalia's, Sebastián's, and Mamá's experiences on the *Esmeralda*; and about Señora Granados and our promise to her to remember the people who disappeared. Then we ask our favor:

Would it be possible for the people of Valparaíso to have a dedicated space in the museum where they can display their memory stones and perhaps build some animitas for the people who died there?

We go on to explain how we want to try to combine the old tradition of the animitas with the new tradition of the memory maps.

"Do you think she'll write back?" Lucila asks, chewing nervously on a fingernail—it's a habit she has yet to break.

"I don't know, amiga, but she might. And that's better than not asking."

News about a
Boat

Late on a Friday afternoon, after onces, I'm out on the roof talking with the owl. I've discovered, quite by accident, that she loves to be talked to. She cocks her head this way and that, as though understanding what I'm saying. Nana is sweeping off the front stoop and is murmuring something about shooing bad spirits away. Hmmm, I wonder if she saw something in her tea leaves this afternoon. Our neighbor Señora Atkinson is calling to her canary in a shrill voice, "Charlie! Charlie! Come back here this minute." The canary chirps in response, and through one of Señora Atkinson's windows I catch a glimpse of bright yellow flitting through the room. As Olivia and I are taking all this in, Mamá pops her head out the window, waving a letter, excited. "Celeste! Señor Pascual just delivered this. It's from Señora Parpadea!"

I nearly fall, scrambling through the window. I snatch the envelope from my mother's hand, ready to rip it open.

"Celeste! What are you doing? You need to wait for Lucila!"

"Oh, of course!" I say, and run for the phone.

"We've got a reply from Señora Parpadea, amiga! Do you want to come here, or should I go there?"

"I'll be right there!" she cries, and I hear the dial tone before I even have a chance to say good-bye.

Within ten minutes, Lucila arrives, breathing hard. It's clear she ran the whole way. We gather around the kitchen table; everyone's on pins and needles.

"You open it, Lucila," I say, thrusting the envelope at her.

She takes it and unceremoniously tears it open. "I can't believe she wrote back!"

"What does it say?" I ask, bouncing my leg up and down nervously.

"Okay, okay, I'll read it," says Lucila excitedly.

Dear Señorita Marconi and Señorita López,

Thank you for your letter and your request. The purpose of the museum is to help our fellow citizens understand what happened aboard the Esmeralda *and to remember the people who suffered there—like your family members and your friends. On that note, I am intrigued by the memory map project and your request to have a space to display the memory stones. After talking with the architect, we have decided to approve your request . . .*

Lucila gapes at me. "She said yes!" Lucila throws her arms around me.

"What else does she say? When can we start?" I ask, stunned.

"Ummm . . . Let's see. . . . She says she also likes the idea of the animitas! . . . And, let's see. . . . She wants us to call her as soon as possible so she can show us the space!"

My entire family claps and whoops. "Well done, niñas!" says Papá. "Well done!"

On Board
the *Esmeralda*

Up close, the *Esmeralda* seems enormous and intimidating; it casts a shadow over us as we approach, and a chill runs through me. Today we are meeting with Señora Parpadea to see the space she has set aside for the memory stones and the animitas. Papá and Mamá—she said she *had* to come—are with us. Mamá and Lucila are fidgety, and I wonder if they really are ready to go back on board.

Señora Parpadea is waiting for us at the base of the ramp. After introductions, she tells us she's eager to show us what they've done so far, and we follow her on board. I glance anxiously at Mamá, at Lucila. Lucila has slipped her hand into Mamá's.

"We've divided the exhibit into four sections," the señora explains. "The first, which we are walking into now, documents the original purpose of the *Esmeralda* as a vessel where the finest Chilean mariners trained. As you can see, we have a number of photographs dating as far back as 1900. Then, over here, we will be displaying some of the tools of the mariners' trade: maps, astro-labes, captains' logs, training logs . . ."

I take a closer look at some of the photographs that were taken from the ship, in which you can see people waving white handkerchiefs. I wonder idly if my family might be in some of those photographs, from back when the ship was simply a wonder to behold.

Señora Parpadea then guides us downstairs. "Now we'll go into the second section of the exhibit. This is the one focused on the appropriation of the ship during the time of the dictatorship. I forewarn you that we have tried to preserve things as accurately as possible so that people will get a true picture of what happened here." Papá and I look again at Mamá and Lucila, but they simply nod solemnly. So the señora nods as well, and opens a door to an inner room.

Mamá stops. "This . . . this is where I was kept," she says in a trembling voice. "I remember how cold it was—the other women and I had to huddle together for warmth at night. . . ." Her face is growing paler and paler. I look at my father in alarm.

"I'm so sorry, Doctora Marconi," Señora Parpadea murmurs.

Mamá draws herself up tall. "I'm okay. It's turning into history—it's no longer the future." Mamá turns to Lucila, checking on *her.*

Lucila points at a place where there's no longer a cell. "I was there—it was just like the one you were in. Look how close we were to each other . . ."

Mamá pulls Lucila to her. "We probably weren't here at the same time, hija, but I know what you mean."

Señora Parpadea quickly points out one of the rooms where the dictator's men did the worst of the worst. Mamá and Lucila prefer not to look inside, and I wish I *hadn't*! Our guide quickly closes that door, and I see relief wash over Lucila and Mamá.

We walk into another space belowdecks that is bright and open, in contrast to the small, dark cells we just saw. The walls have been painted white, and on them are framed documents and photographs. In front of each display there's a bench with hooks on either side and a sign that reads AURICULARES HEADPHONES.

"What are these?" I ask, approaching the first frames.

"These are testimonials. We've spent the last few months talking to people who were affected in one way or another by the *Esmeralda*. Visitors to the museum will be able to read the accounts or listen to them through these headphones."

"Ah, another way to keep them from being forgotten," Lucila whispers into my ear.

Then Señora Parpadea says, "Now let's head back upstairs to the final part of the exhibit, where we've set aside space for the memory stones and the animitas."

We step out onto the deck at the stern of the ship, the outer edge of which is lined with benches. "We thought these benches would be a good place to build the animitas. We haven't installed much lighting out here because the glow of the animitas should be enough for people to find their way around the exhibit, even at night." *Wow, this is going to be a GREAT place for the animitas*, I think. "Now, do you have any thoughts about how you want to display the memory stones?" asks the señora, looking back and forth between Lucila and me.

"This . . . this is more than we could have ever hoped for, Señora Parpadea. Thank you," I say, and look at Lucila. "May we talk to our friends? See what idea might work best?"

"Of course. Let's meet again in a week," she replies.

Ideas in
Bloom

Today my friends and I meet Sebastián after he finishes his after-school job with Señor Barbablanca. As promised, I introduced Sebastián and Nati to him. Not only have they become friends, but Señor Barbablanca offered Sebastián a part-time job!

We head over to a pretty, white gazebo across from the bookshop. Lucila quickly describes our space on the *Esmeralda* and we begin brainstorming ideas. After a short while, Cristóbal says, "What if we build a giant mobile or wind chime with the stones."

"How do you mean?" Lucila asks.

"Well, let me show you what I'm thinking." He pulls a notebook from his backpack and begins drawing what look like clotheslines strung from one side of the deck of a boat to the other, in a kind of zigzag pattern. Then he decorates the lines with fairy lights and adds threads that hang down with the memory stones attached to the ends.

"I see where you're going with this, Cristóbal,"

Sebastián says, excitement in his voice. Cristóbal adds a few flourishes.

"Me too," says Genevieve. "The lines would need to be strung just high enough so people don't hit their heads on the stones, but far enough down so they can still read the names."

"And then when the wind blows," says Cristóbal, still drafting, "the stones will clink together and produce a sound all their own. I was thinking . . . that it could be like the voices of the disappeared."

We all look at him. Cristóbal is still focused on his drawing. When he looks up and sees all of us staring at him, he says, "What? Don't you like the idea?"

"I love it!" says Natalia. "Mamá and Papá's stones will be like they're talking to us, Sebastián."

"I love it too," says Lucila, her eyes wet, but smiling.

And just like that, we know exactly what we're doing.

A **Floating**
Museum of Memories

Señora Parpadea is a woman who gets things done! Barely three months later, thirty animitas have been built, and the mobile of stones has been hung. Tonight we're at the grand opening of the museum! When we walk out onto the deck at the stern of the ship, it's like we've entered an enchanted world. We wander among the dangling stones, the wind clinking them together, inviting us into a space that feels both comforting and sacred.

"Look, Nati. There are Mamá and Papá's," Sebastián says, pointing at the stones that have the names Eusebio and Clementina painted in yellow. He lifts her up so she can get a closer look.

"Hello, Mamá and Papá," she says, touching each stone.

I turn to Cristóbal. "This looks *amazing*! It was such a good idea, Cristóbal." He smiles, warm yet wistful. Because, of course, we can't help but wish that he'd never had to have the idea in the first place.

Lucila is crouched on the opposite side of the deck

in front of an animita—the one she, Marisol, and Doña Estela made. I join her. There's a colorful basket that Lucila made, in which she has placed a letter to her parents. There are also photos of them on their wedding day, and holding a baby Lucila. Abuela Estela put a pair of her son's cuff links in a small dish, along with a necklace belonging to her daughter-in-law. There are also candles and one of the couple's favorite cassettes.

"I think it turned out really well," Lucila says, her voice catching.

"It's *perfect*," I say, looping my arm through hers.

The other animitas are just as moving. I think the people of Valparaíso will appreciate visiting this place and learning about those who died here. And, who knows, maybe the myth of the animitas will come true and the dead will perform miracles. I ponder that for a minute and then decide that the miracle may have already happened: the *Esmeralda* is no longer a scary torture ship but a floating museum of those who are no longer disappeared, not entirely.

Word
from Afar

I'm getting ready to head down to the beach to take an early-morning walk with Sebastián. When I go downstairs to make a café con leche, I find Mamá and Papá sitting at the kitchen table with goofy grins on their faces.

"What's going on?" I say as I sip my coffee. "Why are you smiling like that?"

"We got some nice news," says Mamá. "Why don't you sit down?"

"Sorry, Mamá. I have to head out. I'm meeting Sebastián in fifteen minutes."

I'm about to leave the room when Mamá says, "How would you like to be a bridesmaid?" I stop dead in my tracks.

"What? What do you mean?" I ask, confused.

"We got a call from Tía Graciela late, really late, last night. She's getting married!"

"What? When? A bridesmaid? Is it Charlie? Of course it's Charlie! When?" I blurt out, so happy for my tía, my thoughts all a jumble.

"Well, it's not until next summer, which is good because we'll need time to save up lots of money to go to the wedding. It's going to be on Juliette Cove!" I can tell Mamá is as excited as I am.

"I can't believe it. This is HUGE news! When can I talk to Tía? What does a bridesmaid do? What kind of dress do I wear? Is the wedding going to be in that cute courtyard down by the sea? Will it be at night so Tía can dance in the light of the moon?" I have so many questions, and I realize I'm excited to go back to Juliette Cove. I can see my old teacher—Miss Rose—and Mr. Carter, and I can show my parents all my favorite places.

"We don't know the details, hija. We told Graciela we'd call her back again later today so you two can talk. It will be a big Marconi affair!" says Papá happily.

A huge smile takes over my face. "Thanks, Mamá and Papá. Can I tell my friends?"

"Of course you can! Now go on, or you'll be late," says Mamá, kissing me on the cheek.

As I walk down Butterfly Hill, I realize I'm beginning to feel happiness again like I did before the general tried to ruin everyone's lives. It's about time! It's funny, because now that things are going well, time is zipping by so fast. I forget to look at the calendar Nana Delfina has hanging in the kitchen, because I don't have time; I'm so busy with school, memory maps, literacy classes, and spending

time with Lucila, Sebastián, and my other friends. Before
I know it, another week has whizzed by. Perhaps time
isn't really meant to be measured by days on a calendar,
but by the big events in our lives, and *so* many big things
have happened in my life over the last three years. I also
don't worry about things so much anymore. For instance,
I don't even think about Gloria these days. She's just not
important to me like other people are.

All of a sudden, I feel someone take my hand, and
a happy shiver runs through me when I look up to see
Sebastián. I was so deep in thought
that I made it down to the
water without even realizing

it. As we stroll along the shore, I tell him the Marconi news. We keep walking, breathing in the fresh morning air. The wind blows my hair into my face and tickles my cheeks, and I begin to laugh. Pretty soon, Sebastián is laughing too, and neither one of us knows why. We laugh until we cry blue tears of happiness as we continue along the beach, dreaming about the future that's in the palm of our hands, and we give thanks to life for giving us so much. The future of the past will be our new passion and will guide us toward the truth. Anything's possible on Butterfly Hill.

Acknowledgments

Writing is a solitary activity that requires continuous inner exploration. Nevertheless, writing is also a community activity rooted in solidarity and supported by so many. I want to express my gratitude to the following individuals for their role in my journey:

John Wiggins, my husband and trusted friend.

My children, Joseph and Sonia, who always make me happy when I see them smile.

My mother, Frida, whose faith in my ability to imagine is always with me, and my father who, from heaven and beyond, lives within me, guiding me and advising me.

My translator, Alison Ridley, for an exceptional job translating *The Maps of Memory* from Spanish to English with such love and care, and for the deep friendship that binds us.

Caitlyn Dlouhy, an outstanding editor with an eye for detail and a magnificent understanding of what it means to write for young adult readers.

Jennifer Lyons, my agent, for her unconditional

support and faith in me, and for always being there for me with a generous and kind heart.

There are also so many dear friends who journey with me on the creative process: Vivian Schnitzer, Celeste Kostopulos Cooperman, Carlos Vega, Inela Selimovic, Ilan Perrot, Hugo Krauss, Karen Frederick, Mirko Petric, Roberta Mayerhoffer, Karen Poniachik, Yael Siman, Lori Carlson Hijuelos, Julie Levison, Domnica Radulescu, Cristian Montes, Mónica Flores, and Samuel Shats.